The Demon Ark

Jan McDonald

Raven Crest Books

ISBN-13: 978-0-9934439-7-8

For Bill

Deep beneath the earth of the Plain of Jezreel, just outside the place that had become known as Megiddo, a dark energy was stirring. Waiting for the day when it would be free of the tomb of earth, free to wreak its havoc on this world, returning it once more to darkness and chaos.

(The Sacred Ark)

CHAPTER ONE: MEGIDDO

Josh Hammond was afraid. Actually, if he was honest, he was terrified

Something was wrong; very wrong. He was familiar with evil - with its smell, its feel, its darkness - and evil was emerging right around him. He knew he had to get help and he knew where to look for it.

It hadn't been easy to regain his reputation in the field of archaeology, but he had managed to secure a senior position on the Megiddo Expedition being run by Tel Aviv University, and now he was about to put it all on the line again. His early reputation had been shattered by his conviction that the Ark of the Covenant had held more than the biblical commandments; its secrets were of earth shattering consequence. And he had been proved right, and he had found it. But this was different, and he knew that the Israeli authorities weren't going to listen to his present conviction; that demons were present at Megiddo and that evil was gathering there.

Much had been written in fiction and film script about Megiddo and it had earned its place in horror stories, mainly stemming from the fact that the Book of Revelations had stated that the final battle between the forces of good and evil would take place there. It had become well known that the word Armageddon had its origins in this place but scholars and theologians alike had agreed that this was metaphor and that the world would not end after this battle, nor the apocalypse rain down, but none of them had said that a battle between good and evil would *not* happen. Josh's instinct was that the scene was being set for evil to manifest.

It had started with the storms.

Megiddo is an ancient ruined city on a mound rising sixty metres above the surrounding Jezreel valley in northern Israel. Rainfall at that time of year was not unprecedented, but the region was generally confined to the usual climate of the Middle East. However, as Josh had settled into overseeing the removal of what appeared to be a Bronze Age artefact from the ground, the sky had darkened to indigo, accompanied by thunder and lightning and torrential rain that had caught them unawares. They had scurried to cover the vulnerable part of the excavation but the rain was so hard and heavy that much of it was washed away.

Josh looked up at the lowering clouds and sniffed the air. After such a storm the smell of ozone was to be expected, but he smelled something else; sulphur. The storms came and went for days on end before they finally abated.

That morning at the hill-top dig site, there was unusual activity.

"Josh, come quickly!" A student was waving at him frantically. He took off at speed in her direction.

As he approached he could see a group of students and local workers bending over a senior grad student from Tel Aviv who was on the expedition to complete on her doctorate. She appeared to have collapsed. Josh searched his memory for a name; Ruth, he thought, her name is Ruth.

The group parted as he approached and he knelt beside her inert body, fearing the worst, but relieved as his probing fingers found a pulse in her neck and he could see the steady rise and fall of her chest.

"Someone call an ambulance! What happened?" he demanded.

One of the Israeli students shrugged and splayed his hands in a gesture of confusion. "One moment she was recording the finds and then she suddenly cried out. She was shouting something; I couldn't make it out, it was a language I'm not familiar with. And then she just fell down. By the time I got to her, she was this way."

"Has someone called for an ambulance?" he again demanded as he removed her scarf from around her neck; even though it was loose, at least he felt as if he was doing something useful. As he removed it, he noticed small pustules forming on her neck and throat.

There was a general murmur that an ambulance was indeed on its way.

Josh felt his heart constrict as he pulled the scarf away from her. The veins in her upper chest and lower throat were now visible - and they were black, just as if someone had drawn them on with a permanent marker. As he stared at them, the veins in her neck became visible and black also, and began spreading up into her jawline like inky lace. Several of the students backed away.

She suddenly took in a deep gulp of air and opened her eyes. The remaining students backed off too as they looked down into pools of black in her eye-sockets. Josh felt chilled to the bone, his instincts to drop her and back off, but he was responsible for her, and so he lowered her gently to the ground. As he did so, her eyes returned to their customary blue-green and the black veins faded under her skin. She gasped the air again.

"What happened?" she asked, trying to sit up.

Josh put a supporting hand behind her. "Don't try and get up yet, we've called an ambulance; you should get checked over."

"I'll be fine," she answered, "I must have fainted with the heat, that's all."

Josh didn't like to remind her that the temperature had dropped with the storms and it had remained cool ever since.

That had been days ago and he had kept an eye on her. She had become distant and aloof and, over the last few days, others had succumbed to the same thing. He was worried, even though the Professor leading the dig insisted it was simply a form of 'flu virus. No-one had come to any serious harm from it and the dig was becoming time-sensitive due to the delay caused by the storms.

Days passed as normality returned to the dig. Another layer had been reached, making twenty-five in all. They were at the Bronze Age and Iron Age areas of the site now and the relative sanity that had resumed began to make Josh believe he'd over-reacted.

Then the flies came.

Swarms of buzzing black clouds of fat flies descended, so dense that they obscured vision, landing on their faces, crawling over them, getting caught in their hair. Students were screaming and running for cover, flapping their hands about to try to clear the onslaught of flies that found homes in their open mouths as they ran. A natural phenomenon brought about by the storms, they said. Josh knew better.

The first seismic tremor struck around mid-day the following day, with several after-shocks diminishing in power until they disappeared, leaving behind a magnetic anomaly that sent all the geo-physics equipment haywire. A magnetic field had appeared directly over the epicentre of the first seismic wave and it heralded the rapid appearance of the Israeli military. Jeeps and other all-terrain vehicles arrived, discharging soldiers in olive green field uniforms, all bearing assault rifles and a bad attitude. It had taken less than fifteen minutes to clear the area of everyone other than the army personnel, who were already erecting barricades and posting guards all over the site.

Josh made his first phone call to Mike Travis.

CHAPTER TWO: TEMPLARS

History's reach is long; it's grasp tenacious. Nothing forgiven. Nothing forgotten. Its ghosts play out their roles from generation to generation; some benign, some not so.

On Christmas Day in 1119 at the Church of the Holy Sepulchre in Jerusalem, nine men knelt before the altar in the presence of King Baldwin II and Warmund, the Patriarch of the same holy city. The nine swore vows of poverty, chastity and obedience and to protect pilgrims on their journeys to and from the holy places of Christendom. They would live not as the knights and noblemen that they were, but take up a monastic existence on the Temple Mount in Jerusalem and function as warrior-monks. They would be called The Order of Poor Knights of Christ and the Temple of Solomon, or, as we know them today - The Knights Templar.

And so was born a legend, a mystery, and a conspiracy.

Their leader, Hugues de Payens, was joined by his eight founding brothers: Payens de Montdidier; Andre de Montbard; Archambaud de St Aignan; Geoffrey Bisol; two knights known only by their first names of Roland and Gondemar; and a ninth knight who, throughout history, has remained anonymous.

Until now.

His name was Guy de Nantes – and he had a very different agenda. One that he would nurture until the time came when he would be free to fulfil his own dark destiny.

Ostensibly, the Knights' mission was to protect the pilgrims on their holy journey but, first, they had another task; one that would take eight years to accomplish. They were quartered in the al-Aqsa mosque on the Temple Mount, one of the holiest and most fought-over sites on this earth, built by Muslims on the original site of the Jewish Temple of Solomon, and here they spent those eight years - not just protecting it, but digging under it.

Beneath the Temple Mount were great cavernous openings which had primarily been used to stable King Solomon's horses, but these openings continued as tunnels that burrowed deep beneath the mount itself. These tunnels were systematically and thoroughly excavated by the Templars as they searched for something; something that was never meant to be found. And suddenly, after the eight years of digging, they abandoned their excavations and emerged an extremely wealthy and well-funded organisation. From that moment the Pope granted them almost limitless power and authority with the blessing of the Church. Whatever they had found beneath the Temple Mount had changed the course of their history.

The nine became thirty, became fifty, became hundreds, all fulfilling their original purpose and wielding the sword in the name of Christ. As the Order grew from the original nine warrior-monks that had sworn their oaths of poverty, chastity and obedience, the Templars were forced to evolve into a more structured unit. At the head of the Order was the Grand Master who answered only to the Pope, with his deputy and adviser known as the Seneschal. Hugues de Payens was the first Grand Master and he chose as his Seneschal the ninth knight, Guy de Nantes. It was a choice that would have far-reaching and the darkest of consequences, as Guy kept hidden his true intent, gaining power within the Order, giving counsel to the Grand Master whilst furthering his own agenda that would be answerable to no Pope, but to his master in Hell. His worship was of a different kind and he served only Baphomet; worship of the demon which he insidiously spread to other Knights in the form of a distorted version of their initiation ceremony, growing alongside, and hidden from, the true Knights of Christ.

And, all the time, the Templars were being gifted land

and money in furtherance of their cause. The Poor Knights of Christ were poor no longer.

Speculation was rife but unconfirmed, as it is to this day. Had they found King Solomon's vast treasure? Or had they found treasure of a different kind? Or, perhaps, both? Perhaps they had unearthed the Ark of the Covenant? The Holy Grail? Or was it something far more terrible? Whatever they had found there, it gave them influence and power over Kings and Popes and the dispensation to wage war on behalf of the whole of Christendom.

In 1187, Jerusalem fell into the hands of Saladin and the Templars moved their headquarters to Acre, where they retained control for just over one hundred years, until its fall.

But dreams of recovering the Holy Land weren't over yet, especially in the mind of Jacques de Molay who became Grand Master of the Order in 1293. Despite the fact that Acre had fallen two years previously and the Christian forces were being routed from Jerusalem with relentless vigour, Jacques was determined to raise the Templars to a new crusade. But first there were things that had to be protected, things that must never fall into the wrong hands - things that had been recovered from under the Temple Mount.

He would send the 'treasure' across seas and oceans to the shores of England, away from the clutches of Saracen hands and, to this end, he called Gilbert Belvoir, his Seneschal, to his side. The Knight had served him well and fought with the bravery of a thousand lions, so to him he would entrust the safe-keeping of the most terrible of artefacts. It was a duty that Gilbert would fulfil until his dying day. And beyond.

Jacques dismissed the other Knights present; his words were for his Seneschal alone.

Gilbert Belvoir knelt on one knee, his head bowed low over his sword. "Master."

"Get up Gilbert. You have no need to bow before any man. There is only one before whom we should lower our heads. Walk with me; these walls seem to have developed acute hearing. Only you can I trust."

The Seneschal frowned but obeyed. He had his own suspicions about the security of the Order, feeling a cold, darkness creeping from within their own ranks but unable to identify its source.

Outside the castle walls the winter chill was making its mark with a pall of white hoar frost and the ground beneath their feet crunched with each step. If anyone were to follow them they would surely hear them approach.

"I want you to leave, Gilbert." De Molay raised his hand to quell the instant protest. "I am entrusting scrolls and a ring to your guardianship. You must take them far from here. Acre has fallen and it is only a matter of time before the tide turns against us from Rome. Accusations are growing daily, foul slanders that will be our undoing. Phillip of France is behind them and his power over the Pope is great. You must go now, while there is still time. God forbid the ring should fall into evil hands. It is the ring of Solomon, delivered to him by the Archangel Michael from God himself, in order for him to take control of the demons. I have prayed daily that Michael would come down and take it back, but it seems the burden remains ours."

"But, Master, I would remain at your side to the end. Send someone else, I beg you."

Jacques shook his head. "No, Gilbert. This is your sacred duty. But you must be aware that there is something evil watching. To this end I am sending others on a similar mission to other destinations, each believing that they have the ring and the scrolls; each sworn to secrecy. It will make it more difficult for the darkness to find you. At least it will buy you time. Will you accept this duty? This burden?"

The Seneschal bowed his head again, but not before Jacques could read the sorrow in his eyes. Gilbert's allegiance was obvious and it grieved him to be leaving the Grand Master to face the fate that awaited him - awaited them all - but his oath of obedience would permit him no comfort.

"I will do as you ask, Master. But with a heavy heart."

De Molay nodded his understanding in silence.

"When shall I leave?" Gilbert asked.

The Grand Master reached inside his tunic that bore the familiar red cross and brought out a small hessian package which he handed to the Seneschal.

"At first light. I know the winter is harsh and your journey made more difficult, but that will also be true for whoever or whatever follows you. You are to go to the Temple Church in Paris and from there to London, England. One order you must obey above all else, my brother; never be tempted to wear the ring against the demons. To once put it on your hand will bring about your own damnation. God bless you and God speed."

With these words he parted from Gilbert Belvoir, his most trusted knight.

The ring of Solomon had terrible power, for good or evil, depending on the hand that wore it. It was such a small object to contain such awesome power but it would become the key to the destiny of the world. And the scrolls that had been found among other sacred relics under the mount had the power to blow the lid off the teachings of the Church, the beliefs of Islam, and of Judaism; the three major religions that were in a constant battle to claim the Temple Mount for their own.

Gilbert Belvoir travelled west until he reached the French headquarters in Paris, but his journey wasn't over. He had sensed the dark presence that dogged his steps, and his original and final destination of Temple Church in London suddenly didn't seem to offer the security that he had been expecting. He crossed the English Channel and continued west until he reached the Welsh border and settled into monastic life again in the Templar church and preceptory of St. Michael's, at Garway in Herefordshire; guarding the ring of Solomon, keeping it hidden, even from his fellow Templars and their Preceptor. It was a heavy burden, but his to be borne alone in a place that may have need of it, as legend had it that the Church at Garway was built over the site of one of the closed portals to hell. Its sanctified ground and its atmosphere of holy worship were somewhat of an antidote to its potential.

But a ring that could control demons would not stay quiet, attracting to itself dark entities that would seek to deliver it as a prize to the highest bidder, on earth or in Hell. And then, of course, there were the demons themselves, for what demon could resist the taking of an object that could bring about their own demise, keeping it away from hands that would use it in their destruction?

In Garway, Gilbert Belvoir remained in his daily routine of prayer and contemplation, interspersed with his work; the building of the dovecote and the writing of his journal that would one day be of help to another who sought to quell the demons.

In1294 the Grand Master, Jacques de Molay, suddenly and for no apparent reason undertook the journey across the Channel, bypassing the headquarters in Paris, and the Temple Church in London, travelling on to the small Templar preceptory of Garway in Herefordshire. He now knew his adversary; he knew of the secret Order within the Order. The Knights of the Dark Temple were established and they were strong. Gilbert had to be warned and he could trust no-one; he must make the journey himself.

The Preceptor of the small Herefordshire church and preceptory was flustered; the Grand Master had arrived without warning and - of all things! - seemed intent on one goal; to talk with one of the subordinate Knights, Gilbert Belvoir. Alone.

Gilbert's joy at seeing Jacques was written all over his usually solemn face.

"Master."

"Gilbert. Please don't address me that way, not you. To you, I am 'brother'. You are well?"

"Yes. The better for seeing you. What brings you to this humble place?"

"You. You do. Or rather, I come to warn you. The darkness that we both suspected has revealed itself to me and they are coming for you. They are coming for the ring and the scrolls. I believe them to be close by."

"Then you have come to take it from me? To relieve me of the burden?"

De Molay shook his head. "I must return straight away. Our fate is written, it seems - but the ring, Gilbert; the ring must remain with you and no other until many years from now when its destiny against true evil will be fulfilled. *Many, many* years, Gilbert. Do you understand?"

De Molay's old Seneschal nodded gravely. "I must take it to my grave. And my grave must be occupied sooner rather than later. From beyond the grave I may be better able to protect the artefacts from evil hands." He paused. "Master, I would ask you, which is the greater sin? To take one's own life or to take that of another? How shall we end this?"

"I believe that in the circumstances neither is a sin, brother. Do you wish me to honour you with my sword?"

Gilbert smiled at the Grand Master, his mentor and his friend. From within his tunic he withdrew a small pouch and tipped its content onto his hand. He swallowed the ring, said a prayer and plunged his own sword deep into his body, falling forwards onto it, driving it deep, passing from this life into death.

Jacques de Molay prayed for his Seneschal and remained at Garway while Gilbert's iron coffin was forged by the local blacksmith. Iron to withstand the demons. He commissioned the stone tomb to be placed in its own crypt beneath the Garway church, refusing to leave until he had overseen its construction and his friend's entombment; his friend who would be forever watching, forever on guard.

11

CHAPTER THREE: JACK'S DEMON

Mike Travis had a fierce grip on Jack's arm, staring at the raised, livid marks above his friend's wrist; it looked as if he'd been branded. It was the demon Bazaliel's seal that had previously been on his shoulder, before Mike had killed the demon in hell.

"*What in God's name ....?* How the *hell* did this happen?" He couldn't hold back the anger in his voice as he demanded an explanation from either Jack or Ben.

Jack Carter and Ben Lovecraft were his best friends; Jack it seemd forever as they had served as comrades-in-arms in the Royal Air Force. They had been together in Iraq and Afghanistan, where Mike's helicopter crash had taken his life for a breath-holding amount of time before the medics had brought him back from the realm of death. Since then, Jack had been by Mike's side as he recovered, helping him come to terms with his new-found gift of being able to see spirits and other entities.

Benjamin Lovecraft, a huge, red-headed, red-bearded, bear of a man; ex-priest, exorcist and biker, had come to Mike's aid when he had been out of his depth with a demon on his hands. Recently, he had revealed his true identity: he was the fallen angel Seraquel. As if that hadn't been enough for Mike to get his head around, Ben had also told Mike that he was there to mentor him, teach him, guide him and in the process find his own redemption.

Mike wasn't in the mood to back down. "*How? How* did this happen?" he demanded again. "Bazaliel is dead. I bloody well killed him myself! So how the hell is his seal still on Jack's arm? Someone explain this to me." This last directed at Ben.

"Easy, Mike. It was Jack's decision. His choice."

Mike's eyes widened in amazement, but his grip on Jack's arm didn't lessen. "***What?***" His eyes returned to Jack. "You mean to tell me you allowed this to happen? *Why?*"

Jack's voice remained steady. "Not allowed - invited. As to the why; I was having a massive heart attack, Mike, and, when it came right down to it, I didn't want to die. Right at the crucial moment, that's when you killed Bazaliel - or thought you had - I had a split second to understand what I needed to do to stay alive. And I did it. Free will. My choice. Let me remind you that you had put him in me in the first place. Why is it so different when it was my decision?"

"Oh ... I don't know ... ***because he's a friggin' demon, maybe?***" He ground his teeth together in a familiar gesture of anger and frustration as he felt his fury rising into the red zone, a gesture that always emphasised the long scar along the length of his cheekbone, a souvenir from his crash. When he trusted himself to speak, he said, "Ben said it was a minor heart attack and that you were going to be all right."

"It *was* a minor heart attack only because Bazaliel stopped it. I was set for the bone yard, Mike. I'm sorry if you would have preferred that, but I didn't. Why are you so angry?"

Mike tried to swallow back the bile of his anger. "*Angry* doesn't come close, Jack. The demon is a scumbag. How do we know it wasn't him that caused the heart attack in the first place? Insurance, maybe? He was about to betray us all to save his own filthy skin. And in case you were absent that day, demons lie! Lovecraft's Rule number one: Demons friggin' lie!"

Jack's voice didn't waver, although the hurt in his eyes spoke loud and clear. "I have his seal, Mike. I have control."

Mike made an impatient sound in his throat. "Clearly!"

Jack continued, "You got a second chance, Mike, and

so did I. Well, a third chance in fact. I wanted to do the same for him, maybe help him back into the light. And like I said, I didn't want to die. Do you think you could let go of my arm, now? You're cutting off my circulation."

Mike flung Jack's arm away from him and stood up abruptly, leaning against the table. "I think someone cut off the circulation to your brain, too."

Jack looked away. "I think maybe you should go."

Mike appealed to Ben, "Can't you get some sense into him, for God's sake? Am I the only one who sees the problem here?"

Ben put a hand on Mike's shoulder. "We would have lost him, Mike. Really. And he made the decision himself. Perhaps no-one is past redemption. Not even a demon. Bazaliel wasn't spawned in hell - he fell. Like me. But *his* crimes were such that he went straight down there. You're exhausted, Mike. You've had more on your plate in the last few years than most people have in a lifetime. Go easy on him. And yourself."

Mike wavered, and suddenly it seemed as if his own spirit had left his body, and he sagged against the table. His head fell forward and for several minutes he couldn't speak. When he could, he lifted his head and Ben could see the trauma reflected in his eyes.

"What happened, Ben? What happened to me? I was happy investigating paranormal phenomena, helping people find peace, both living and dead. Suddenly I'm a goddamn demon hunter! I mean, what's that about? Why me? There are other hunters out there, so why the hell me? Why can't I have peace? And it's not just me, there's Beth and Addie; it puts them in the firing line too."

Ben smiled at his friend, "Because you're good at it. Because the world needs people like you who will step up to the plate to get rid of the scumbags, the devils and the demons. Because at some level you agreed to it. But, most of all, because you're a good man, Mike, and good men take on the crap. A*nd, most of all,* because you're of

Michael's bloodline. That's the heaviest heritage. Beth and Addie know that too, and that's why they let you get on with it. Go home. Get some rest and let things settle in your head. Jack's alive and with us. If he had chosen to die, then we would be mourning him right now, wondering what could have been done to prevent it. And we *would* have been asking ourselves that question, Mike. Well, Bazaliel prevented it. Time will tell if Jack really has control of him, in the meantime, he seems to have. Go home to Beth. Things will seem different after a good night's sleep."

Mike refrained from saying that he thought he would never have a good night's sleep again. He seriously doubted it. Instead he simply laid his hand on Ben's arm. He looked back to Jack who was deliberately avoiding his gaze.

"I'm sorry, Jack. I mean it. I'm really sorry. I'm knackered, but that's no excuse. We'll talk again in the morning. Right now, there's a bottle of scotch with my name on it, and I intend to empty it."

Jack's relief was obvious. He had been hurt by Mike's anger but he knew that the root of their deep friendship was unscathed. They would sort it out. He smiled and nodded.

"I'll have one with you. They said I should refrain, but they don't know about my secret weapon." He instantly regretted his attempt at humour and looked anxiously into Mike's eyes, waiting for another heated outburst.

Mike hesitated momentarily and then grinned. "Well, I suppose if you have to have a demon inside you, he might as well be useful, right? Just don't get him wasted until you know his limit. See you tomorrow. Beth wants to come over as soon as she can, but she was exhausted and I put her to bed."

Relieved again, Jack took hold of Mike's hand and gripped it tight. "Night," was all he could manage.

Mike sat in his car, his dark mood descending again. He

thought of his wife, Beth, already sound asleep before he had left for Ben and Jack's place. After all she had been through, dragged, literally, to hell by demons, where he had followed her and brought her back to him, to them all, he wondered how she could sleep. Maybe she was stronger than he was or, more likely, it was sheer exhaustion that had taken her consciousness into the oblivion of sleep. He hoped she wasn't having bad dreams.

He switched on the ignition and threw his car into gear, leaving Ben's cottage on the edge of Skenfrith in a cloud of gravel as he stepped too hard on the accelerator. At the junction his phone rang just as he pulled the car to a halt. He was in no mood for conversation and a glance at his watch showed way past midnight. He didn't recognise the number so he hit the call reject button. It rang again almost immediately. He hit the call accept button.

"*What?*" he demanded of the distant voice. There was a momentary hesitation at the other end.

"Mike? It's me, Josh. You said you'd call me back. It's the ..."

Mike interrupted him. "Not now, Josh. Bad time."

"But, Mike it's ..."

Something deep inside Mike snapped, and he felt the rush of anger and frustration, mixed with a hearty helping of fear, hit him somewhere in the middle of his head. "I said, not now, Josh. Are you dying? Is Maddie or Grace dying? No? Well, like I said, not now. I'll call you in the morning."

He didn't wait for further conversation, switching his phone off and throwing it onto the passenger seat. He paused; turning left would take him home, but on impulse he turned the car right and headed towards Abergavenny. He was all too aware of the fragility of his healing PTSD, unsure if he wanted to scream or punch the living daylights out of someone. Right then, he didn't care which. He needed to speak to Beckett.

Instinctively he glanced at his watch again, and then

allowed himself a rueful smile. The time didn't matter. In the normal run of things, vampires didn't sleep.

CHAPTER FOUR: KNIGHTS OF THE DARK TEMPLE

Dark, dank cellars and black hooded cloaks are not for the Knights of the Dark Temple; their headquarters are as breathtakingly opulent as their regalia.

Templemore Manor sat on a hill overlooking the spectacular Malvern Hills; built by the Knights Templar in 1215 it became the main preceptory and administration centre for many of the smaller Templar enclaves until the dissolution of the Order, when it passed into private hands. Those hands belonged to Robert de Lacy, the Grand Master at that time of the blasphemous and secret arm of the Templars – The Knights of the Dark Temple. From that day forward the Dark Knights met in secret, performing the evil rituals of their sinister cult in the shadow of the Templars who knew nothing of their mysterious and murky existence.

The Knights of the Dark Temple existed only to worship Baphomet and subsequently other - more powerful - demons. Originally said to be the object of worship by the Templars, by those that sought to discredit them, Baphomet became the symbol that the Knights of the Dark Temple chose to represent their own foul deity, evolving as it did into the more familiar goat-headed, female-breasted, winged and cloven-hoofed figure with a flame between its horns. This image of Baphomet became the God of the Dark Temple Knights and so it remains, as does their brotherhood, acquiring vast wealth and power within the halls of government, financial institutions and industry. Their web is vast and their reach, global.

Anathema to the Templars, this devil worship thrived alongside and inside their ranks without their knowledge and therefore without censure, growing like cancer from the mind of their first Grand Master, the ninth knight, Guy de Nantes. Templemore Manor was now a preceptory again, but serving a different deity. Its ownership always passed from Grand Master to Grand Master and is currently owned by financier Richard Vermont.

In the Great Hall, with its black and white chequered floor, walls covered in medieval tapestries and vaulted ceiling, the Grand Master of the Knights of the Dark Temple sat enthroned on the ornate carved chair, raised on a plush carpeted platform, looking down on the brotherhood. In direct contrast to the simple tunics and tabards of the Templars, Richard Vermont and his assembled knights wore evening dress which in no-one's imagination came 'off the peg', over which they wore tabards which were heavily encrusted with rubies and gold thread woven into the sigil, or seal, of Baphomet. Their ease with their opulent surroundings spoke of their individual wealth and collective power, and the entire assemblage appeared as if it would bankrupt a small country.

In front of the raised platform stood a marble altar adorned with a bejewelled, gold chalice; a gold statue of their beloved Baphomet; and a lethal, ceremonial dagger.

The Knights stood in a semi-circle around the altar awaiting the signal from their Grand Master that the ceremony should begin. He gave it, and the door to the great hall opened as if in response to the silent gesture. Two Knights entered, one each side of a blindfolded, naked man who stumbled along between them, leaning heavily on their guiding arms.

The initiation ceremony began.

The naked man fell prostrate before the altar and at the feet of the Grand Master, breathing heavily and hardly daring to move.

The Grand Master stood and, with slow, deliberate steps, he descended from the platform and stopped just inches from the prostate initiate.

"Who are you, and why do you come here?"

The naked man took a trembling breath. "I am nothing but a vessel and I come here to serve the Infernal Master and become a Knight of the Order."

The Grand Master did not respond for several minutes, allowing the heavy silence to settle around the gathering, building the atmosphere of anticipation.

Eventually, he spoke. "What is your name, and who am I?"

Another trembling breath from the initiate. "My name is Wormwood and you are The Grand Master, chosen by Baphomet."

The Grand Master took a step backwards and nodded to the two escort knights. They bent forwards and pulled the initiate to his feet, supporting him in front of their master. The Grand Master circled the naked man, collecting the ceremonial dagger from the altar as he passed. Once in front of the initiate again, he moved in close and pressed the dagger against the naked flesh over his heart, piercing his chest and smiling as the red stream began to flow down towards his abdomen.

"It is better for me to kill you now with this sacred blade, than you should betray this Order and your brother Knights. How say you? Shall you live or die by the sacred pact?"

"I shall live by the pact."

The Grand Master smiled with satisfaction, this was indeed a great prize, but a prize that had to know his place - only then would he prove useful. He also knew that, although an initiate now, this man would rise through their ranks to become his successor. But not yet.

He pressed the blade further into the man's flesh, drawing a gasp of pain. Then, with practiced ease, he drew the blade through skin and superficial tissue, creating the sigil of Baphomet in flesh, deep enough to make the initiate pass out as the blood flowed down his abdomen and his thighs. He nodded once again to the escort knights, who responded by allowing the initiate to fall to the floor in a naked, bleeding heap.

Richard Vermont, the Grand Master, picked up the gold chalice and bent over the unconscious man, allowing the freely-flowing blood to run in rivulets into the cup. Then, towering over him once more, he proceeded to make a cut in the palm of his own hand and held it over the chalice where his own blood flowed and mixed with that of the initiate. And in that moment he allowed the form of his master to become visible to the assembled knights, who collectively fell to their knees.

Richard Vermont's eyes became black holes that emitted a power so evil, none of the kneeling knights dare to look into them. All heads were bowed, in respect, in awe, and in fear. The demon stood before them in all his foul presence. Momentarily his bestial nature shimmered before them, before resuming the human form possessed by Richard Vermont, Chief Executive Officer of one of the Europe's largest banking institutions.

He raised the gory chalice to his lips and drank deep of the blood within. With another silent gesture he indicated to the escort knights to raise the initiate to his feet. They did so, rousing him into consciousness again, to stand before the demon, who had temporarily returned to the form of their Grand Master.

One of them grabbed the initiate's hair and yanked his head back, forcing his mouth open to receive the unholy sacrament. Vermont poured the remaining blood into the back of the man's throat, allowing him to choke violently as he clamped the man's mouth shut, forcing the gore down his throat. When the choking ceased, one of the escort knights removed the blindfold and the initiate opened his eyes; now, his black eyes mirrored those black holes in the face of the Richard Vermont. The invitation had been received and accepted as the Grand Master raised his hand and a bolt of something akin to lightning shot from his raised palm onto the chest of the initiate, burning the bloody sigil into a permanent brand, claiming him for his own. There was no return now for the junior Cabinet Minister.

There was a sudden sound of rushing wind, though the room remained still. It was the signal for the next part of their ritual; the summoning of the Demon Ark. They had been drawing it to them for several months, ever since they had gained access to the archives in Rome. As one, the Knights of the Dark Temple, in every preceptory, would be synchronising their ritual, drawing the Demon Ark from the depths of hell towards the surface of the earth where it would manifest in the place known as Megiddo. Already there had been random seismic activity as it came closer to the surface with every ritual. The demons were gathering, ready to leave the confines of the underworld and come into this world to claim it for their infernal master and all the denizens of hell.

CHAPTER FIVE:GETTING HIS HEAD STRAIGHT

Mike pulled his car to a slow halt outside The Cedars, the home and consulting room of Dr Paul Beckett, his counsellor, shrink, and friend - who just happened to be a vampire. Beckett's was a long story, better kept for another day, but right then Mike needed to make sense of his own rapidly disintegrating world.

In the space of what seemed too short a time, his life had been turned upside down as he had been catapulted from investigating what now seemed like routine paranormal phenomena, into becoming a demon hunter with blood on his hands and his name high on the demons' hit list. He had lost a friend and mentor in Dai Bricks; allowed his best friend to be possessed by a demon in an effort to save his life; his wife had been taken into hell by demons and he had followed to reclaim her. Now, when things should have been returning to some form of normality - if ever they could, and whatever that was - he had discovered that Jack had once again allowed the demon in, the same demon that he had believed that he had killed during his sojourn in hell. His head was spinning; he felt that he was losing control of everything and, that he had somehow been responsible for all that was rapidly becoming his own endless nightmare. And, on top of all that, it seemed as though there was to be another harsh call on him. He couldn't bring himself to return Josh Hammond's call, knowing he wasn't ready to deal with whatever else was coming his way until he had got his head straight.

Ben's first ever words on the subject were loud in his consciousness – *You have a choice, Mike. Run or fight.*

Personally, I recommend the first option. Right then, he wished he had chosen that door. Instead, he had walked through the other door into a world of demons and darkness that seemed to have chewed him up and spat him out. And he knew that he had changed, hardened, become something else, something that had a piece of the darkness in his own soul. He knew that Ben wasn't the one to find some order in the mess that was his mind right then, and for this reason he had turned his car towards Beckett.

Mike was unsurprised that Beckett opened his door before he had even reached for the doorbell. His friend's lean and handsome face, that would never age, was grave as his eyes drove through into Mike's subconscious, even before he greeted him.

He stood away from Mike, appraising him. "You look like hell. Unsurprising, as I see you've been there. Come on in, Mike. Let's talk. And, before you say it: no; no couch, no probing into your head, I've seen enough to know what's in there. Just come in and talk to me."

Mike felt some of the burden fall from him. He couldn't talk to Beth about all of this, she'd been through enough and that was part of his problem. Whatever he did from here on in affected them all, so he had to do it right, before anyone else paid the price. He didn't know if he could do it.

Sitting on Beckett's sofa in front of a blazing fire, Mike smiled; he was on the shrink's couch after all. It was just heavily disguised as a soul-warming piece of comfortable furniture.

Beckett read him and grinned back. "So sue me! You look in need of a drink, my friend. And before you say no, I'll drive you home in the morning. It's too long since I've seen your beautiful wife anyway." He was pouring a very large measure of single malt whisky into a crystal glass that defied Mike's attempts to guess at its age. He hoped he wouldn't drop it, he really felt that weak.

"You know I've seen your thoughts Mike, but if you

want to talk anyway, that's good too. Whatever you want, whenever you're ready; it's your dollar, as they say." He laughed his silky, deep laugh that could calm or seduce, whichever he felt like at the time. "Don't worry. No charge for a friend. It's my privilege to help you, and besides, I'd like you to have a reason to think twice if you are ever tempted to cut off my head."

The incongruity of this statement made Mike take a large swig of the whisky. He was sitting on the sofa of a vampire whilst searching for some kind of redemption. He remained silent for several minutes.

He put the whisky glass down onto the centuries-old table at the side of the sofa. "How do you do it, Beckett? Come to terms with what you are now, I mean. You were human not so long ago, and now you are a supernatural being that can only survive by drinking human blood. I know you don't kill or harm anyone, but there are those of your kind that do, and I know you make it your business to go after them, but how do you come to terms with your loss of humanity?"

Beckett raised an eyebrow. "Well, I didn't see that question coming. I'll refrain from doing the obvious in turning the question back at you. I guess it's a matter of acceptance. Unlike you I had no choice; it was taken out of my hands. You are wrestling with this because ultimately it was your decision to go down this road. I know that life, fate, or destiny - whatever you wish to call it - has put those circumstances in your path but you could have walked away and, deep down, you know that if you had done so, you wouldn't be sitting here right now."

"OK, no need to sugar-coat it! I didn't expect you to be so blunt, but you're right. I blame myself for all of this shit."

"And thereby hangs the problem. You aren't looking at the big picture nor at what you are actually doing; standing up to evil and doing your best to rid this world of it. Not exactly a run-of-the-mill occupation, however you look at it. But what's actually putting a bug up your arse is the fact that on some deep level you take satisfaction in killing the bastards. Am I right?"

"Lovecraft's Rules."

"I'm sorry?"

"Lovecraft's Rules – Ben's rules for dealing with the demons and staying alive to fight another day. Once the demon fully possesses a human at the deepest cellular level there is no coming back for that person - their soul has been plundered and no exorcism will restore their humanity – but, they were human once, someone's father, brother, mother or sister. And I stick the Crucifixion blade into them or cut off their heads and walk away with no regret and, yes, with some degree of satisfaction. Does that make me as much a monster as them? Because I feel tainted, Beckett, bloody well tainted. There's something dark in me that wasn't there before. I'm changed. And I'm scared."

Beckett kept his expression neutral as he waited for Mike to continue and when he didn't, Beckett leaned forwards, his hands crossed into his lap.

"You won't want to hear this, Mike, but you're wrong. Every single one of us has a piece of darkness inside us somewhere; it's what we do with it that makes us a monster or not. If you didn't have that inside you, we'd be having this conversation in a padded cell right now. It's that tiny piece of darkness that is your strength and your salvation. Without it you wouldn't be able to do what you do, and thank God that you can. These doubts are natural and in some way healthy. You are examining your inner being and questioning your killing instinct, but I'm afraid you need to accept that part of yourself. You have killed before, or been part of it, when you were in Afghanistan, but that had the badge of duty on it, making it easier to accept - cleaner somehow - and even then you didn't come out of it unscathed. But this life that you find yourself in now; it's no different, Mike. This world is at war. The demons and the monsters are out there and you are standing against them, you just don't fly an attack helicopter or wear a uniform now, that's all. Accept it, or prepare yourself for a serious stay in a psyche ward."

Mike took a deep breath. "It's not that simple though, is it? There's Beth and Adain, Jack and Ben, you … and there was Dai. Would he be dead now if it hadn't been for me killing Astaroth? That's down to me."

"I'm not sure that's fair on Dai or you. Dai was a part of this fight before you climbed aboard. He knew the risks and still he did what he did. And Beth? You think she doesn't know what the risks are? And yet she still stands behind you, accepting those risks because if no-one fights this fight, we're all screwed. As for Adain, she's in the safest place I can think of. Though you must know that when she's older and her abilities are fully developed she'll be back here fighting alongside you."

Mike fell silent and picked up his glass, examining the sparkle of the firelight in the exquisitely cut crystal, tilting it until the amber light of the whisky inside was also filled with the reflection of the flames.

Beckett continued. "Not all monsters are ugly or misshapen beasts with horns, Mike. You know that. Most of them that are already here are handsome, beguiling devils that capture our imaginations and seduce us into apathy. It's harder to stick that blade into a handsome or beautiful face than that of sickeningly hideous monster. But remember that's what they are, deep down in their stolen bodies: monsters. You're not the monster, Mike, you're the white knight. Yes, you have changed, and it's that change that is going to make you live to fight another day, and we need that. The hero of the story always lives to fight another day."

Mike had no words; he simply swallowed the whisky in one gulp and leaned back into the sofa. Eventually he spoke, his voice weary and low.

"A friend once told me I had a choice, run or fight. In

my arrogance I chose to stand up to these evil bastards, without a thought for Beth or Adain, or any of the others that I care for. I was going to be the hero, the white knight, as you put it. But I've seen what that arrogance has brought. First Jack, then Beth - who next? It's bigger than me; bigger than all of us. It's too much, too bloody much, and I'm going to walk away and take Beth and Adain with me, far away, then no-one else will pay the price for my pig-headed arrogance."

Beckett searched his friend's eyes, his mind, and his soul, sensing and feeling the exhaustion and the pain in the slow acceptance, and he did the only thing he could do to help him; he used his vampire powers, piercing his gaze and reaching deep into his consciousness and sending him to sleep.

He took the glass from Mike's loosened grip and covered him with the exquisite throw from the back of his own Queen Anne chair. He turned the lights down low and closed the door quietly behind him. Mike would sleep, untroubled by his raging thoughts, until morning when acceptance would have had a chance to creep in and overcome the doubts. He let his vampire sight travel to Beth, seeing her sound asleep, exhausted too. He would watch over them both and call her as soon as she woke to let her know that Mike was all right and would be home as soon as he woke. His hypnotic voice would soothe her and calm any anxiety, even from a distance.

His regret lay in the knowledge that, despite his reassurances to Mike, something was coming that would take him to the brink and back again. He firmly hoped that the 'back again' part of that hope would be fulfilled.

CHAPTER SIX: BLOODY BIBLICAL

GCHQ, CHELTENHAM

A young, blonde woman looked up and signalled the General, standing in the centre of the room.

"Sir, we've picked up some chatter between NASA and the International Space Station. I think you should hear it. Keyword is Megiddo."

She relinquished her headset and he put the earpiece against his ear. She replayed the recording.

The voice of Commander Rod Tyler was clear. "NASA, are you seeing this? The video file is downloading to you now. It's over the Plain of Jezreel according to sat info, in the area of Megiddo. Can you see this? What the hell is it? We can't identify."

The reply was equally clear and equally intriguing. "Roger that, ISS, we have the file. We don't have an answer as yet but stay on coms, I'll get back to you."

"Roger that, NASA."

Static followed for several seconds then NASA broke its silence. "Commander Tyler, this is NASA Flight Control Room 1, CAPCOM, go to black coms. Now."

"Roger that NASA." Then the line went dead.

General Ryan nodded at her. "Good work. Send the file directly to my desk. And keep this on highest clearance until further notice. The highest, understand?"

She nodded and returned to her listening post, on alert for further broadcasts, tuned into the frequency that had caused the initial hit, but knowing that if NASA and the space station had gone dark there would be little else to hear.

The General turned on his heel, already speaking into his cell, his voice low and outwardly calm but the frown on his brow told a different story. He had a sudden desire for retirement; he had a feeling this was the one that would get messy. To the voice on the other end of the call he said, "I'm initiating Protocol 218. Who do we have out in Haifa? I want them on the line in less than five minutes."

CIA HEADQUARTERS, LANGLEY, VIRGINIA

"Sir, this was relayed from our station in Jordan. You should hear it."

The Chief of Staff listened intently to the recording then nodded at the young agent. "Send it to me and then delete it."

"Sir?"

"Delete it. As in: remove it, wipe it, how else do you want me to say it? Am I clear?"

"Sir."

The Chief of Staff stood for a moment, contemplating his next move, and as he did so, his eyes flickered into their more natural colour. Black.

*

Mike's phone rang, bringing him out of the deep sleep that Beckett had induced in him. His eyes were blurred and for a second or two he was totally disorientated, then, as he took in his surroundings, Beckett entered bearing a steaming mug of coffee. Mike acknowledged him with a brief nod and hit the accept button on the call. He couldn't put Josh Hammond off any longer. Beckett pointed to the door, querying Mike's desire for privacy. Mike shook his head, so Beckett sat in the Queen Anne armchair that he had occupied the night before, crossed his legs and waited in silence.

Mike sipped the hot coffee, making a face as it burned the back of his throat. He was awake now, right enough.

"Josh. It's still not a good time, mate."

"Mike, don't cut me off again! You need to listen!"

Mike closed his eyes as if to blot out what was probably coming next, then, realising that Josh would just keep on phoning him until he took his call, said. "OK Josh, I'm all ears. Go."

"I've just come from the dig in Megiddo. Well, 'come from' isn't really how it was; more like evicted from. Something is happening there, something wrong. Everything has been pear-shaped for weeks now; local storms - big storms, flies, bloody swarms of flies; people have been falling sick for no apparent reason; and there has even been the odd minor seismic tremor. Bloody biblical, Mike. Then suddenly the military arrives and we're all out of there faster than you can say 'dig'."

Mike was silent for a moment. "And that's my problem, why?"

"Because of something an old friend of mine told me. He said something was coming to the surface - God alone knows where from, but something is coming - something dark. That's all he said at first, then, as things got worse he told me to look at an old scroll. Maddie translated it, well, what was left of it; it hasn't aged well. It spoke of The Demon Ark. Now, call me reactionary if you like, but that doesn't sound good in anyone's language. And, given your help in the past with the other 'Ark' and with what this thing is called, well, I thought you'd be interested."

Thoughts and memories tumbled around Mike's head until rational thought took over. "Who exactly is this old friend of yours, Josh? Is he a reliable source?"

"Rabbi Eli Rosenburg. I've known him for years, Mike. I trust him. I trust him and his information and I'm worried about him. He's missing; no-one has seen or spoken to him for a few days and it's not like him to just take off."

"Josh, I ... I'd like to help, really I would, but, you're too late. I've shut up shop. I'm out of the game. And in any case, if, as you say, no-one is allowed on the site, I don't see how I can be of any help."

"I thought you'd come." Josh said in a muted voice. "I thought after last time, you'd come."

Mike sighed, he could sense the agitation and the disappointment in his friend's voice, but what could he realistically do, even if he was willing? And what, if anything, was happening there? And if there was something, what did it have to do with anything he would want to get involved in? But, there was the little niggle that said anything called The Demon Ark was probably something that shouldn't see the light of day. He sighed again.

"I'm sorry Josh."

"Mike, I wouldn't be asking you unless I thought it was a big deal, given the way things have been happening and Eli disappearing at the same time. All I have is what Eli told me and the scroll; he was going to fill me in more after Maddie had translated it and I'd read it. When he said it was coming to the surface, that's literally what he meant. There's a huge object underneath the dig site that is throwing back a magnetic field picked up by geophysics and, from what I can gather, the distance between it and the surface is getting smaller - slowly, but daily. At the rate it's rising they estimate a week before it breaks through the ground. Mike, there is a military and science presence everywhere, but the advantage of living out here is getting to know the right people. I think I can get us access."

Mike frowned, "I'll see what I can find out for you, maybe come up with some more information, but that's it. I'm sorry, I can't help you this time."

Beckett had been listening to the conversation, his vampire hearing allowing him to listen to both sides.

"Interesting," he said.

Mike scowled, "What is?"

Beckett nodded. "I thought you were made of stronger stuff. I understood why you felt that way last night but I thought after a deep sleep you might feel differently. I'm surprised, that's all."

"So you think I should stay in the game and put everyone around me in the firing line? That Jack's present situation, which we all know is a direct result of my actions, isn't enough? I told Josh I'd try and help by getting him some more information and I will. But that's it. Do you know anything about this 'Demon Ark'?"

Beckett should his head. "No, but I'll ask around."

Mike smiled. Beckett's contacts among the ancient vampires understated his 'asking around'. "I'd be grateful. Josh Hammond isn't given to knee-jerk reactions - conspiracy theories, yes, but in my experience his instincts are usually sound. He arched his aching back and downed the rest of the coffee. "Thanks for the ear, Beckett. And the coffee; I'll never know how a vampire can make such good coffee! And I'm guessing you already spoke to Beth?"

Beckett nodded. "Yes and you're welcome. And before my 'transformation' I drank so much coffee it was either get really good at brewing it or spend a fortune in coffee shops. Now, as much as I would love to spend the morning with you, you should get your arse off my sofa and go home. Glad to be of service. I'll call you if I get to know anything about this 'Demon Ark'. I'll start with Mihai."

Mihai was one of the ancient vampires classed as one of the good guys. Mike knew of him only what Beckett had told him, but it was enough to satisfy him that if anything came back from him, MIke could rely on it. He stood up and arched his back again and headed for the door as his phone rang again. He put it to his ear and waved his goodbye to Beckett.

"Morning, wife!" he said to Beth. "I'm sorry, love, I had a rough time with Jack and Ben and needed to clear my head of a few things. Beckett put me to bloody sleep. He does that you know." He gave a half-hearted laugh in an effort to defuse the anxiety that he knew Beth was feeling.

"It's okay, Mike." Her voice was distant, dreamy even. She put her fingers to her temple, gently rubbing, trying to get rid of the bad headache she'd had all night. "I was out for the count as well. Beckett called me early so I wouldn't worry. Jack called too." She waited for his reaction.

"I guess he told you we had a difference of opinion, then."

"If that's what you'd like to call it," she replied in her still-distant voice. "He told me what had happened. It was his decision, Mike, and we weren't here, *you* weren't here. If you're honest, you'd made the same decision for him once and it's probably because you weren't here that you feel guilty and it's turned to anger. You should go to him, Mike."

Mike swallowed emotion. "I've just left one shrink, I'll have you know. Beckett may not like competition." He paused, aware that his feeble attempt to distract her had failed miserably. "I love you, wife. Beth … are you okay? You sound … I don't know … far away."

"I'm fine, still tired I guess and I've a bit of a headache. In fact I'm thinking of going back to bed, so go over to Ben and Jack's place and listen to Jack before you go off on one again. Or I may have to impose sanctions!"

He laughed then, really laughed, and felt the grapefruit-sized lump in his chest begin to disperse. He'd been an asshole to Jack and he knew it, but Beth had brought a perspective to his emotions that had lifted the darkness that had descended on him way before the Jack issue. "I'll be home as soon I've put things right with Jack. If you're sure?"

"I told you, I'm going to take some paracetamol and go back to bed."

Mike tried to dismiss Josh's call, determined not to get involved. This was the beginning of the end for him; no more putting loved ones in danger for the sake of - what? His own misguided sense of duty? But it didn't take long before the maggot that had been planted by Josh began to wriggle. What was the Demon Ark and why did he have an inbuilt conviction that, whatever it was, it wasn't going to end well? Whatever, he wasn't going to get involved.

CHAPTER SEVEN: REMEMBER ME NOW?

Mike was deep in thought as he took the road out of Abergavenny leading to Skenfrith, where he hoped to make his peace with Jack, and come to some kind of peace about the fact that his best friend was again being kept alive by a demon possessing his body. Surely there was another solution? A heart attack was one thing, but people got over that - even the big ones that were meant to pull the plug permanently. He got it; Jack didn't want to die. Well, he didn't want that either, but had they been too premature in allowing Bazaliel back from hell and into Jack's body? He would have to have a long talk with Ben; they would look for an alternative solution together.

As if to match his returning dark thoughts, the sky became overcast, darkening rapidly, and then, from nowhere, the heavens opened and a deluge of rain came down in stair rods, overpowering his windscreen wipers and obliterating the road ahead from his vision. He swore, stepped onto the brake and guided the car to a halt at the side of the road. The sky turned to midnight.

He pulled his phone from his pocket to call Beth; there was no signal. Then his phone died completely. He swore. And the engine died as a thick black cloud descended over the car.

"Bollocks," he said, with feeling.

"Charming."

Mike spun around. "Who the hell …?"

In the darkness of Mike's car, the dark skin, hair and clothing of the man in the rear seat faded into the general background, but the eyes were bright and penetrating. Mike could feel the other's presence in his head. He turned and tried to open the door just as the lock engaged.

His fury was uppermost now. "Who the hell are you? Get out of my car!" Then the rationale of the situation hit him. It was a demon in his car and, apparently, in control of it. Thoughts of Jack's 'accident' rose to the surface.

"Wrong department, Michael. I'm from the other place. And you need to listen carefully to me. Do I have your complete attention? Or do I have to take you someplace where you will have no alternative but to listen to me?"

Mike's breathing steadied; he still felt threatened but the threat didn't seem immediate.

"Whoever you are, and wherever you're from, release my car now and get the hell away from me."

The man on the back seat sighed. "OK, we'll do it your way."

In an instant, Mike's consciousness was in a whole other place. He was standing on nothing that appeared solid and was surrounded by a blinding light that was accompanied by a high-pitched whine that reached into the deepest recesses of his entire being and then some. He closed his eyes against the burning light and tried to shut the noise out of his brain. Neither action worked. He opened his eyes again to a tall, coloured man who could have had a career as a Hollywood star. His urbane manner annoyed the hell out of Mike who simply wanted to punch him in the face. He refrained because, deep down, he knew that such a course of action would be futile. From his surroundings he knew that he was in the hands of a supernatural being, although the fact that the eyes were bright and clear, and not black holes in the face, made him think twice about his demon assumption.

"Okay, you have my attention. Now say your piece and sod off!"

"So much anger. To be expected I suppose. You have changed somewhat since our last encounter, Michael. You were more … malleable … back then."

Mike frowned and stared harder into the man's eyes.

There was a glimmer of recognition but nothing on which to pin it.

"Who *are* you? Where do I know you from?"

"I'm hurt! I thought you would have no problem remembering me. Perhaps I can make this easier." With no warning he raised his hand and placed two fingers in the centre of Mike's forehead.

The high-pitched whining stopped, leaving a sharp pain in the centre of his head that was fading rapidly. He felt himself relax one notch from several thousand. And then he was right in the middle of a memory that had been tucked away in such a deep, dark recess of his mind, that even Beckett had trouble locating it when he first treated Mike for the PTSD.

He felt as if he was flying, then floating, and in a state of confusion. From his elevated position, he was looking down on the mangled wreck of his helicopter. Sirens were blaring and people were running from all directions. It was hot - blazing hot – and, outside the military base there was nothing but desert. He felt the relentless grip of fear that he had experienced back then, as he descended lower and watched as the medics struggled frantically to resuscitate his dead body.

"Oh, God," he groaned as recognition slapped him squarely across the face.

The scene appeared to shimmer and take another form. This time he was in a similar situation to that in which he now found himself, except all was silent; too silent. Then suddenly the man from the car was standing in front of him, all smiles and calm authority. A far cry from the suave and none-too-patient being that stood beside him now. And he knew who he was dealing with.

On this recognition, he found himself back in the present.

"Remember me now?"

Mike nodded, his eyes wide, his mind racing for the finish line. This was it then; he was dead somehow. Had he

41

crashed his car and died so suddenly he had no recollection of it? Confusion was rapidly giving way to something else, something darker.

"Yes, I recognise you, though I'm damned if I remember your name."

"That's just it, Michael, you're not damned. Not yet, anyway, although that may change. But it's come to our notice that you are about to break our agreement. And that's not very nice, now is it? After all, we gave you back your life and you agreed to do something in return, but we hear that you are about to walk away from that. Mission unaccomplished. Oh, I know you've made a start, but now the heat is on you think you can renege on our deal? I'm afraid it doesn't work like that. There would be consequences you see. The order of things would be out of sync, as it were. Oh, I know you have free will, and you have; and if you choose to walk away then, like dominoes falling, the consequences will take a different direction. That's all. But I think it only fair that you should see the big picture before you decide to change the course of your life. *And the lives of others.*"

The last sentence was given maximum emphasis, ensuring its impact on Mike's mind.

He sucked in his breath. "What do you mean by that? If I walk away, and I'm seriously considering it, it's *because* of the effect my actions are already having on others; others that I love."

"Of course, and that is natural; a human response. But have you considered that the die is already cast? That, even if you walk away, the demons will still hunt you and your loved ones? They don't forget and they don't forgive. The deed, as they say, is done. So, walk away, by all means, but you will walk away forever looking over your shoulder."

"And if I don't? Walk away, I mean. And, while we are on the subject of reneging on our deal, I don't recall any deal involving demons and other filth from the pit. I remember the bit about helping trapped spirits, investigating the paranormal to help the living and the dead; I think the demon clause must have been added afterwards. And you still haven't told me your name!"

The man made an impatient gesture and there was a rustling sound and a huge and dark shadow from behind him spread outwards. A wing-shaped shadow.

Mike gave a wry smile. "Oh, I see - an angel. I heard that some of you lot were sons-of-bitches!"

The angel drew himself up to his full height, which made Mike gasp. "Have a care with your tongue! I will have respect!"

Mike's bridges were well and truly burned now and events of the previous days lit the touch-paper as he allowed himself full rein of his emotions. "Respect? Respect has to be earned where I come from, and you can show yourself to me as tall as the Eiffel Tower as often as you like, it will make no difference. And I think I've earned a little respect too, you bastard. Now if there's nothing else, I'd be grateful if you put me back where you found me. If I'm not dead, that is."

"Be assured, Michael, that if I were to allow my true presence to become accessible to your senses, your mind would be lost in a feeble heartbeat. I am giving you a chance to do the right thing by standing and facing the demons. They are about to be given the opportunity of universal free passes out of hell and into your world, and if you can walk away from that, then you don't deserve what little comfort you would get in your short-lived peace. For short-lived it will be – for all. There's a darkness rising that is so ancient it is beyond imagination, and if you can't stop it, your world will change forever."

Mike gave his all in the attempt at looking and sounding unimpressed, though the opposite was true.

"No pressure there, then. Okay, so, what if I stay? How can I take on the entire population of hell? You said it yourself; I am only human. How about a bit of help down there? It doesn't look as though there is much going on *here*? Or is it beneath you? And why me? What's so special about me?"

The angel threw his head back and laughed. "Oh Michael, does your arrogance know no bounds? You're not special, you were convenient, that's all, and you agreed to it - a long time ago. "

Fire flared then in his eyes, which he quelled with obvious difficulty. It wasn't a difficult assumption that Mike wasn't his favourite human right then. He sighed.

"Angels just don't get the respect we had in the old days; people believed in us and were grateful for our help. As for helping you, well, I'm here aren't I?"

Mike was on a roll. "I'm guessing the store is bare in the respect department because, from what I've seen, some of you are assholes, and on second thoughts I don't need your help. I have what I need in that way down there after all; one of yours that you chose to kick out of here. He's got more angel in him, ironically, now that he actually has none, than any of you lot put together."

"You speak of Seraquel. You would do well to not put too much trust in him. He is a rebel with a cause. His own cause. So be it! I have warned you as was my duty, and now you must return to fight the fight that you agreed to - and you did agree to it - and one day you will remember that or walk away from your destiny; either way your fate with the demons is sealed. How you deal with that is up to you. If you decide to stay, you will find the help you need when you need it, even though you might think you don't. That's just your arrogance. The time is drawing near when that decision must be made. As for my name; you can ask your friend, I am certain he will know it."

He made a sudden motion and put two fingers on Mike's forehead again.

Darkness. Falling. Nausea. And sudden and stark awareness of his surroundings; sitting in his car at the side of the road.

He took a deep breath and turned the key in the

ignition. The engine roared into life and the car was suddenly filled with the light of mid-morning. He threw the car into gear and moved off towards Skenfrith - where his destiny awaited him, one way or the other.

The angel, on the other hand, was pissed. He couldn't trust the human that they were pinning their hopes on; maybe he needed some insurance, some form of leverage. It meant going off-programme and going it alone, but he considered the risk worth it.

The angel found Beth about to leave for Ben and Jack's house. She looked fragile and more than weary; there was an embryonic something going on in her head. He felt a stirring of compassion, unusual in him, and decided on his next course of action. He needed leverage but there was no need for torment and what he could see brewing was best handled away from there, in the initial stages.

He materialised in front of her, making her start.

"Hello, Beth."

CHAPTER EIGHT: THERE'S A TEMPLE IN MEGIDDO?

Richard Vermont had dismissed the main gathering, taking time with his newest initiate, enough to reassure him and confirm in him that he was special - which indeed he was, because now The Grand Master had access to the highest echelons of government and able to bypass secretaries and advisors. He allowed himself a brief but contented smile.

Only his Seneschal, William Marshall, remained. Named after his ancestor, an Earl of Pembroke, Marshall had his eye on the Grand Master's throne. Right then, he knew where his allegiance should lie, but he knew he was no match for Vermont, yet. That day would come.

Richard took a silk handkerchief from his pocket and wiped away a remaining smear of blood from the corner of his mouth. He put a hand on the Seneschal's shoulder.

"It is time for us to leave, William. Our duty now lies in Megiddo. We must be there to provide the energy for the Demon Ark to complete its journey into our world and to welcome our Master when he arrives. You have done well, my friend, and you shall be rewarded. I had the ear of the Prime Minister's secretary yesterday. It appears that your family title may soon be restored to you. Your family lands and property won't be a problem, they too will return to you."

"I'm gratified, Grand Master. Thank you. But I am simply happy to be of service to you. Always."

Richard Vermont eyed him carefully and then allowed his naturally urbane expression to become wreathed in smiles. "The Demon Ark will surface in a week, when the dark energy is at its height. But we will leave in the morning to make preparations in the Megiddo Temple."

A shadow played around the Seneschal's eyes. "There is a temple in Megiddo?"

"Of course, it is one of the most potent temples on this earth - or rather, under this earth. Beneath the ruins that have been the centre of archaeological interest for many years it has remained, undiscovered and protected. We must open it once again. I have every expectation that, as it has remained untouched for centuries, it will be intact when we open it again. We have the manpower to make it happen and meanwhile the local officialdom has evicted the archaeologists from the site and is protecting it with their military. The signs are there, William; The Dark Ark will soon become a part of this world again and then the powers of darkness will be restored to their former dominion, and the demons will once again walk the earth with impunity and power. Our time has come, Seneschal."

"That will be a great day, Grand Master, and to know we have assisted in the resurrection of the demons is satisfactory. Is there anything I can do to assist you further?"

Vermont shook his head. "No. Leave me now; I wish to commune with the Master alone."

The Seneschal bowed his head and left the room, but remained just outside in the corridor to listen and watch, unwilling to miss anything.

The Grand Master returned to the marble altar and once again lifted the ceremonial dagger to his palm and re-opened the healing cut made earlier. He lifted his closed fist on high and allowed the blood to flow into a small copper bowl. To this he added several herbs and a black powder. He lifted a lit candle from its gold candlestick and touched the ingredients in the bowl with the flame. At once there was a foul smell permeating the air and thick pungent smoke surrounded him in a dark cloud. For a moment the cloud circled above him before settling above the altar.

Burning red eyes pierced the cloud and looked out

from the centre. The temperature of room fell suddenly and then a guttural voice spoke; a voice that seemed to emanate from every corner, crevice and curtain.

"You have served me well, our numbers are swelling and we have people in the right places for when the moment comes and people will look to their governments for answers and protection, but they will already be ours. You should have caution, however: there is one that envies you and seeks to replace you when the opportunity arises."

Richard Vermont appeared to freeze and then slowly, very slowly, he turned to the open door. His eyes closed and when he opened them again they were black holes in his face. He sniffed the air, and then his mouth twisted into a cruel smile which vanished as soon as it had appeared. William Marshall felt a chill run through him and turned tail and left in a hurry. The voice continued.

"There is one preparing to thwart our efforts. It would be well if he was prevented from doing so."

A heavy silence descended as the Grand Master communed in silence with the demon. After several minutes he rose from the altar and turned off the lights in the Great Hall. Foul-smelling smoke continued to curl up from the incense burner and the sulphurous candles were left to burn out to their sockets. Richard Vermont had been given a task which was time-sensitive; the Demon Ark would see the light of day in about a week. He would be on a plane with his Seneschal to Tel Aviv the following morning where he would transfer to a private jet which would take him on to the small airstrip at Megiddo itself. Israeli officials that had been well paid would ensure the transfer was without issue. But there was a maggot of doubt in his head now. Who was the one who sought to take his place? He had sensed the presence of William Marshall near the door, listening, but was that enough to damn him? He probably wouldn't take the chance. There would be others to step into the Seneschal's shoes. It would be better to strike first without proof than to put himself in danger. Megiddo would be a better place to dispose of him.

CHAPTER NINE: SANCTIMONIOUS BULLSHIT AND WINGS

Mike was rattled. The angel encounter had left him wanting to lash out at someone as long-buried memories had begun to filter into his consciousness. He recalled his death and the greeting as he entered the afterlife; the one who had greeted him then had just vacated the back seat of his car. He heard the distant voice that had offered him a return to life with a gift; the gift of seeing spirits that were bound to the earth and how he could help them pass over to the afterlife. That had sounded good, noble even. Then as his memory expanded to include a darker suggestion - the suggestion that some spirits were just pure evil, and that he may encounter them as his experiences progressed - he cursed aloud.

It had been veiled as a faint suggestion and he had agreed to it. The terms were put in such a way that loose interpretation was inevitable. But he *had* agreed. If it had been suggested that he would become a demon hunter and descend into hell, probably on more than one occasion, his agreement may have held some provisos. Sneaky bastards.

There was no turning back now; too many people had been hurt and he wanted payback. His last encounter with demons had opened up something dark inside him, but he realised that it was this very darkness that would see him through. One thing was certain; there was no way that Beth was going to become involved on the front line. No way. Despite her insistence, he would walk away from it all before he would allow that, and he knew she wouldn't want that either. He knew he would have a fight on his hands, but he also knew that it was one he would win. He wasn't about to back down. He was a demon hunter now, and inexperienced he may be but that would change - he just didn't know how rapidly and with what necessity.

The torrential rain followed him to Ben's place and, even though he ran the fifty yards from the car to the front door, he was soaked through. Glad of the fire blazing in the hearth he stripped off his soaking clothes and dried off in front of the flames, picking up an old dressing gown of Ben's that was way too big for him, wrapping it around him and fastening it with the old cord belt; Jack's offer of something more 'Jack' didn't look as though it would warm a flea.

Ben passed him one of his steaming coffee mugs and Jack poured him a healthy measure of his best scotch.

Mike took a swallow of both before meeting Jack's eyes. "I'm sorry. I didn't mean to be a jerk, it's just …"

Jack interrupted him with his characteristic grin. "Just that you're a jerk. I know. But it's what makes us love you. Jerk."

Mike allowed himself the first real smile for what seemed like an eternity. "Yeah. I'm a jerk. Seriously … are you OK?"

"As okay as possible with a demon wrapped around my soul. Look, Mike, I know you're worried but you know what? There's more to it than just staying alive. I was aware of the bells and whistles and general chaos when the old ticker stopped and aware of the most god awful pain. I thought; here we go again. Maybe this time I'll go for good. Then there was this voice in my head. Bazaliel, saying you had taken off his head but he had been too quick for you, and he was there in my head saying he could keep me alive, like before, but now he had no demon body to go back to. That if I evicted him he would be good and dead, the real thing, his soul damned to the darkest regions forever. But he was different, or he seemed different; he said he would prefer to stay here and help you. Well, I'll help you through him, though I still don't know how it will work. But, you know, inside information … that sort of thing. I can hear him when I want to, Mike, and when I don't, I can shut him out. All I do know is that without him, I'm a goner. And if I can turn it around to something good, something useful, then that has to be good, yeah?"

Mike turned his eyes to Ben, who had remained unnervingly silent throughout. He gave nothing away, so Mike returned his attention to Jack.

"And you're OK with all that?"

Jack nodded. "Yeah, yeah, I think I am. It feels weird sometimes, but I'm getting used to it. And I've got his seal burned into my arm so deep, only amputation will get rid of it. He agreed to that."

Mike sighed and slowly nodded his head. "Then I guess I'll get used to it too. I mean, you're still you, right? No demonic tendencies? No black eyes?"

If he had any doubts about that they vanished as Jack turned on his usual sassy charm. "Well, apart from a deep-seated need to be by an open fire and a strong desire to spit pea soup, I think I'm still me."

Peace made, Mike allowed a frown to cloud his forehead. "I picked up a hitchhiker on the way over. Bastard just appeared on my back seat. One of your lot," he directed at Ben. "All sanctimonious bullshit and wings. Wouldn't give me his name; very precious about that he was. It seems they got wind of the fact I was considering a change of occupation, and they didn't like it. Apparently I agreed to all this when I met him last, back when I died, though the contract seemed very open to interpretation if you ask me. Basically he said that if I walked away there would be consequences and if I stayed on the job there would be consequences, so I'm stuffed either way and unless I can stop the demons so is everyone else. If I hadn't seen the wings I'd have him pinned as a demon. And I'm beginning to think there's not a whole lot of difference sometimes. No offence Ben, but I can see why you left the club."

"He wouldn't give you his name?" asked Ben.

Mike grimaced and shook his head.

"What did he look like?" Ben quizzed.

"Denzel Washington on steroids."

Ben frowned, the reference going over his head. Jack laughed at him and explained.

"African American, handsome beyond belief, ripped, and Hollywood superstar written on every pore. Quite fancied him at one point."

Ben nodded his recognition. "Sebastian," he said. "Sebastian is a gateway angel, one of the meet and greet team, which is why you remember him, though he's got ambitions for higher things, no pun intended. He's an asshole."

"That's the one!" Mike agreed. "I had an overwhelming urge to knock his perfect teeth down his angelic throat."

"Yep, he tends to evoke that reaction, though I don't recommend it; he has all the angelic powers of his rank and he'd kick your arse into next week. What his business is down here I have no idea but you can guarantee one thing; that whatever it is, it's in his own interest. Did he say anything else?"

"Not directly, but he hinted at knowing about my phone call from Josh Hammond. Josh has got his boxers in a knot about something happening near the dig he was working on in Megiddo. Apparently all the archaeologists have been given their marching orders and its now under Israeli military control. Josh has a scroll in his possession, which may or may not relate, about something he calls the Demon Ark. He said it was rising, whatever that means, and it would probably only be a week or so before it broke through the ground. All sounds a bit muddled to me."

Ben's face paled at the mention of Israeli military and, on hearing 'the Demon Ark', his expression became grave.

"The Demon Ark?" he demanded. "Are you sure?"

Mike nodded. "Positive. You know about it?"

Ben was already pulling the rug away from the trapdoor that led to his cellar and tunnel, where his most extensive arcane library and Mike's weapon store was housed.

"Come with me. I know about it in theory and it's a theory I hoped would never be tested." He disappeared down the stone steps, flicking lights on as he went, Mike and Jack in his wake.

At the bottom of the steps Ben halted in front of an iron door.

Mike raised an eyebrow. "This is new."

Ben was unlocking the iron padlock that held it closed. "Yeah, iron, it keeps demons out. I ordered it a week ago from an artisan blacksmith and it was delivered and installed this morning."

"Don't tell me - you built him a bike."

"I build bikes for a lot of guys, Mike. Come on."

In the cellar, he strode over to a bookcase with glass doors. He flung them open and selected a heavy volume of obvious antiquity, handling it with appropriate care. He placed it with almost reverence onto Mike's desk and flicked on the reading lamp.

After leafing through its pages he finally stepped away from the desk. "Here, look. I'll translate, it's Enochian, the language of the angels, and perhaps it's better not to ask where I obtained it."

Mike peered at the text, which he didn't recognise, frowning characteristically. His eyes fixed on the faded drawing in the centre of the page. It looked like a black version of the Ark of the Covenant and the entire drawing had a sinister quality to it.

"The Ark of the Covenant?" he asked.

Ben shook his head. "No, Mike, that is the Demon Ark. And if that's what they are digging up out there I can see why Heaven is twitchy, and why there seems to be an increase in demon activity, and why assholes like Sebastian are moving to cash in one way or another."

Mike didn't speak, his querying glance was enough. Ben placed his finger on the text.

Ben continued, "The Demon Ark is prophesied to rise

from hell in advance of what John of Patmos wrote about in Revelations, however much it is clouded in metaphor."

Mike understood immediately. "The end of the world?"

"As we know it," Ben replied. "Academics and theologians differ in their opinions but whatever the outcome, it's not good news. Not the end of the world as such, or maybe not even the apocalypse, but if the Demon Ark appears in our world and is allowed to activate then it might as well be."

Mike made a gesture to Ben for him to explain.

He obliged. "If the Demon Ark is activated, then every portal to hell will open and every demon in the pit will have a free pass to this world. *Every* demon."

CHAPTER TEN: EVERY DEMON

Sebastian stood in the doorway of the bedroom. His greeting startled Beth. She gasped. "Who are you? How did you get in here?"

Then, as immediately as her words were from her lips, her mind had grasped the situation; not getting it quite right, but close enough. "Get away from me, Demon!" She began the opening words of exorcism. "Exorcizamus te, omnis immundus spiritus, omnis satanica potestas, omnis incursio infernalis adversarii, omnis legio, omnis congregatio et secta diabolica…" (We exorcise you, every impure spirit, every satanic power, every incursion of the infernal adversary, every legion, every congregation and diabolical sect …)

Sebastian grinned at her and then allowed himself to laugh aloud as her puzzled expression turned to obvious fear.

"Now that is no way to treat a guest, Beth. And while I commend your effort, it is wasted. I am not a demon. And no," he said, reading her, "I am no ghost or wandering spirit. Try again. Here's a clue." He allowed his true form, although not his true size, to manifest, including the huge wing-span.

Beth's face remained impassive as she acknowledged him. "An angel? What do you want from me?"

"Excellent, straight to the point. Actually, nothing; it would be more accurate to ask what do *you* want from *me*. Your husband is about to embark on something that has a very good chance of killing him - and you, mainly because he will be distracted by the fact that you are in danger. He can't afford to be distracted. So, if you want to protect your husband, you will come with me where you will be safe."

Beth was backing away, "I'm not going anywhere with you. Now, get out."

Sebastian sighed, right in front of her, in her face again. "Oh well, I tried to do this the easy way, but I can do it your way. So like your bloody husband."

He raised his hand and touched Beth on the forehead before she could blink. She fell into his arms and he remained still for a moment, contemplating what he had sensed when he touched her head. He touched her again and looked into her mind; what he saw there alarmed him before he disappeared with her.

*

In Ben's cellar, Mike was silent and white-faced. "*Every* demon?"

"Yes," Ben said. "Every single one of them, from the lowest, slimiest, slithering worm to the big guns, including Morning Star."

"Morning Star? You mean Lucifer? Satan? The Devil?"

"Those are some of the names that have been given to him over time, but his name is Morning Star. If the Demon Ark is activated, then it's game over for humanity."

Jack interrupted, "What do you mean 'activated'?"

"My next question," said Mike.

Ben pulled out his tobacco pouch and began rolling a cigarette, a sign that all was not well in his head. "I don't know much more than that, but I will. My Enochian is a bit rusty, so it's going to take me a while, so leave me to it and don't disturb me."

As if to emphasize his point he turned away from them and began leafing through the book once again.

Mike inclined his head to Jack, indicating the steps, and headed up into the kitchen. They went up in silence.

Once in the kitchen, Mike turned on Jack. "*You see?*

You see what crap I'm into, what crap I'm bringing down on you all?"

By way of reply Jack just looked helpless, something that unsettled Mike even further. He grabbed his phone and dialled his home number. The answerphone kicked in; Beth was obviously on her way over there. Once again, thoughts of taking her as far away as he could played with his mind, in between hearing Sebastian's voice telling him that basically he was damned if he did and damned if he didn't, and so was everyone else. The die was cast. The only way out of it was to fight his way out and take as many demons with him that he could, kill, slaughter or maim. He felt a burning inside of him, something smouldering that would take very little to ignite.

Ignition came sooner than expected.

There was a sound of a distant rushing wind and before he could say 'angel', Sebastian stood in front of them. Jack made a rush towards him and Sebastian's raised hand sent him flying across the room into the far wall, where he slid to the floor, unconscious.

Mike followed suit and received the same treatment. Sebastian then turned his hand towards the trapdoor and it slammed shut and the bolt slid across effectively trapping Ben below. Mike groaned and tried to stand.

"Michael, I just want to tell you that Beth is safe. I have her in a place where she believes she is with your daughter. She sees her, hears her, and in her mind, she is with her. And you are there too. She is happy. Have no fear that I will hurt her. You just need to know that she is safe. That's what you want, isn't it? For her to be safe? Well, there is no safer place. When you have completed your task and prevented the Demon Ark from activating, I will return her."

Mike was on his feet, however unsteady, and lunging towards him. "You *bastard!* I will rip your heart out and feed it to the dog! *Where is she?*"

Sebastian frowned, and with a flick of his hand sent

Mike sprawling again. "I have no heart; you have much to learn. Perhaps you aren't up to the job after all. It would be a great pity. For some reason which is beyond my understanding, you are Heaven's choice in this fight. But I wouldn't put any money on you right now. Do as you are destined and Beth will be returned to you, having no memory of anything other than a pleasant vacation with her family."

Jack was suddenly wide awake and the black that hovered in his eyes made Mike's heart sink. Jack leaped towards Sebastian.

The angel took a step back and held up his hand, palm forwards, towards Jack. The air crackled and Jack appeared to be battling something invisible that was holding him back.

Sebastian snarled, "Back demon, back Bazaliel. Michael, you must learn to muzzle your mongrel!" And with the now familiar rushing sound, he was gone.

Ben was hammering on the underside of the trapdoor. "*What's going on?* Mike? Jack? Let me out!"

Jack's eyes faded back to their usual hazel colour and he slumped onto the sofa. Mike's eyes were blazing as he yanked the bolt back on the trapdoor, releasing Ben's bulk back into the kitchen.

"Mike?" He looked at Jack's ashen face. "What the hell?"

Mike spoke through gritted teeth. "Not hell, Ben, heaven. Sebastian paid us a visit to inform me that he was 'keeping Beth safe'. I swear to God, if there *is* such a thing, that I will kill that bastard. Why can't they leave me alone?! *Where is she?*"

Ben's voice was deliberate and low. "Heaven and hell don't mind their own business, Mike, that's Catholic thinking, and sometimes there isn't much to choose between them. But, if it's any consolation, Sebastian won't harm Beth. I'm guessing he's taken her for leverage in the first instance but he is, after all, an angel and he won't hurt her."

Mike ignored him and was furiously dialling their home number. It rang unanswered. It rang unanswered because where Beth was, no telephones rang.

Mike's fury found vent in kicking the table and sending it over onto its side. "If that's supposed to make me feel better, it bloody well doesn't! You know what? They can shove it, I'm done! I'm going to get Beth back from wherever the hell he's taken her and then I'll do whatever I have to do to send that bastard to hell with the other pieces of shit!"

Their attention was suddenly claimed by Jack who had rapidly recovered; too rapidly.

"I think something's wrong," he said, a slight tremor in his voice. "I lost control of the demon. Only for a moment but it felt as if I had no hold on him."

"Oh, well, that's all right then! As long as it was only a moment! Jesus, what the hell is happening here? Angels are supposed to be on the side of the good guys! Or am I wrong? Tell me!" Mike exclaimed. "And not that I didn't say it was a bad idea with Jack, but *hey*, it was a bad idea!" He cast a hopeless glance at Ben.

Ben tried to remain calm. "It's okay, Jack. We'll figure it out." He turned to Mike, "You know you aren't going to walk away, because you know it's the quickest way to get Beth back. Come down with me, I think I found something."

Mike's reply was more of a growl, "It better be good."

"Depends how you look at it," Ben replied. "In this scenario there is no such thing as good, it's more like differing degrees of bad."

CHAPTER ELEVEN: A VERY NICE STORY

General Ryan closed the door of his GCHQ office behind him, a signal to the occupants of the huge room outside that he didn't want to be disturbed. It didn't happen often but when it did, they knew better than to approach within ten yards.

He was listening to the voice of Jon Barclay in Haifa, and what he was hearing gave him no comfort. Outwardly a decorated senior officer in the British Army, General Ryan had another vocation; one that wouldn't go down well with the powers that be.

The Strazca was a secret organisation, birthed in the twelfth century in Slovakia during Ottoman rule, when Transylvania became a part of the Ottoman Empire, and vampires from the remotest regions of Transylvania were emboldened to leave their lairs and travel into Hungary and beyond. The Strazca travelled with them, setting up safe-houses in most of the European capitals and in New Orleans, some of which eventually evolved into the country's headquarters. Their role was to watch the vampire population; to study them and curtail their activities whenever necessary. By 'curtail' they really meant stick a stake through their hearts, remove them and take their heads off. This they did with skill and without hesitation when any vampire within their radar became an actual threat to the general population – which was often.

At the beginning of the thirteenth century, The Strazca expanded their interests to include anything of a supernatural or paranormal nature; watching, reporting, studying, and investigating each such phenomenon or creature that came to their attention, keeping step with a developing world, embracing each modernity as it raised its head. In this technological age, their libraries were creaking with ancient volumes and sacred scrolls, but they existed alongside banks of computers.

General Ryan had been a part of The Strazca since the Berlin Wall came down, his role to listen and report any activity that could be of interest to the organisation. What was happening in Megiddo definitely fitted into that category, especially since the location had also been flagged in a phone conversation in which the Demon Ark had been mentioned; a conversation between Josh Hammond and Mike Travis.

Jon Barclay was already en-route to Megiddo. "Keep me updated on this number today only, it's a burn-phone and I'll be changing it daily. I'll call you at eight-thirty tomorrow morning if I've heard nothing from you. Is there anything else?"

General Ryan hesitated, and then made a decision; it was time to cover his own arse. "Yes," he said. "There's a name that keeps cropping up lately, ever since the Ark of the Covenant issue, someone who we already have an interest in: Mike Travis."

"Where is he?" It was a question that required an immediate answer from the General.

"He's not involved further than an initial contact as far as I know but I'm running a search on phone conversations and internet searches as we speak. He's low-profile but he has the potential for trouble."

"Watch him and report. Get a full profile if we don't already have one."

"Will do. How are you going to get access to the site?"

Jon Barclay had limited patience at the best of times; today it was stretched to twanging. "My problem. You just do your job and leave me to mine." The sound of a hang-up came through the General's phone. As much he respected other members of the Strazca, Barclay's attitude pissed him off. But there was a bigger picture; one that was dark and full of nightmare. He sighed; it was getting close to the time when he asked for a research job - retirement wasn't an option for someone with the access to the information that he had, but the alternative seemed attractive.

He opened his door and beckoned to the young operative that had alerted him to the NASA conversation. She appeared in his office immediately. He closed the door behind her.

"General?"

"I want you to run something for me. Full background, full screening. The name is Mike Travis. I want a full dossier. Problem?"

She shook her blonde head, flushing at the thought that she had been selected to do something that obviously had the potential to develop. Why else would he call her into his office and close the door to task her with it?

"How far back?" she queried.

"As far as it goes. All contacts, family and friends, locations, conversations, the works. Most importantly I want a trace on his phone and I want it routed directly to me; directly, understand?"

She did; it meant breaking protocols, but she knew from the General's expression that even she would not be party to the telephone chatter.

General Ryan continued, "I want to know where he is and where he's going. I want to know what he's thinking and doing, what he had for breakfast, and when he goes for a piss. And it goes without saying that this is classified. I will arrange to upgrade your clearances; you can consider this a promotion."

She flushed again. "You can rely on me, sir."

He cast an eye over her name badge; I Reeves. "Ingrid isn't it?"

"Yes, sir."

"Well, Ingrid, don't let me down."

He turned away from her, effectively dismissing her, a

message that was received loud and clear. She hurried across to her station; head down, on a mission.

*

Down in his cellar, Ben was poring over the ancient volume, reading aloud the Enochian text as he translated it as best he could. Mike and Jack faced him from the opposite side of the desk, listening intently and trying to follow what Ben was saying, but Mike's mind was full of Beth and where Sebastian had taken her.

"The Demon Ark is basically the evil twin of the Ark of the Covenant," Ben explained. "Where the Ark of the Covenant's purpose was to keep the earth safe, by enforcing the energy grid around the planet and housing some pretty hefty God-energy - for want of a better word - the Demon Ark's purpose is to bring darkness and chaos into the world by countering the protection of the grid and opening every portal to hell at the same time, thereby allowing all the demons a way here. This much I knew. What I didn't know, is that there is mention of something called the Lapsit Exillis, a name given from the condensed Latin, *Lapis lapsus ex caelis*, literally translated as 'the stone fallen from heaven'." He picked up another book and opened it at a page marked by a scrap of paper as Ben wouldn't risk the consequences of leaving it open and straining the spine.

Mike and Jack stared down at the text – again, futile, as this time it was in Latin. Ben continued, "This is the story of Morning Star's fall from Heaven. In the narrative, it describes a green stone that fell from his princely crown during his fall. The stone fallen from Heaven." Ben could see Mike's growing impatience and his desire to just get on with it, although he was trying to keep a lid on the molten lava that threatened eruption. He gave him a look which said, *'Wait, I'm getting there'*. Ben carried on, though he continued to glance at Mike.

"Apparently, the stone, the Lapsit Exillis, landed on the earth a long way from Morning Star, who then continued his descent into hell. Because of its origin, it is a stone of great power."

Mike lost his hold on his patience. "A very nice story, but what the hell has it got to do with what's happening?" he demanded. Jack moved to put a steadying hand on Mike's arm but the look that Mike threw him made him back off.

Ben picked up yet another book. "This is another one in Enochian, it tells how the angels were sent to earth to find the stone and return it to Heaven. This they did, where it was fashioned into a ring; a powerful ring that could control demons. This ring was given to King Solomon, and I held it in my hand! I bloody well had it in my hand. I knew Solomon wouldn't be able to resist the temptation to abuse its power and I refused to give it to him. Michael came and took it from me and they gave it to Solomon before I was put into my holding cell for so many centuries, I almost lost count."

They all fell quiet until Mike broke the silence with the obvious question. "So, what is it, a magic ring to control demons? What? What else?"

"The Lapsit Exillis, the Ring of Solomon, can control demons, yes. But it can also shut down the Demon Ark. It's the only thing on this earth that can."

CHAPTER TWELVE: THE TRAPIST MONK

Mike and Jack in stereo: "So, where is it?"

Ben's face clouded over. "I have no idea. There is no further mention of the ring except for a text that refers to the Demon Ring. Because of its context, I believe that to be the Ring of Solomon. The text lists it among other 'treasures' that were kept under the Temple Mount, under Solomon's Temple. If that is the case it is long gone. Those tunnels were excavated in the twelfth century by the Knights Templar, if it was there, they removed it. There is no further mention of it."

Mike strode past Ben and began picking random books off the shelves. "There must be! Here, look! Look again!"

"Put them down, Mike. I know every book on every shelf, and I know that there is nothing more to find here. I know you're desperate, but mate, if this goes south, we're all shagged. I get how important this is -- to you, to Beth -- to all of us, but, ranting and raving and going about like a headless chicken is what will get us killed. All of us. I said there was nothing more here, but that doesn't mean there is nothing anywhere else. It's a long-shot, but if he's still around, there's someone I used to know who is a Templar expert. I'll see if I can contact him, but it's not that simple."

"How so?" demanded Mike.

"Because he's a Trappist monk living in a monastery on an island. Fortunately, off the South Wales coast. He lives, or lived, in Caldey Abbey, on Caldey Island."

"What do you mean by 'or lived'? Mike persisted, still on the brink of a precipice that threatened to engulf him.

Ben allowed himself a brief moment of anxiety.

"Brother Bernard was eighty-four when I last saw him over ten years ago. He's well into his nineties now, if he's still alive. I need to make a phone call. While I'm doing that you need to familiarise yourself with your weapons. You're going to need them; it's not just demons that would give their eye-teeth to get their hands on Templar artefacts, or 'treasure' as they see it. Jack, leave him and come with me. He needs space to calm down." He left unspoken the words, "And the presence of Bazaliel, however controlled, won't help him."

The grapefruit-sized lump was back in the middle of Mike's chest and he was finding it hard to swallow. There were beads of sweat on his brow and he knew that Ben had been right; he needed to calm down and focus. He tried deep-breathing but the lump in his chest refused to budge, so he tried shifting his focus onto something he could control; his weapons.

Unlocking the cabinet that held the most lethal, and therefore highly illegal, brought a past military training back to the fore. He felt the grapefruit shrink to an orange. That was the key: restore his military mentality and he would restore his calm. Half ashamed at his lack of control, he decided there and then that a new Mike Travis needed to emerge if he was going to be any use to any of them, especially Beth.

He strapped the wrist-activated blade above his right hand and practiced operating the mechanism by twisting his wrist. Satisfied, after several minutes, that he had that one down without losing any fingers, he moved his attention back to the cupboard, his eyes alighting on the box containing the Crucifixion blade. Beckett had obviously agreed to a long-term loan.

He took the box out and placed it carefully onto the desk; there was always a sense of awe and reverence in him when he handled the blade, wrought as it was from one of the nails used in Christ's crucifixion. He opened the box but didn't lift the blade from it; just seeing it reassured him.

His attention was claimed by a loud, rumbling noise from outside that penetrated his sanctuary in Ben's cellar. He took the stairs two at a time and emerged into the kitchen to see Ben taking a set of keys from a guy in overalls and high visibility jacket. Ben signed a paper and closed the door.

He turned to Mike. "I hired an excavator; it's time to put a driveway into here - it should only take me an hour or so - I need to get your new vehicle into the workshop. Plus, when I'm done with it, it won't be safe to leave it out there on the road. I managed to get a great deal by the way, but it means losing your Volvo."

Mike frowned; he loved his car. "What have you done?"

"Part-exed yours for it. I told you, you need a different vehicle; it will be perfect once I've customised it. I've agreed the balance in some customisation of his kid's bike."

Mike just nodded, it seemed an inevitability that Ben's magic with bikes would be involved somewhere in the deal. He couldn't begin to imagine what Ben had in mind for the new vehicle, but knew he didn't just mean a spray job. He sighed, the runaway train had left the station and he had to ride it. He turned to Jack, suddenly saddened at the rift that had opened up between them; a truce there may be now, but Mike knew that Jack still felt the wound.

"I could use some help down there, if you'd care to get off your demon-arse." He threw a customary grin at Jack who responded in kind and followed him down the steps into the cellar.

"This was as much a surprise to me as it was to you, you know. And I've been living on top of it."

Mike was glad to get Jack alone and he went straight to the point. "Tell me honestly, are you okay? I mean, what does it feel like?"

"Having a demon inside me, you mean? Honestly?

Weird at first, but now, I don't feel any different."

"What about up there, when you lost control of it? Come on, Jack, we need to talk about this, and you need to be honest. Ben told me that once full possession occurred the host was lost, so why is this different?"

"It's the seal. I have his seal forever branded into my wrist. I don't know how I lost control of it, though I think it had something to do with being threatened. I know that sounds bizarre but it really felt as if Bazaliel was protecting me."

Mike wasn't mollified. "You still had no control over him and that could be serious. We need to have this out with Ben."

Jack nodded. "If for a second I believe he's a threat, I'll evict him and take the consequences."

Mike didn't voice the thought that, if that happened, Jack may not be strong enough to evict Bazaliel whether he wanted to not. Instead he turned his attention back to his weapons.

"I was always good on the range on our annual test. Let's hope I'm still as good."

"I always beat you," Jack replied. "Though, what the hell use a gun is against a demon I don't know."

Mike picked up a box of hollow-point bullets that had been 'modified' by Ben. "I think the secret is in the ammunition."

A nagging thought that had been tapping on his consciousness for the past minutes became clear. He turned a puzzled look on Jack. How could he be down there with the iron door in place? It's supposed to keep demons out after all, so how did Bazaliel get past it?

Ben appeared at the entrance to the cellar, cutting off his thought process.

"I just got off the phone to Caldey Abbey. Brother Bernard is still there, and if I call back in an hour they'll take a phone to him; he's very frail and doesn't leave his room, apparently. I have to call then as it's a silent order between the hours of seven and seven and, before that it's vespers and compline. If anyone knows anything about the Templars having the ring, it's him. Whether he'll tell us about it is something different."

Before Mike had chance to reply, Jack gave a small cry and put his hand on his forehead. "Christ, that hurt!"

Ben was at his side immediately, guiding him to the chair. "What is it?"

Jack shook his head painfully. "Damned if I know, but there was a blinding light and a pain in my head as if an axe just went through it." He paused for a moment, eyes distant, then he said, "They will come. You need to ward this place."

He was on his feet and over to the bookshelves at the head of the tunnel. He ran his finger along their spines, allowing them to rest on one with old, dark leather binding, and pulled it from the shelf. "Here, this one. This one contains the warding sigils. We need to do it now. And you need to speak to Brother Bernard before it's too late."

Neither Mike nor Ben were under any illusion that they were listening to any other than Bazaliel.

CHAPTER THIRTEEN: THE STRAZCA

Ut Canis In Custodiam In Occulto – We are the Watchdog of the Occult; this is the motto of the Strazca, and as mottos go, it fairly says it all. They dutifully monitor and record all paranormal or supernatural activity; they study it; they collect it and its artefacts; they document it; they are experts on it; and, when it steps out of line, they deal with it; without prejudice, without hesitation and without conscience.

The British headquarters of this secret organisation are hidden in plain sight -- in your face, so to speak. Linwood House, near Alderley in the heart of rural Gloucestershire is a spectacular country house built in extravagant Jacobean style, with its stone stacks and pointed gables under a Cotswold stone roof; it wouldn't look out of place in the most opulent period drama. It is built over three floors with sweeping staircases and high-ceilinged rooms that would grace any royal apartment, including an extensive library on the ground floor. The cellars, far from being there to house old boilers and wine racks, cover the entire footprint of the house and extend outwards underground into a vast network of rooms that serve as archives, museums and vaults. The top floor, underneath the pointed gables of the roof, is one huge room furnished with desks and computer terminals and their own private servers that beep and whir continually. The first floor comprises bedrooms and suites for visiting members and those in permanent residence.

In short Linwood House is set to draw the eye from a great distance; strange, one might think, for a secret society. Surely a nondescript office building would be more in keeping. The Strazca, however, has a good cover:

Linwood House belongs to a reclusive billionaire who runs his empire from his magnificent home. It's an 'almost' truth, as Roman Woolfe is certainly a billionaire, and most definitely reclusive. He is also the Eldritch, the head of the British arm of the Strazca.

Roman Woolfe's parents escaped persecution from Bratislava during the Second World War and settled in England, where his father made a good living from his skills as an excellent watch-maker. Roman was educated well and soon became a self-made man with a small fortune. Nothing to cause any concern one might say, but Roman had a secret - his grandfather was a lycanthrope, a lycan or, in plain English, he was a werewolf; fortunately the condition had not been passed down as it was an acquired condition from the bite of another lycanthrope and not hereditary. Mention of such a thing in England usually resulted in folk tapping the side of their head to indicate the insanity of such a belief; in Slovakia it resulted in folk crossing themselves *and* the road. Belief in various aspects of the supernatural is subjective, dependant on personal experience and cultural heritage.

It was his deep-seated knowledge of supernatural lore that brought Roman to the attention of the Strazca; they nurtured him, finished his education and mentored him throughout, and finally took him into their society as a researcher, then a field operative, until he found himself sitting on the council. Now, Roman Woolfe is the Eldritch, his word is final, his judgement sound and sometimes severe.

Jonathan Harcourt, a senior council member sat with Roman in one of the sitting rooms, both of them facing a bright blaze in the ornate fireplace, grateful for the heat and comfort on a dark autumn day.

Roman spoke with quiet authority, "I think it's too early to bring him in. I want to see how this plays out. Do we have anyone out there, just in case?"

"Yes. He's been notified and is ready. His instructions

are to watch and wait. We have the dossier for the council's consideration."

Roman Woolfe nodded his approval, "Good. And the other matter?"

"It would seem that there has been celestial intervention."

Roman sighed. "There's an angel involved? What is the source of the information?"

"One of our own; a sensitive."

Roman Woolfe scowled; infrequent for him, believing in an economy of emotion and expression. "I don't like it when the angels interfere; you can't always trust them. Do we know which one?"

"No, although it doesn't appear to be one of the big boys. Roman, I'm concerned for the other party."

"Which one? There are two that give cause for anxiety."

"Mainly for the woman. She has been touched by evil once too often, I fear for her mind."

Roman nodded. "Duly noted. Now, if there is nothing else. I need to speak to the translator," he said, as he left.

*

Brother Bernard's room in Caldey Abbey was more than the usual monk's cell; it housed his bed, a table and chair and row upon row of books and journals. He was too frail now to go to the library to work on his research and translations, and so his work had been brought to him. His meals were served to him in his room and his prayer vigils took place there too. At ninety-six, Brother Bernard was under no illusion that his life was rushing towards its end and he contented himself with passing the time immersed in his passion: the Knights Templar.

A young novice tapped respectfully on his door before entering. He loved Bernard and spent many hours listening to him as he shared his research and knowledge of the

Templars, and he had been glad that he had been on telephone duty when the call had come in.

The old man appeared shrivelled and weary, and the novice hoped that the call wouldn't exhaust him. He had warned the caller to be brief but they had insisted it was urgent.

"Brother Bernard, you have a telephone call," he proffered the phone. "They said it was important, urgent even."

The old man looked up from the depths of the volume he was working on, puzzled, his eyes cloudy with age. "What can an old man like me possibly have to do with important or urgent? Who is it?"

"He didn't give a name, but said to tell you it was about *Lapsit Exillis* - I think that's what he said."

Brother Bernard narrowed his eyes. "Tell them I don't know what they are talking about."

The novice did as he was bid, then turned to the old man, "He said you were … I'm sorry, Brother, these are *his* words … always a stubborn old man who probably knew more than was good for him."

Bernard's thought processes were slow now, but always deadly accurate when they caught up. His wrinkled face suddenly animated, and he held up a hand for the phone, waving the novice away with the other. "Thank you, lad. Come back for this thing later," he indicated the phone and his need for privacy.

After he had heard the novice's retreating footsteps he put the phone to his ear. "Benjamin? Is that you? It's been a very long time since Rome."

"Hello, Bernard. Yes, it is and I'm sorry."

"What can be so urgent you need to speak to an old man sitting in a monastery just waiting for his maker?"

"I heard the boy tell you what I wanted, Bernard, and I'm sorry I don't have time for polite conversation, but I need to talk to you about the ring. You know the one I mean. Lapsit Exillis. And it's about Megiddo."

Ben heard the old man's sharp intake of breath then, "Not over the telephone. Can you come here?"

"Yes, but it will take a couple of hours. I definitely won't make it before seven and the silence. It will be very late before I get there."

"I'm an old man who doesn't sleep more than a couple of hours at night. I will arrange it, and I still have some influence with the Abbot; he indulges me because he thinks it may be my last request." The monk chuckled at the thought, and then continued. "The novice you spoke to hasn't yet taken the vow and I will break mine for this. Come here as soon as you can, the hour doesn't matter. I told you, I sleep very little now and the boy is young enough to do without it. I will look out the relevant texts." He went to disconnect the call and thought better of it. "And Benjamin ... be careful."

He disconnected the call, only for it to ring immediately. The young novice had gone back to his duty station and so he had no choice but to answer it.

"Hello?"

A cultured voice answered him. "Hello, I wish to speak with Brother Bernard if that's possible, please."

Bernard hesitated momentarily. "This is he."

He hadn't lived this long, immersed daily in arcane documents or locked in contemplation of the divine not to know spiritual evil when it threatened. What had Benjamin Lovecraft become involved in? Whatever it was, he felt the need to pray.

His knees and hips were arthritic and his back ached from a lifetime of bending over books and documents, but he fell to his knees at the side of his bed to commune with his God.

CHAPTER FOURTEEN: WARDING THE COTTAGE AGAINST DEMONS

Ben pored over the book that Jack had retrieved from the shelf in the cellar, nodding occasionally and then, obviously satisfied, he called Mike and Jack.

"These are powerful protective symbols to ward off demons, no doubt. But there is one thing above all else that makes them so."

Mike raised a quizzical brow.

Ben continued, "They have to be applied directly to the doors and windows and they have to be drawn in blood. Try not to make too much of a mess; everything you need is downstairs. There's a canula, collecting bag and tourniquet in the cupboard to the left of your desk."

Mike noted the 'your' desk and was about to say that it was his fault and therefore it should be his blood, but Ben cut him off.

"Preferably Jack's as it now contains the essence of a demon. It will make it more powerful against its own kind."

Jack nodded a silent agreement.

"I'm going to Caldey Island. Your vehicle will be here later, don't forget that Mike. I'm guessing I'll be gone for several hours. It's a couple of hours from here to Tenby on my bike, but then I've got to find someone to take me across to the island and I don't know how long I'll be with Brother Bernard."

Mike nodded. "Sure you don't want me to come with you? "

Ben shook his head, "No." He cast a meaningful glance at Jack, "Look after things here, Mike."

Minutes later, Ben roared away on his bike leaving

Mike staring at the excavator as if it was an alien being. He needed to get on with finding Beth; it was his priority, not some Demon Ark manifesting in the Middle East, it was Beth and only Beth he cared about. But Sebastian had made it clear she was safe and would be returned as soon as he complied. He kicked out at the wall with such savagery, that, Fred, Ben's Rottweiler, moved to the other side of the room, huffed and lay down again.

Jack had remained silent while Mike adjusted to his situation. After several minutes he spoke quietly. "I'm sorry, Mike. I know I haven't made things any easier for you, with this demon thing, but I'd agreed to it in an instant without time to think. If you think it better I evict Bazaliel now, I'll do it. I'll do it while Ben is away and then he won't have to watch."

"Watch you die, you mean?" Mike snapped. "Well, that's not something I care to witness either. We'll make the best of it, Jack. Christ, you've seen me through enough. Do you think I'm going to walk away from you just because you've got some unholy virus squatting in you?"

Jack appeared to swallow something large and hard in his throat. "Thanks, but if I think for a moment that this demon is a threat to any of you, I'll choose that option and immediately."

Mike sighed. "You know, Jack, I think we're all screwed anyway, so what the hell. Come on, let's get this blood-letting over with, then we've got some artwork to do."

In the cellar, Jack settled into an old leather armchair while Mike gathered the necessary equipment. He stretched the rubber tourniquet around Jack's arm and felt around for a suitable vein. It took three tries before the dark red blood started to flow into the bag.

"Sorry, Jack, I'll keep the day job, but you're going to have one hell of a bruise." Then he laughed aloud at the absurdity of his words. A bruise was nothing compared to what he thought might come their way. "Sit still while I put the kettle on. Tea and a biscuit is the usual after a blood donation, I think."

They both looked up together as they sensed a change in the atmosphere of the cellar; both tensed. Mike was the first to relax as the spirit became visible to him. The old cap was pushed to the back of his head and Dai Bricks stood before them in all his comforting familiarity. Mike breathed out his relief.

"Hello, old friend," he said, the warmth of his greeting reflected in his previously cold eyes. "I didn't know when we would see you again."

Dai's voice was distant but Mike could hear every word. Jack's usual grin when Dai was around was absent.

"Mike, I know it's Dai, but things inside me are going haywire, my heart is racing; Bazaliel is twitchy because he knows that Dai can send him hellwards."

Dai frowned at Jack, "Jack, you're an idiot, I know what you did, look. And whether I think it was right or wrong, I wasn't here, so I can't judge, isn'it. But I won't do anything to harm him if that would mean you too. Not unless I have to, though I'm guessing Mike'll be quick off the mark anyways. But I'm sensing there's something not quite right with that seal on your wrist. Because I can feel that demon as sure as I can feel you, so I'm sure you don't have complete control, see."

Jack went pale. With Bazaliel inside him, he could see and hear Dai as well as Mike could. "I know. But I honestly don't think he's a threat. If I did, I would do what I had to straight away. I would."

Dai pushed his cap further back on his head, "Aye, I know, lad. Still, he needs watchin'." He turned to Mike then. "More to the point, see, is I've come to tell you I've seen Beth."

Mike took two steps towards Dai, his hand out. "Where? Is she all right?"

"I think so; she's well protected by the angel. Piece of

work, he is. Wouldn't give him the time of day, but he seems to have some influence up there."

Mike's eyes narrowed. "Up there? You mean …?"

"Aye. Sebastian took her to heaven's waiting room, isn'it. And no, she's not passed over, but she's weak, Mike, you should know that. It's no good me pretending she's not. Going to hell and back has left its mark, see; left its mark on her mind."

Mike swallowed the rising panic. "What are you saying, Dai? … You saying she's lost her mind? Because she was perfectly rational when I spoke to her earlier." He paused as he remembered her words, spoken in a dreamy, distant voice. "She said she had a headache and she was tired."

"Well, at the moment she seems to be in her own world, so to speak. I couldn't get close enough to see, but I get the feeling she thinks she's with you and Adain, no sense in changing that right now. But I wanted you to know."

Mike's face hardened and his eyes darkened. He'd been here before. Heaven or hell, what was the difference? "What can I do?" he asked Dai. "You know about Megiddo?"

Dai nodded. "I do, and I wish I didn't. It's right what they're saying. This Demon Ark will set all the demons free, all of the bastards. That's all I know. Where's Ben?"

Mike told him what they had found out and where Ben had gone, looking for more information, hoping to find the answers they needed to obtain Solomon's ring. It could be anywhere in the world and time was running out. It was time they caught a break.

Dai nodded. "Aye. If it's to be found, it's the Templars that will have had it for sure. He looked at Jack's anxious face. "I'll be off now then; I can see me being here is making that thing edgy; which is appropriate, isn'it, because it belongs in the edges. But I'm watching, see. Make no mistake."

His spirit shimmered and faded.

Jack looked miserable. "I'm sorry. This isn't going to work." As he spoke, his eyes turned to the black pools that Mike had previously seen in Jack's eye-sockets.

Bazaliel spoke. "There is something you should know. The demons that are already here are gathering in the place called Megiddo, and others; others that will help birth the Demon Ark. And they know of you. You should ward this place."

Mike was reluctant to engage with the demon, but instinct told him to. "How will that affect you? Surely if no demon can cross the sigils, then how can you?"

"Because I have the permission of my host. I can be of use to you, you know."

Mike snarled, "Lovecraft's Rule number one, mate. Demons lie. So before I change my mind and send you to the pit, shut the fuck up." He picked up the book and began studying it, blanking out Bazaliel. "Jack, you'd better start keeping that thing under control or I swear I'll … well, I will! Come on, we need to start painting."

An hour later and the walls, inside and out, of Ben's cottage were covered in deflecting sigils that were intended to ward off every legion of hell before they returned to the fireside, exhausted but too wired to sleep. They both looked up at the sound of an engine. It was followed by a loud knock on the door.

Mike answered it.

The driver of the car transporter was pale as his eyes darted from one bloody sigil to the other, still wet and red on the door. He thrust a set of keys to Mike, followed by a clip board.

"I aint seen nothing like this before and I don't want to know what they are. Just sign here and I'll be on my way. You got keys for me?"

Mike took the keys and signed the paper, then wordlessly handed over the keys to his Volvo. It felt like a loss.

He stepped outside and watched as the driver ran hell

for leather back to the cab of the transporter and lowered the ramps. He didn't give the cottage a backwards, forwards or sideways glance as he unchained the black four-by-four, shiny in the moonlight, like a huge lumbering beetle. And when it was off the bed of the truck, he stowed the chains and drove away leaving Mike's car in the middle of the narrow road.

CHAPTER FIFTEEN: CALDEY ABBEY

Two and a half hours later, Ben brought his bike to a halt on Tenby Harbour. All was quiet and the tide was full in. He cast around looking for a likely place to find someone to take him to the island, and settled on a pub on the quayside that looked more as if it was the haunt of regulars and locals, than tourists. No neon lights or flashy signs, just a weathered old board, announcing its unimaginative name of 'The Harbour Inn'. He parked the bike and headed for the bar.

It was six-thirty and already full dark; there would be no chance of the normal ferry taking him to the island, but if he could find a skipper who was planning some night fishing he may get across and, as Ben could pay him more than he'd get for the mackerel he'd catch, he was hopeful.

Judicious questioning of the barman gave him the address of one Jim Talbot, who apparently would take no great deal of persuasion to accept the fee for the journey. The fishing boat was his father's but, as that said parent was usually half-asleep, half-drunk, by seven, he should find the son amenable to the fare. There was no-one else that he could think of that would take a boat over to the island so late in the day at that time of year.

The harbour-side cottage looked well overdue for a coat of paint and the curtains at the window hung precariously from over-stretched wire. *Just like I feel*, thought Ben, as he knocked on the peeling door.

From the speed at which he heard movement inside, he knew that it would Jim Talbot that opened it. He was right.

The young man in front of him was as unkempt as the house, dressed in jeans that were torn - not as a fashion-statement, just torn – and, neither could the three day growth on his face remotely be classed as designer stubble.

"Yeah?" he demanded.

Ben was straight to the point, finishing with, "How much?"

Jim Talbot said fifty quid, Ben said thirty, and they agreed on forty.

"I'll meet you on the quay in ten minutes," Jim said. "You did say cash, right? Up front?"

Ben eyed him. "Twenty up front, the other twenty when you bring me back."

"All right, but I'm not waiting all night. I'll be coming back after an hour. Right?"

Ben nodded his agreement and handed over a twenty pound note. If he couldn't get the information from Brother Bernard in an hour, he would have to stay the night and return on the normal ferry the following day. Either way, he felt relief at the thought that within an hour he would be with the old monk who could hopefully point them in the right direction at least.

The crossing was cold, choppy and comfortless, but they landed on the jetty in Priory Bay on the north side of the island without incident and Ben began the short trek inland to the Abbey. He glanced at his watch: seven-twenty. The abbey would be in silence; he hoped Bernard had managed to arrange his out-of-hours visit.

The white building with its arches, towers and spires looked ethereal in the shadows given off by the meagre lighting as he approached the raised entrance. He had anticipated a huge iron knocker or bell-pull but was disappointed as the huge old door was opened as he approached it. A young novice smiled at him and answered Ben's unspoken question.

"I was instructed to watch for you, and to take you straight to Brother Bernard to minimise any disruption to the silence."

Ben smiled back at him and simply nodded.

The abbey was indeed swathed in silence and their

footsteps seemed to echo too loudly as they made their way to the back of the abbey. In deference to his failing mobility over the years, Brother Bernard's room was on the ground floor.

As they approached, Ben knew there was something wrong, something very wrong. Apart from the silence, the air was heavy with something else, something that smelled of copper. A considerable amount of blood had been spilled in their immediate vicinity, but the young novice strode forwards as if he couldn't smell anything, even though it was overpowering. Ben felt inside his pocket for the vial of holy water he always carried; the irony hit him, he was in an abbey, desperately fumbling for holy water about his person.

At the end of the corridor a door was open. Ben knew this would be where he would find what remained of the old man, but he walked on; unwilling to give the boy the advantage, he played ignorant, but he was prepared for the events of the next few minutes.

The novice stood back from the door for Ben to enter, stupid being its primary state if it truly believed Ben hadn't smelled the blood. The boy had been completely and irrevocably possessed, and there was nothing left of the smiling young novice inside. The corridor was remote and housed only Bernard's room and some store rooms; along with the hour, it was understandable that no-one else had raised the alarm.

Ben entered the room that had recently had its walls splattered with Brother Bernard, who lay spread-eagled on the floor, his robe slashed away from his body, his abdomen open with its contents spilling out.

Ben spun around and flung most of the contents of the vial into the face of the demon that began howling and spitting profanity from its blistering lips. Ben followed through with another dose as he began the exorcism.

"Exorcizamus te, omnis immundus spiritus, omnis satanica potestas, omnis incursio infernalis adversarii, omnis legio, omnis congregatio et secta diabolica."

We exorcise you, every impure spirit, every satanic power, every incursion of the infernal adversary, every legion, every congregation and diabolical sect.

The demon lunged at him, screaming. Surely someone had heard that piercing the silence.

"Ergo, omnis legio diabolica, adjuramus te...cessa decipere humanas creaturas, eisque æternæ perditionìs venenum propinare..."

Therefore, diabolical legions, we adjure you ... Cease to deceive human creatures, and to give to them the poison of eternal damnation; ...

He heard running footsteps at last, but the demon was on him. They fell together onto the floor and Ben made a grab at the knife that was still sticking out of Brother Bernard's entrails and, in one smooth movement, he plunged it deep into the novice. It wasn't enough and he knew it as he continued the exorcism,

"Vade, satana, inventor et magister omnis fallaciæ, hostis humanæ salutis...Humiliare sub potenti manu Dei; contremisce et effuge, invocato a nobis sancto et terribili nomine...quem inferi tremunt...Ab insidiis diaboli, libera nos, Domine."

Be gone, Satan, inventor and master of all deceit, enemy of man's salvation ... Be humble under the mighty hand of God; tremble and flee when we invoke the Holy and Terrible Name at which those down below tremble ... ... from the snares of the devil, deliver us, O Lord .

Two brothers appeared at the door, aghast at the sight within. One of them crossed himself and the other vomited into the corner. Ben grimaced; as if the smell wasn't bad enough already.

"Someone better fetch the Abbot," he said tersely. "And tell him to bring the biggest knife he can find." It was enough to dispatch the two and it was no surprise to Ben that minutes later an alarm sounded throughout the abbey.

The Abbott appeared flanked by the two biggest monks housed in the abbey. Ben allowed himself a wry smile. He prepared to defend himself but was pre-empted by the Abbott, whose keen sense of events was smack on the money. The Abbott raised his hand to quell the reaction from the accompanying monks and indicated the door. His glance said, 'Wait outside'.

Inside the room he stared at Brother Bernard and then at Ben and then crossed himself before he broke his silence and spoke.

"It seems you have arrived too late. What evil has stalked these halls? Brother Bernard was insistent you be allowed in regardless of the hour. I sensed in him a great unease and he told me your purpose."

Ben was surprised at that. "He did?"

A nod. "He was also worried that others might also be coming, but it seems they were already here."

"Something was," Ben replied, "something that got inside that lad. I suppose you know what I have to do now?"

The Abbott nodded. "I do. Sometimes evil must be dealt with by evil means. But please, allow us to care for Brother Bernard in our own way. We are subject to the law of the land here - but how do I begin to explain this? Two savage deaths within the confines of our abbey?"

"Perhaps it would be better not to have to try?"

The Abbot frowned. Ben continued. "I have a friend in the police force, Detective Inspector Gareth Jones, who deals particularly with things such as this. We are way out of his jurisdiction here, but I think maybe we can leave it to him. You will have done what is required of you by the law and can bury Brother Bernard in peace. The lad went crazy and attacked Brother Bernard, who managed to defend himself with the knife before the boy finished him off. The lad died from the wound before help could be summoned. I believe that's the way things happened here."

After a moment the Abbot spoke again. "It will take a

great deal of prayer to be able to come to terms with this. You must bear a huge burden."

Ben sighed. "I get by. Usually. But if I hadn't contacted Brother Bernard, he'd be sitting here with his books right now. It's a burden all right, and one that just gets harder. But the bigger picture is even worse. Pray for me, Father Abbot."

The Abbot looked directly into Ben's eyes, into his very soul. "Not many know the correct way to address an Abbot," he said. "I sense something of the clergy in you Mr Lovecraft."

"Ben, please. Benjamin Lovecraft, ex-Father Benjamin Lovecraft to be precise; ex-priest and exorcist at your service."

The Abbot beckoned the two monks waiting outside. "Get a stretcher and take our Brother to the infirmary, and care for him, prepare him for burial. Benjamin and I will take care of the boy; he too needs care and blessing." As the two brothers retreated, he returned his steady gaze to Ben. "You should come with me to my office, Ben. Brother Bernard left something for you. I told you he was afraid of something, but I hadn't decided whether or not to give it to you. I have decided now. I will do what is necessary for the boy. I understand. Only decapitation will finish off the evil. Allow me to take that burden from you."

CHAPTER SIXTEEN: NEW FACES

Ruth Weiss was twenty-eight and pursuing her doctorate at Tel Aviv University with a promising career in the world of archaeology. Rising stars in the field were few and far between; most caring more for the past than their own futures, academically or in the rarefied atmosphere of university politics. Ruth had the knack of combining all aspects and was ear-marked to take over from the retiring Chair; her star, as they say, was in the ascendant.

Except that Ruth Weiss was, herself, history. Resident now in her body was a demon; one of many that were gathering over Megiddo in readiness for the main event; the rising of the Demon Ark. They would be ready to welcome all the other demons out of the pit, especially the high-rankers who would be looking for their second-in-commands.

Josh Hammond watched from a distance as the grad students, volunteers and qualified archaeologists gathered for the daily meeting that had taken place since they were evicted from the site in the bar at the kibbutz. Ruth had been the first casualty, but there had been others that had fallen sick in the same manner: a sudden onset of collapse and the spread of the black veins and then, the fever, and the plague-like pustules, all followed by a rapid and unexplained recovery. And he had seen the demons in the black eyes of them all. Now there was no-one he could trust except Mike Travis and he was thousands of miles away. He had pleaded his case and hoped that Mike would come but he hadn't heard from him.

Now three students were missing and all Ruth would say was that they had taken the opportunity to see more of Israel while the dig was suspended. Josh knew better; that the demons were behind the disappearances. He just couldn't prove it and he certainly wasn't going to draw their attention by speaking out. He waited and watched.

New faces stood out from the crowd and Josh's interest was piqued when a man he hadn't noticed previously approached Ruth Weiss. And he would have noticed him, as his attire was a far cry from the boots, jeans and old T-shirts that were the usual clothing at the dig; his tailored linen shirt alone would have taken care of Josh's salary for a couple of months.

They spent several minutes in deep conversation and then left together, Ruth leading the way. Who was he and where were they going? Josh had watched from a distance until then, but now he needed to follow them. His gut was doing the fandango; he was no coward, but preferred to keep his own soul intact. Following demons could get you killed. Or worse.

He was surprised as they made their way towards the dig. The military were allowing no-one within a hundred yards and had actually cordoned the area off, with guards posted at regular intervals. The last time that Josh had approached, he was left in no doubt that they meant business; the black eyes told him so.

At the cordon Ruth simply bobbed under it and approached the armed black-eye with a confident step. There was no way that Josh was going any closer. He would try and watch from this distance. Low profile. The further away that Ruth and her visitor went, the calmer his heart-rate, until they came to a sudden halt and Ruth turned, slowly and deliberately, to face him. And looked him straight in the eye.

She took a step towards him and Josh felt the rising nausea; could he bluff his way out of the situation? He doubted it. It wasn't put to the test though, as Ruth's visitor grabbed her arm with obvious impatience and, after a brief hesitation and keeping her black eyes locked onto Josh, she eventually turned back and they carried on.

Fighting the desire to empty his bladder, Josh gave himself a moment to recover then moved forwards to try to see which part of the excavation they were heading for. The answer perplexed him.

Ruth and her visitor stood before an unexcavated mound way to the east of the dig, which had so far been left untouched as there was no reason to dig there. He frowned. Most odd.

His instincts had been that they were headed for Megiddo's Great Temple which dated back to the Bronze Age and was ten times larger than a typical temple of the era. They had found evidence of ritual animal sacrifice in uncovered corridors that were used to store the bones, but nothing more sinister than that; certainly nothing that would draw demons to it. Or had they missed something?

As he watched them, he was suddenly aware of the approach of several vehicles. They stopped at the site in a dust cloud that obscured his vision temporarily, but when it cleared, what he saw made his heart sink. It was clearly a party of diggers, all carrying state of the art equipment, including what he believed to be explosives. No. They couldn't. They wouldn't. Would they?

The entire dig would be blown to fragments of rock. What could they possibly be looking for that hadn't already been found? He searched his memory banks for an answer while his fingers were pushing out Mike's number on his phone. Before the number had finished dialling, he eyes locked on to Ruth's visitor and the flash of steel as he cut her throat and stepped back from the fallout and mess.

Mike answered on the second ring, obviously after checking caller ID. "Yes, Josh, I'm coming. But there's something I need to do first. Something I need to find that …"

"Christ, Mike, there's demons here, Mike. A shitload of demons! Killing people! What shall I do?"

At the other end of the conversation, Mike's eyes narrowed. "Stay the hell away from them and if you can't, then protect yourself. Any way you can. Try and find your Rabbi friend, he'll help you. I'll call you when I can. Looks like I'll be flying into Tel Aviv, you can meet me." He looked across at Jack. "I'll have company." He disconnected the call before Josh could tell him that he'd found his Rabbi friend; he was right there in front of him, his wrists bound behind his back and being pushed forwards by the muzzle of an assault rifle.

Jack nodded at Mike. "About time," he said. "About bloody time."

"Are you up to it? I mean …"

"Yeah, I know what you mean; can I trust Bazaliel? Yeah. Yeah, I can."

Mike continued. "Having one of them on our side will be an advantage they won't expect but, you have to be sure that it won't dump you and join this friggin' demon army and take us with it."

"I don't know why I know, I just know."

"Hope you're right, I don't want to bury your arse in Israel."

CHAPTER SEVENTEEN: GILBERT BELVOIR

No sooner had Mike disconnected the call from Josh than his phone rang again; his screen told him it was Ben.

"Hi, Ben."

There was a long pause as Ben gathered his thoughts and raging emotions. Mike gave him the time. Eventually Ben said, in a voice that sent chills down Mike's spine, "Brother Bernard is dead."

"Hold on, Ben, I'm putting you on speaker."

Jack looked up at the significance of that as Ben continued.

"It was a demon attack; the bastard sliced him open like he was nothing … I killed it. Fortunately, the Abbot is one of the good guys and, thank God, he has knowledge of the evil that we are all facing. He told me to leave and not look back, that he would deal with what happened. And I believed him, trusted him, and I left. But not before he gave me a package from the old man. Brother Bernard knew he was in danger and he left it for me."

His voice, his normally booming voice, lost some of its strength then; breaking as his emotions got the better of him.

"He was in his nineties for God's sake, an old man who couldn't defend himself, and he knew it was coming, because I called him and I took this to him!"

Mike took his time to reply; there were no words that would make Ben feel any different and he knew it.

Jack's only thought was for Ben, "You okay? You're not hurt?"

They could both picture Ben's expression softening with his voice, "No, I'm fine. It wasn't a powerful demon;

probably one that was just watching him. It had taken up residence in a boy, a novice, for God's sake. I had no choice, the boy was long gone." He took a deep breath as the thought of the boy's head rolling away from his body sickened him, despite the fact he knew that the demon had possessed the boy long ago and he was essentially gone.

"I haven't had time to read everything, just the letter that he left attached to a translation of a journal belonging to Jacques De Molay." He sensed the questioning expressions at the other end. "Jacques De Molay was the Grand Master of the Knights Templar; in fact he was the last Grand Master before his execution for heresy. He was elected to the position in 1293 while serving in the Holy Land and, one of his first acts was to send his Seneschal, his most trusted knight, Gilbert Belvoir, back to England. He makes veiled references to Belvoir's duty to protect what was entrusted to him. Then, in 1294, right in the middle of their persecution at its height, with no explanation, De Molay travels from the Holy Land back to England, bypassing the most important of the Templar sites, Temple Church in London, and heading for the westernmost preceptory to visit Gilbert Belvoir. And then return to the Holy Land, again without pausing at any of their important holdings." He paused again, allowing the irony in his voice to have full effect. "Oh ... and while he was with Belvoir he ordered him to kill himself."

Mike was the first to speak. "What does all that mean?"

"It means that I know where to look for Solomon's ring."

"*Where?*" In stereo from Mike and Jack."

"Garway. St Michael's Church, Garway, in Herefordshire. Almost on our own bloody doorstep!" He paused. "The journal tells how De Molay stayed at Garway long enough to see Gilbert Belvoir interred in a stone tomb, and he supervised the entire construction. His tomb is underneath what was the original circular nave, which would make perfect sense as Garway Church is supposed to have been built over a portal, which is why it was dedicated to St Michael as protection. Snag is, the entrance is not inside the church as you might think but from outside. Bernard speaks of a large rectangular stone tomb in the churchyard, but that's all. You'll have to find it for yourself. Have you got the stomach for grave-robbing Mike?"

Mike looked troubled. "Herefordshire? Solomon's ring is in a tomb in a churchyard in Herefordshire?" The disbelief in his voice was all too evident. "I mean, you'd expect it under the Temple Mount, or in Ethiopia, or Temple Church in London, but Herefordshire?" His scepticism was apparent on every pore. "Not buying it, Ben. He tells Belvoir to kill himself, and he does? Just like that?"

"It's not me that's selling it, Mike. This is direct from De Molay's journal."

"Actually, it's from a translation of the journal made by Brother Bernard. Could he have got it wrong?"

Ben shook his head. "He died for this, Mike. Gutted like an animal. He didn't get it wrong."

"So, just like that, I open the tomb and the ring is there? Sounds too easy," Mike mused.

"I'm sure it won't be that easy; the journal doesn't say where the entrance to the underground crypt is," Ben replied. "And no doubt there will be obstacles and precautions."

"Booby traps?" Mike questioned. "Jesus Ben, I'm no Indiana Jones and I have to tell you, at the risk of cliché, I have a bad feeling about this."

"I'm on the way home," Ben said, "We'll talk later. In the meantime you'd better prepare for a long trip. Pack what you can." Mike knew he meant – *'Pack what you can get through security at the airport.'*

Jack stood up suddenly and grabbed the phone from Mike's hand and switched it off. "Bazaliel said that we're being tapped. Don't know how he knows, but he does!"

Mike raised an eyebrow as he gave vent to his anger and anxiety once more.

"Jesus, Jack! I thought you had that thing under control! Now you're listening to it!"

Jack took a moment to look pained. "Mike, you said yourself it may give us the advantage. Well, how can it do that if I don't listen! And if it can sense things like this, I'd call that an advantage, wouldn't you? And more to the point, if he's right, then whoever it is that's listening in knows what we know now."

Mike put his hands to his temples. "Christ, this is a mess. That means I can't wait for Ben to get back; I need to grab some gear and go now. You'd better stay here."

"Why? Because of Bazaliel?"

"*No,*" Mike snapped. "And I wish you'd stop calling that thing by name as if it's human. I want you to stay here and tell Ben what's happened and why I can't phone him back. And you'd better not answer the phone again either. Not until we can deal with this. And, besides … I want someone here in case … in case Beth comes back."

There was a long pause of unspoken uncertainty between them, and then Jack nodded his understanding.

"OK. I'm sorry, Mike. Let's not allow this thing to come between us. Please?"

"Course not, it's just … well, I guess I have a lot to learn about these bloody fallen angels and the demons some of them become. Until then, don't pay me any heed. We'll work this out. It's just … right now … right now, it's too much; too bloody much."

"Yup. And, Mike, don't forget what you promised me. I meant it; every word."

Mike knew immediately that Jack was referring to the promise he made to take his life if he lost control of the demon, or if there was any sign that Bazaliel had betrayed them, and especially if it harmed Jack in any way whatsoever.

"Let me talk to it. Can you do that?"

Jack lowered his head and steadied his breathing. When he looked up, his eye-sockets were like black ink, and when he spoke, the voice that passed over Jack's vocal chords was deeper than his friends and was possessed of an accent; probably Eastern European, Mike thought.

"So, Michael, still you don't trust me? What must I do to show you? I have just warned you that I sense another soul listening to your conversation and another source of electrical impulse. I believe you call it, being hacked; though I have to say, that expression has other connotations for me. Unpleasant ones."

"I guess it's going to take a bit more than that. In the meantime, I want you to know this: that if for one second I think that you are harming Jack in any way, or that you are betraying us, I won't hesitate. And if you really know what he's thinking, you will know that I mean it, because I made a promise to my dearest friend, and it's what he would want. Are we clear?"

"Crystal, Hunter."

"Don't think that by calling me that you will bait me to anger, because you know what? It's what I am now, and what I will always be from here on in until I get my wife back. Don't make me prove it to you."

"You will have no need. I admit, that when Azrael brought me out of the pit the first time I would have betrayed Jack Carter in a heartbeat, and I planned to do as much, expecting to be free in this world but, in the seconds it took for me to do that and you to kill me, I knew I still had a connection to Jack and that I only had a heartbeat, if you will pardon the pun, to save him as his heart seized. I made a choice, Michael, and I won't change my mind. I will remain in Jack's body for as long as it takes for me to heal him. Not all of us fallen ones lose our powers completely. I can do this, where Seraquel cannot. What you do to me after that is up to you."

Mike's expression of loathing flickered momentarily, and then as his memory of Bazaliel's earlier betrayal flooded back, it returned. "So be it. As long as you know I won't hesitate, not even for one beat of my heart. I will take Jack's head off to free him from you."

"So be it."

Jack's eyes flickered momentarily and suddenly they were his own again. He swallowed hard. "Thanks, Mike. I know I can trust you to do what's necessary now. I know you promised before, but I know now that you will keep that promise."

Mike's voice was gruff as he replied, "Well, I can't stay here getting all mushy! I've got to get to Garway before whoever it was listening to me. St Michael's again, did you notice that? Let's hope he's still watching over me!"

*

GCHQ, Cheltenham

General Ryan put the headphones back on his desk and picked up his private cell phone. He dialled and listened to the answering voice before saying just one word, "Garway."

The cultured voice at the other end replied in like fashion, "Thank you."

End of conversation.

In the huge room outside the General's office, Ingrid flicked a switch disconnecting her earpiece from the General's private phone along with the incoming trace, and left the office. Once outside, she dialled a number from her own phone.

"I have the information; Garway Church in Herefordshire."

The Strazca Headquarters, Linwood House, Nr. Alderley

Roman Woolfe's expression was grave as he replaced the telephone in its cradle. He did nothing for several minutes and then picked it back up and dialled.

It obviously didn't ring for long, as he spoke almost immediately.

"Lizzie, it's Roman Woolfe. Listen to me carefully and then get yourself over to St. Michael's Church at Garway."

CHAPTER EIGHTEEN: MORE ANCIENT THAN YOU CAN IMAGINE

As Josh watched in abject horror, his old friend, Rabbi Eli Rosenburg was repeatedly shoved, stumbling forwards, by the butt of the gun being held by a burly thug in khaki uniform behind him. Eli was an elderly scholar who spent most of his life in libraries or in his office poring over old scriptures and at the next shove, he fell forwards. The guy with the gun yanked him to his feet and yelled something at him before slapping him hard across his face and shoving him again; even from where Josh was standing he could see the trickle of blood down the old man's face and the broken lens in his spectacles. Fury demolished common sense and he rushed forwards to try and help him.

Surprise did help him initially, as he was able to grab the gun and smash it into the thug's face. He went reeling, but before Josh could do anything more, two others were on him, ripping the gun from his grasp and shoving him face down into the dirt. One held him down with a heavily-booted foot and the other yanked his hands behind him and snapped handcuffs around his wrists. The one that Josh had attacked was back on his feet and heading towards him with a murderous look. His boot connected with Josh's ribs and there was a loud crack, followed by a yell from Josh and a gasp as he tried to suck in air past the fractured bones. The boot went back for another shot.

"Stop!" What the hell do you think you're doing?" Richard Vermont demanded. "No more bodies, I said. Not yet." He strode over to Josh who was gasping in agony at the assault on his rib-cage. "Who have we here?" He put his highly polished, shoe underneath Josh, eliciting another groan and gasp as he turned him over to get a look at his face. "Do we know who he is?"

One of the armed guards on the perimeter of the site had joined them. "He's one of the archaeologists."

Richard Vermont tilted his head on one side. "Is that so? You fancy yourself the hero, archaeologist? You wish to save the old man? Then perhaps you can take his place. I need someone to open the Megiddo Temple for me. If you can do that, he is disposable and you can take his place. If not, then you are disposable. It's your call."

Each breath brought exquisite pain to Josh's chest as he tried to speak, knowing that his words would decide the fate of them both. "I can do that, but I need his help. Look at us; we're both injured, thanks to your goon! And you should know, the temple area has already been excavated."

The demon, in Vermont's body, threw out a hand and the pain in Josh's chest was amplified a hundredfold. He bit his tongue in an effort not to cry out.

"I'm talking of a temple far older and sacred to a deity more ancient than you can imagine, and I believe you can imagine a lot." He paused, as if having an internal conversation. Then he said, "All right. With two of you, it will be done a lot quicker. The old man will guide you through the inscriptions and you will open the temple. For that reason I will take away your pain." He raised his hand again and threw his energy at Josh. This time the pain was from his shattered ribs putting themselves back together as Vermont's demon continued, "Next time I raise my hand to you, will be to extinguish your life. Do you understand? If you try to escape, or to deceive me - and I will know if you try to deceive me - I will do it. And then I will kill the old man, only more slowly."

Josh nodded a dumb acceptance as the handcuffs were removed from both of them. His mind was in overdrive. How could he set Eli free without getting them both killed? What the hell did the demons want from them, that they didn't just waste them there and then?

They were both hauled in rough haste towards the spot where Josh had seen the man open Ruth Weiss's throat.

Vermont grabbed Eli's arm, "Show him! Tell him!"

Eli's eyes were filled with deep sadness as he reached into the inside pocket of his jacket, bringing out a sheaf of notes that he had made over many years of study. He handed them to Josh.

"It's true," he said in a voice that was barely audible. "It's true, Josh. There is a temple under here that was built by the Sumerians to an ancient God; ancient beyond imagination. And it's here, intact, under our feet; the entrance is under that mound."

Josh narrowed his eyes. "Eli, you know how long I've been digging here. That just doesn't make sense. The Sumerian temples are in what used to be Mesopotamia, now Iraq. There was no Sumerian worship here. And their temples were huge ziggurats, built like pyramids above ground."

The old man sighed. "I know, but it's true nonetheless. What is under there should never see the light of day again. Believe me, Josh, that temple should be left buried for all eternity."

"You can't leave it at that. Why? What is down there?"

"Evil; pure evil. It is the place that will birth the Demon Ark."

Richard Vermont interrupted further talk. "Enough. Now you will begin to open the temple. My men will help you with the physical digging."

Josh nodded towards one of the 'men' who was carrying a box that was clearly labelled 'Explosives'. "Well, for a start we won't be using those. Unless of course, you want to blow the temple into gravel. And we'll need geophysics data to locate the void."

"It was done yesterday. This is the location. It was confirmed by Ruth Weiss. Shame about her; pretty girl, an impressive host for a demon, but sadly it was not to be.

She believed she was more important than was in fact true."

Josh swallowed his fury and his disgust. "Let me see it."

One of Vermont's men stepped forwards with the map and thrust it at Josh. "Get on with it. And, just so you know, I'm an explosives expert; I can blow the dick off a gnat and still leave the rest intact. Just do your job once the entrance is exposed."

Eli's expression was a mixture of great sadness and terror, his face tinged with varying shades of grey. Josh put a steadying hand on his arm as the old man swayed in front of him.

"Eli? Are you OK?"

The old rabbi nodded and put a hand to his sweating brow. "Yes, yes. Don't worry yourself over me. Do as they say, *chabibi*," he said, reverting to his native Hebrew term of affection for 'my friend'.

Vermont approached them. "You will confirm the exact location. Ruth Weiss thought she would play me for a fool, and you know I didn't take that kindly. So, Archaeologist, is this the entrance?"

Josh looked at the map several times and paced the ground in front of him, measuring with well-established strides. "I think so. But I'll need a laser-measure to be sure."

Vermont eyed him carefully. "You're sure." He nodded to the demon with the explosives, and then turned his gaze back to Josh. "Step away, please." Another nod brought another of his men with handcuffs again, and they were marched to a safe distance. Josh was increasingly concerned about his old friend, with good reason; the old rabbi was about to have a heart attack.

As the first of the explosives brought a muffled bang amid a cloud of dust, Eli fell to the floor, semi-conscious. Richard Vermont stepped closer to him, allowed his demon to the fore and made an assessment and a decision, and then with one wave of his hand, brought the old rabbi's life to a close.

"You'll have to do this on your own, then."

At that moment, another seismic shock hit the site, accompanied by a darkening of the sky that could only been a portent of approaching evil. In response, the black eyes of Vermont's demon glowed incandescent red before returning to the black holes that were now a permanent feature. Josh was left in no doubt that the nearer to the surface and to being activated the Demon Ark got, the more power it gave to all black magicians and demons already walking the earth.

Richard Vermont appeared gratified. "Morning Star is impatient," he said. "You must hurry, Archaeologist."

CHAPTER NINETEEN: GARWAY

It was fully dark as Mike drove past the entrance to the church in Garway. He almost missed the sign that was semi-buried in a growing hedge, pointing down the lane to his left. He reversed his car and turned into the lane. The church was down a dirt track on the left and he quickly realised that any headlights of an approaching car would be seen a mile away. There was no way he would negotiate the track without headlights, especially as immediately adjacent to the church was Temple Farm, private land now, but once part of the Templar preceptory, and his headlights would be as beacons through the dark. He drove past it and as soon as he could, he turned the car around and drove back through the village and into the car park of The Moon Inn, where he quickly lifted the holdall containing an array of tools and weapons from the boot; unsure of what he'd need as a rookie grave-robber, he'd thrown an assortment of likely hardware into the bag. He proceeded on foot back to the church, preferring the anonymous approach that wouldn't bring the local constabulary on his case. Neither did he want to announce his presence to any lurking demon.

He was reasonably confident that he would reach the church before any other agency, demon or otherwise, would have the chance after being notified by whoever had been listening in to his conversation with Ben.

The dark did little to allay Mike's worries about entering a churchyard and desecrating a grave. He figured it might be something that would happen more than he would be comfortable with in the future, but for now he had to find Gilbert Belvoir's tomb with only the light of his phone, and even that would shine out like a landing light in the darkness. He negotiated the dirt-track by feeling his way along the hedge; the gate opened at his first attempt, and he fervently hoped that no-one had seen the quick on-and-off of the light on his phone for him to get his bearings.

Shining the light from his phone directly down onto the uneven ground minimised the glare, and at least it meant that he didn't fall over any flat gravestones. Not for the first or the last time, he wondered what the hell he was doing; he should have taken Beth and Adain and disappeared.

He stopped and held his breath. There was a low, creeping shadow moving behind a gravestone directly ahead. He waited, peering through the darkness.

The shadow moved again, creeping slowly; it seemed to be crawling low to the ground. He felt his pulse rate spike and slowly lowered his holdall to the ground. Whatever was coming towards him through the darkness was silent. It stopped ahead of him, its eyes glowing.

And then it began to purr, as the large black cat came up to him and rubbed against his legs.

Mike exhaled loudly and then stroked its sleek black coat. "Stupid cat! You nearly got yourself killed. Don't you know it's dangerous to be in a graveyard at night? There's no telling who or what you might meet, you know, grave-robbers or something." The purring got louder as the cat appreciated the attention.

"Yeah, well, it's time to go home now. Go on, shoo!"

The cat remained unimpressed and continued to rub against Mike's leg. He gave it a gentle push. It backed away but it stayed close. Mike decided that ignoring it would probably send it on its way, so he bent to his holdall and took out a crowbar, hoping he would find the tomb quickly and that he wouldn't need to vandalise it too badly. He grimaced; this was going to be gruesome and just plain wrong. But if Ben was right and it really was where he would find Solomon's ring, then maybe the end might, just might, justify the means.

A quick flash of the beam from his phone located a likely looking tomb. He crept forwards to get a better look, and was relieved to find that the top of the tomb bore the Templar seal carved into it. Two knights on one horse under the Templar cross, well-worn with age - but its condition was a good thing, as the stone top may give way with brute strength and the crowbar. He mentally crossed his fingers.

The cat meowed loudly at him as he leaned into it, placing the crowbar just under the lip of the lid.

"Shoo!" he hissed at the cat. It hissed back at him, arching its back, its fur on end. He sighed. "You think I want to do this? Push off and chase mice or something, you flea-ridden tomcat!" He heaved against the lid of the tomb. The cat was hissing and yowling loudly and Mike was afraid it would attract the attention of the occupants of the adjacent farmhouse. He let go of the pressure on the crowbar and turned to the cat, which was now all business and obviously pissed off; hissing and yowling constantly at Mike.

"Yeah, I get it, cats are psychic and stuff and you don't want me messing around in a bloody graveyard over what was believed to be a portal to hell. Well, I've got news for you: it's not my idea of a good night out either, and once I have what I came for, I'm gone. I won't disturb him any more than I need to. And why I'm trying to explain myself to a cat in the dark, in a graveyard, is beyond me, so shoo! Please!"

The cat remained unimpressed and equally pissed off. Mike decided to ignore it and carry on. He leaned against the crowbar and heaved. The lid gave a fraction. He heaved again and it gave an inch or so. Another heave moved it out of alignment enough for him to think he may be able to shove it to one side; a better option than removing it, because it would make it easier to replace. If he removed it completely, it was either going to shatter in the fall to the ground, or stay there because he had no way of lifting it back into place. He dropped the crowbar onto the ground where it landed with a soft thud that made him shudder. He turned his attention back to the tomb and began to shove the top inch by inch to one side; the grinding sound went through him and he tried to shut it out and focus on why he was there.

Suddenly he stopped, alert, listening, acknowledging the fact that the hairs on the back of his neck and his forearms were at attention. There was a feeling of nausea slithering around his stomach and he felt the muscles of his bladder tighten. He didn't move or breathe, afraid the sound of his breathing would attract whatever was moving towards him, wafting its stench on the chill night air as it approached.

Suddenly galvanised into action, he made a grab at the holdall at his feet, reaching for a small machete, thankful that he had strapped the wrist-activated blade under his jacket. He spun around, dropping his phone onto the ground, which lit up enough ahead of him to see what was bearing down on him.

At one time it may have been human, though there was no humanity remaining in the desiccated, skeletal thing with jagged teeth, drooling mouth, and nails like talons protruding from clawed fingers; it was barely clothed in stinking rags.

Mike took a step back as it made its leap towards him. He flexed his wrist and the blade emerged with a whooshing sound which continued as he flashed it through the air.

The thing kept coming, undeterred by the blade that had already sliced into its exposed, emaciated chest. He swung the blade again as the thing's claws bit into his arm and it cocked its head ready to sink the jagged teeth into Mike's neck. The machete connected with bone and the thing made a mewling sound, hesitated then lunged at him again.

There was an unearthly scream and a frantic hissing sound, as the black cat leaped onto the back of the thing that was doing its best to take a bite out of Mike. It drew the thing back enough for Mike to swing the blade again and follow it immediately with the machete, but not before the thing closed its jaws and made the cat howl in pain. Mike's machete connected where it was aimed and sliced through the thing's throat like a hot knife through butter.

There was a sound like tearing leather and another sickening soft thud as its head toppled from its body onto the soft earth. And then, silence. Mike allowed himself to breathe. The cat had gone behind a gravestone and he wanted to make sure it was all right; the feline had made the difference between him taking the thing's head off and becoming its next meal. The word 'ghoul' played around in his head as he made a vow that, before he stepped out again from Ben's cellar, he would be armed with much more knowledge - then he checked himself; there wasn't going to be a next time. He was determined now to do what he had to and that was that. He quit, and the angel, Sebastian, could shove it where the sun didn't shine once he had Beth back.

He moved quietly towards the gravestone, not wanting to scare the already terrified moggy.

"Here, kitty. Here puss," he said in his best crooning voice.

The voice from behind the gravestone stopped him in his tracks. "You couldn't look away while I get my clothes on, could you?"

He started, his heart skipping at the shock, "What the f …?"

CHAPTER TWENTY: LIZZIE LEE

There was a scuffling sound that took several moments as Mike's brain asked more questions in the space of seconds than he could cope with. Couldn't be. Impossible. Fiction. Wasn't it?"

She stepped from behind the grave; a beautiful young woman who looked to be in her very early twenties, tossing her sleek black hair out of her face; her lithe, slim, feline elegance, was enhanced by her tight black jeans tucked into high black leather boots and her large amber eyes shining out through the darkness.

Puss in boots, Mike thought and then shook himself out of the notion.

"The name's Lizzie Lee and, in case you didn't know, that was a ghoul; it stepped out of that broken tomb back there. Must've been living there for years. You breaking open the tomb drew him out for a meal, I guess. They're small potatoes in the hierarchy of supernatural evil, mostly brain dead. And, for your information, I have no fleas and as you can see, I am not a tom. Oh, and you're welcome by the way."

Mike was still processing the events of the last moments; although occupying only minutes they played out as hours in his confused brain. He fought for something clever to say in reply but all that came out was, "Thank you. Er ... are you okay?"

"The thing dug its claws in me but it didn't break the skin. I'll have a bruise made in hell but I can live with that. Are you going to stand there all night, or are you going to get on with what you came here for? It's OK, I'm one of the good guys. Time for explanations later."

Mike was irritated now by her attitude. She'd helped,

yes, but *he* had slain the beast. He picked up the crowbar again, trying to focus, but the questions remained: how did she know what he was there for, and what the hell was she? Cat? Woman? And there was, unnervingly, something familiar about her. He let the insanity go and turned back to Gilbert Belvoir's tomb and with a mighty shove the top slid to one side with a grating noise.

Mike grabbed his phone and shone the light inside, expecting to see the grinning skeleton of the knight at the very least, instead, all that was illuminated in the dim light of his phone was a black void and a couple of stone steps. He shone the beam onto the top step and played it downwards.

The steps disappeared into the blackness of the stinking, damp void.

"Of course they do," he muttered to himself. He picked up the holdall and straddled the wall of the tomb, feeling for the top step with his boot. Lizzie Lee stood motionless yards away; he shook his head, "Thanks for the help, but I meant it when I said 'Shoo!' so, if it's all the same to you, you should push off now. I don't know where the hell this leads to or what in God's name is down there."

He felt for the next step and slowly, step by step disappeared out of sight. Lizzie Lee sat on the soft turf, watching and waiting.

Inside the tomb, the steps led down into a narrow tunnel that smelled of damp earth and rotting timbers - among other things best not dwelt on. Tendrils and fingers of old roots and spider webs touched his face and hands as he moved forwards, and then, to his relief, after a couple of yards the tunnel walls and roof were made of brick and stone. In the pitch dark, the dim beam from his phone shone reassuringly like a beacon, illuminating the tunnel.

After thirty yards or so, the tunnel arched, framing a doorway into a vault. A quick calculation on distance and direction told Mike he was directly under the original circular knave of the Templar church. He moved slowly through the doorway into the vault, his beam resting on the centrally-placed stone tomb; the only tomb in the vault.

He moved closer to inspect it, dropping his holdall onto the floor. It was more elaborate than the tomb above ground, bearing the Templar crest, an effigy of Gilbert Belvoir on the lid, and an inscription. Mike played the light over it, brushing away the layers of dust with his free hand.

Gilbert Belvoir, Seneschal. Forever watching. Forever guarding.

"Sorry to disturb you, Gilbert, but you've got something we need."

He leaned against the tomb lid, his fingers searching for a place to insert the crowbar. There was nothing.

He shone the beam directly against the join of tomb and lid. It appeared solid.

"Great. Hope you're having a laugh!"

He walked around the tomb, searching in the circle of light for something that would indicate an opening. There was none. He played the light over the effigy of the knight again, pausing over the knight's left hand, over the ring on the middle finger.

Could it be that simple? Sometimes simple was the most obvious answer. He pressed on the ring, half expecting to hear the grinding of stone on stone as the tomb opened as if by magic. Nothing happened. So much for Indiana Jones!

He took a step back and played the beam around the vault again.

In the far corner stood a statue of a knight with a threadbare tabard over chainmail, showing the faded remnants of what had once been a red cross. The statue was leaning on his sword, head bowed, both hands crossed over one another; the entire statue was covered in centuries of dust and cobwebs.

He moved the beam around the walls of the vault, searching for something, anything that would give him a clue how to open the tomb. On the opposite wall, the circle of light picked out another inscription. Mike made his way over to it.

Like the inscription on the tomb, it was layered with dust. He raised his hand to brush away the detritus of the years, his shadow grotesque on the wall.

The sound from behind him was there and gone before he could spin around, light beam scanning the vault. He turned back to the inscription. This time the sound was immediate and close.

He spun around in time to raise his arm against the swiping sword wielded by what he had wrongly believed to be a statue of Gilbert Belvoir. He connected with the underside of the descending arm, turning a potentially nasty injury into a glancing blow which did damage all the same. The inscription on the tomb *Forever watching, Forever guarding*, suddenly took on a whole new meaning.

Gilbert Belvoir swung his sword again, pushing Mike back towards the wall. There was a clash of steel against stone as the sword missed Mike's head by inches. He ducked under the raised sword just as it came slashing through the air again.

"This is new!" he gasped. "Hey! Gilbert Belvoir. Put up your sword! You've been guarding the ring until it was needed. Well, pal, it's needed. Boy is it needed."

The sword slashed through the air again, narrowly missing Mike's ear.

"Didn't know ghosts could do that. No, really. So, if you can hear me, hear this!" He began to recite the Roman ritual of exorcism. "Exorcizamus te, omnis immundus spiritus, omnis satanica potestas, omnis incursio infernalis adversarii, omnis legio, omnis congregatio et secta diabolica ..."

What had once been Gilbert Belvoir hesitated, for a second only, and then came forward again, slashing through the air with the ancient steel blade.

Mike carried on reciting the exorcism, backing away all

the time, desperate to reach the holdall.

Belvoir slowed again, enough for Mike to fall to the floor to avoid the descending sword and roll out of the way, grabbing his bag as he did so. He thrust his hand inside and brought out a rosary, and without hesitation he threw it at Belvoir. The knight raised his free hand and caught it and held it; there was none of the expected reactions, such as burning, sizzling flesh or a cry of rage. Instead he raised the sword again as Mike took a step to the side.

Mike was speaking his thoughts aloud again. "Of course not, stupid! The guy isn't evil; he's protecting the ring *from* evil! Belvoir, listen!"

Gilbert Belvoir was obviously not doing any such thing as he slashed with the sword again, driving Mike against the wall of the vault, pressing his long-dead body against Mike and, making him gag with the stench of the grave as he pushed the Templar sword against his throat.

Mike shut his eyes, waiting for the bite of the steel into his flesh, trying with his last breath to get through to the one who had guarded the ring for hundreds of years.

"I know about Jacques de Molay and what he made you do. He wrote a journal; we have it. It tells everything, about you, about the ring and about the Demon Ark. But we need the ring - the Demon Ark is about to be unleashed and, in case that doesn't sound crappy enough, it will open every portal to hell. Does that do it for you, eh? Does that rock your boat?"

Belvoir hesitated and Mike felt the pressure against his throat ease. He dared to open his eyes. The knight was staring at him with sightless eyes, but there was something in his demeanour that made Mike understand that he was listening.

"In Megiddo - you know where that is - the Demon Ark is being brought onto the earth and every demon in hell will be free to walk this world. *Every* demon! The ring will stop it. Please, listen. Jacques de Molay wanted you to guard the ring for this reason. Give it to me and I swear by every God in every Heaven that I will use it to stop the Ark and destroy it."

Gilbert Belvoir lowered the sword and stepped back. Mike stood still, a perfect target for the knight's sword, but he figured he needed to show trust to gain it. He closed his eyes again and swallowed hard.

When he opened them Gilbert Belvoir no longer stood in front of him and the corner where he had once stood guard was empty.

And the tomb was open.

He hesitated, only for a moment, before leaning into the open tomb. The grinning skeleton of Gilbert Belvoir lay inside, the rotted cloth of the white tabard bearing the red cross of the Templars was dust long ago and inside the ribcage was a ring with a green stone.

He reached inside the tomb and picked it up with his fingertips, almost afraid to touch it lest it should somehow taint him, and put it into the pocket of his black leather jacket. His glance fell back into the open tomb and rested on a scroll clutched in the clenched finger bones. Would it crumble to dust if he touched it? But if he left it, what then? Was it important? Of course it was, otherwise it wouldn't have been buried with this awesome guardian. He decided that the risk should be taken; perhaps he owed it to Gilbert Belvoir to take his legacy and pass it on. Whatever it was.

Gingerly, he reached back into the tomb and touched the ancient parchment. It didn't crumble, but there was a brittle cracking sound as he pulled it free of the skeletal hand. It came away in several pieces, but essentially repairable. He laid it carefully on top of the contents of his bag

He took a moment to look back at the grinning skull. "Rest in peace, Gilbert. You've done your part. It's my responsibility now, God help me; God help us all."

CHAPTER TWENTY-ONE: NO PARTY TRICK

Sebastian was worried. His initial glance into the mind of his leverage proved alarming. Such great trauma had taken place, especially during her time in Hell; so much fear and heartache in what was essentially a strong mind, the toll it had taken was massive.

Beth Travis had retreated into a world of sunshine and happy, family days spent with her beloved Mike and Adain. He watched her thoughts manifest in the part of her mind that was essentially the place of dreams. He had intended to place her into a state of no fear, keeping her there until her husband had done what was required of him; had fulfilled the part of his bargain made at the time of his death.

Now, Beth had taken herself there. And there was no bringing her back from behind the wall of safety and happy dreams, unless he unleashed the tide of horror that she was protecting herself from. He watched her thoughts as if they were playing out on a TV screen.

The sun was shining, all colours were vivid and vibrant, all sounds were crisp and clear. The sound of childish laughter filled her head as a smile spread across her face, serene now. A man's laughter joined that of the child and he could see the source of their joy. Something simple. He would never understand humans and their capacity to find immense joy in such simplicity.

Up in the bluest of skies, cloudless in its perfection, a kite danced in a gentle breeze. He followed the line of the string that anchored it precariously to the earth, into the young girl's guiding hand. She was running along a sandy stretch of beach with the man running close beside her, watching her lest she fall, waiting to move quickly to prevent her from hurting herself should that happen. Mike and his daughter, Adain.

Sebastian looked again, making sure that his initial thoughts were correct. There was no bringing her out of this; the result would be catastrophic. She had to emerge from the protective shell of her waking dream in her own time, however long that took. However he looked at it, there was bad news coming for Mike Travis when he returned her to the earth.

But there was a bigger picture, one with far-reaching consequences. Mike was about to walk away from his destiny, quit his new role as demon hunter, and take his family far away. But that couldn't happen; he couldn't allow it. The so-called free will that had been granted to humans had only led to chaos and destruction. They needed to be tamed. Too much depended on it. Most of it affected the humans that infested the earth but some of it affected him and his aspirations. If he was the one seen to bring Mike Travis to heel, then his boring position as part of the induction team would give way to something much more interesting; something with more authority, something more suitable to his intellect and potential. Something that would take him closer to the creator of all this chaos.

He allowed himself a wry smile. No wonder so many of the humans had trouble believing in a God, any God; the angels had the same problem. At least the ones on the bottom rung of the celestial ladder did.

But once he had the ring of Solomon in his possession, the rest would be easy; before that, however, he had to prevent Mike from keeping the Demon Ark at bay. The more demons walking the earth and the more chaos and destruction down there, the more the humans would have respect for the angels. And when he returned the ring that could control them, well, his future suddenly looked a whole lot better. It would be one in the eye for Michael, at any rate; God, how he disliked that one. So smug and self-assured - the humans even had a special prayer to him, invoking his protection. Well, once he had the ring and controlled the demons, they would pray to *him*.

And if Mike Travis succeeded in destroying the Ark and he managed to get the stone from him he would almost certainly be in for a higher rung on the celestial ladder. It was win, win.

He watched her for several more minutes before deciding that it was safe to leave her, lost in her own world; he needed to keep an eye on his future.

Sebastian materialised in the graveyard and stood back in the shadows, just another angel among the granite ones on the tombstones - bigger that's all. He stood there, waiting, and watching.

A subtle movement to his left took his attention.

A beautiful woman, tall and slim with sleek black hair, walked with feline grace towards the open tomb. He frowned. This wasn't in his plan; something was going off script. If anything was guaranteed to add to the chaos down here it was humans interfering in heaven's plans. In this case: his plans.

The woman stopped, looked around, listening, searching the graveyard with amber eyes - eyes that had no place in a woman's face. And then he understood, as she fell to her knees and cell by cell transformed into a large black cat. A black cat that was launching itself in his direction, a hissing ball of angry black fur and lethal claws. Felines, apparently, had even less respect for angels than humans do.

So, there was a shape-shifter butting in. He would have to deal with that, but right then he had no wish to lose any dignity and, in the same instant, in a flurry of dark feathers, he disappeared. The cat landed on the adjacent gravestone with an angry hiss and something akin to a low growl. Her prey had eluded her.

She returned to her naked, womanly shape, dragging on

her clothes again as Mike appeared from inside the tomb that was essentially the entrance to the underground vault. He looked away, blushing.

She hurried towards him. "That part is a pain in the ass," she muttered without a blush. "We should get out of here, quickly. It won't be long before others arrive. Others who won't hesitate to kill you and take what you have found down there. Come with me, I'll take you back to your car."

Mike's face was a mixture of surprise, annoyance, and confusion. "Look … sorry, what did you say your name was?"

"Lizzie Lee. You can call me Lizzie."

"Look, Lizzie, as much as I appreciate your kind assistance and your more than impressive party trick, I'm fine. Thank you. And I have absolutely no idea whether I'm speaking to a woman or a cat or even if I saw what I think I saw. But you shouldn't get involved any further. Go home."

"Better than shoo! But still churlish. You did indeed see my transformation, and I'd rather we call it that than a party trick; the latter implies choice and deliberate trickery. I have no such choice and, yes, you're correct I am what is known in the supernatural world as a shape-shifter. Now, will you please come with me, before we both find ourselves in a fight that neither of us wants? Your car is in the car park of The Moon Inn, I take it? You're bleeding, by the way. Did you know?"

Mike's opinion was better unspoken, but in reality, he would appreciate a lift back to his car, whether he believed an attack imminent or just a ruse. He refused to look down at the blood that he could feel pooling around his wrist and hand. His thoughts were still racing between weird and random, and he was beginning to feel light-headed as he got into her car at the end of the lane, and he was still plagued by the thought that she was familiar. He couldn't place it, so he let it go.

She read his thoughts. "You're losing a lot of blood. But I'll stop that when I get you out of here."

He stared hard at her. "Who the *hell* are you?"

"I told you; Lizzie Lee. Christened Eliza after my maternal grandmother actually, but everyone calls me Lizzie." She paused, as if assessing how much to tell him. "Have you heard of the Strazca? No? Well, that's good, that's how it's supposed to be; it's a secret organisation, so it would be a bit of a worry if everyone had heard of it, wouldn't it? I only tell you, because you are about to learn a whole lot more about us."

"Us?"

"Mr Travis, or can I call you Mike? It seems only fair as you call me Lizzie, don't you think? Now, here's your car. I want you to follow me so I can deal with your wound."

"What are you? A doctor, or a nurse, or …"

"A cat? It's all right. I'm a herbalist, qualified I assure you, but it's in the blood. I'm a witch; not the New Age, take-your-clothes-off, harm-none Wiccan type; I'm more your traditional badass, you-deserve-your-ass-kicked-you-get-it type. You knew my grandmother."

Recognition fell into place; he knew why she was familiar. "Mam Thomas was your grandmother."

She tossed her sleek black hair out of her face. "She was."

Mike fell silent for a moment. "I have a lot to be grateful to your grandmother for." His mind travelled back to Mam Thomas and how she had given her own life to help him save Beth. It all seemed so long ago.

"Yes," she said, in a solemn voice, "So perhaps you'll trust me now, hmm?"

She was suddenly alert and pushed Mike hard so that he fell behind a gravestone, just as a shot rang out and pinged a chunk of granite from the sheltering headstone. Another shot and another, each one finding its home in the slab of granite that was barely covering Mike. This was it then, he had no weapon to hand against a gun, but if he could get close enough he could possibly get a repeat of the ghoul's fate. At least he wouldn't go out cowering behind someone else's epitaph.

He put his hand to the ground and connected with soft fabric and denim. Lizzie's clothes.

There was a sudden hissing and yowling and a muffled scream followed by a shot, which appeared to have been fired randomly as there was no sound of it hitting anything, and even though it was dark and he hadn't yet seen his enemy, it was obvious to Mike that whoever it was, was a crack shot.

Another scream of agony and yet another shot, and then, "My eyes! You filthy moggy!"

It was Mike's cue for action and he took it without hesitation, twisting his hand and operating the mechanism that ejected the blade at his wrist.

In the half-light of the beam from his phone, he could see the man writhing in agony on the floor, blood pouring from his eyes and his gun, impotent on the ground beside him. Then, a second later, a foul stream of words spoken in a language so ancient it was almost just guttural sounds in the back of his throat, came pouring out as he tried to stand.

Mike's blade was accurate and unforgiving, severing the demon's neck from his torso in a blinding rush of adrenaline and rage. He fell to his knees, blood- spattered and breathing heavily.

Lizzie Lee stood naked in front of him. "Pass my clothes, Mike, if you wouldn't mind."

He was dazed, and realised he'd been staring at her - not with lust, but fascination. He turned away quickly and grabbed at her clothes, passing them to her behind his back, grateful that in the dark she wouldn't see his discomfort.

She smiled to herself as she dressed; she had seen his blushes in the dark with her feline eyes just before they returned to their human shape.

"Come on, I need to stop that bleeding. Not all of the blood all over you belongs to that piece of shit."

"Where are we going? I have to get back home; I have to get on a plane."

She glanced down at his arm. "Well, then. You should let me see to that and I'll tell you what I can while I fix you up. There's something else you need to do before you do anything else. Someone you need to meet. But we'll do it your way. I'll meet you at your friend's house."

He narrowed his eyes. "You know a worrying amount about me. I'm not sure that's a good thing."

She smiled, her young face illuminated in the lights of the Moon Inn and he could see just how young she was; barely twenty, he thought.

"You'd better let me put something temporary on that, or you'll pass out while you're driving. Then we are going in there," she nodded towards the pub, "and before you argue, don't bother, you are going to have a pint of Guinness to replace the fluid and iron you lost. Come on, and, before you ask me, I'll have a pint of real ale - not milk."

He smiled at her; Beth was going to love her.

CHAPTER TWENTY-TWO: PAZUZU

Josh Hammond's fears that the whole dig site was going to end up as gravel didn't manifest. He was amazed at the skill of Richard Vermont's men and relieved that the entire Megiddo site was still intact. Only then could he afford the time to mourn his friend Eli and to allow the shock to set in at his murder, and for what?

Still no-one knew for sure what was beneath the mound; supposedly a Sumerian temple, even though there had been nothing to indicate that above ground, but he couldn't deny the geophysics data showing a void. And a Sumerian temple was way out of place in Megiddo. Part of him dreaded what they were going to uncover because of the nature of those that sought it, and part of him - the archaeologist part - was excited. Whatever was under the mound would be revealed within the hour; already they had exposed the doorway, and the Sumerian texts and artwork that he had been allowed to glimpse had set his heart racing. His thoughts were interrupted as one of Vermont's henchmen grabbed him roughly and cut through the ropes that bound his hands and feet together whenever he wasn't being 'useful'. He was dragged unceremoniously to the temple entrance and what he saw took his breath away.

The entrance was flanked by pillars which descended below ground level on either side of steps, hewn out of the bedrock. This was so untypical of the Sumerian period temples it made his brain buzz. He would have descended those steps without the encouragement of Vermont's thug.

At the bottom, he was greeted by a massive granite statue of Pazuzu, the Sumerian demon of the south-west wind, the most terrible of all demonic entities, having the power to spread plagues, pestilence and all manner of loathsome diseases. He was known as the bringer of storms, locusts and drought. Josh considered the conflicting history of the demon: some sources stated that he had begun his existence as an angel; one of the fourteen who became Lucifer's chief lieutenants when he led a rebellion against Heaven. Cast down into hell as a demon with the others following Lucifer's defeat, Pazuzu, became one of the Annunaki, gods worshiped by the Sumerians and the Babylonians alike. Mainstream historians and archaeologists insisted that Pazuzu only came to power during the Assyrian period, long after Sumer had come and gone, but Josh had never confined himself to the boundaries set by scholar-puppets and had seen the evidence for himself. Now, more evidence reared up before him.

The clay statue in front of him was typical of the depiction of Pazuzu: standing a massive seven feet in height, with the head of a dog and the body of a man with four wings, the right arm pointing skywards and the left pointing down, the tail of a scorpion and a snake for a penis. Josh shuddered at the image.

The statue stood on a clay plinth which was covered in its entirety by strange markings and sigils. Josh had seen similar before in other ancient temples. They were magical markings designed to keep the demon's spirit contained within the statue itself or confined to the temple, unable to cross the threshold.

Overnight, Vermont's extensive team had opened the temple and cleared away fallen debris and checked the security of the roof and walls; their agenda was to open the temple with complete disregard of the layers of history above it, and so they had ripped their way in. Once inside, they had seen the improbable state of preservation and bowed before Pazuzu - for who else could have maintained the temple in this way? The temple was open now and it was spectacular. As he fed on the splendour he pondered the unbelievable preservation; there was no logic to the temple being intact after millennia. The whole was illuminated by torches on the walls, fed with oil from channels connected to a central oil cistern.

His awe was interrupted by the unwelcome question: if they had accomplished what they set out to do, then why did they still want him; why was he still alive and not the victim of the same treatment as Eli? He wasn't sure he wanted to speculate on the answer.

It was supplied without asking, by Vermont. "Magnificent isn't it? I'm sure you would love to spend time here and I am inclined to grant your wish. In fact, you are to be an honoured guest in the ceremony that will take place tomorrow night. In the meantime I will allow you to remain here to enjoy this magnificence while you can. Perhaps I can draw your attention to the large stone construction in the centre?"

He nodded to his entourage who, all save two, left the temple. Vermont smiled, and it reminded Josh of a snake that was about to bring bad news to something small and insignificant.

A glance over his shoulder at the huge rectangular stone made his blood run cold. It was approximately seven feet long by four feet wide and had deep channels running along the sides into what Josh knew would be a drain. A sacrificial altar; and now he understood his role as a guest of honour.

As he turned back to Vermont, one of the heavies planted his fist squarely under Josh's chin, turning his lights out, before leaving him in a heap on the floor to come to whenever his body dictated. Josh didn't hear the door slam shut, nor the heavy bolts and locks secure him inside.

He was out for half an hour and when he woke his head was pounding and, on careful exploration of his jaw, he decided that, on the whole, he'd been lucky. He'd seen the size of the fist that travelled towards him at a speed that defied any preventive manoeuvre; he worked his jaw side to side and up and down, concluded it was intact, and hauled himself to his feet, allowing the room to spin itself to a stop.

Josh could never be accused of being slow on the uptake and he was all too well aware of his situation and its probable outcome. All that remained was to decide between spending the remaining time in studying the temple as his heart craved, or trying to find a way out. Common sense pulled him in the direction of the latter. He wanted to go home to his wife, Maddie, and their autistic daughter, Grace, more than he wanted to learn the secrets that the temple was bound to give up.

He skirted the sacrificial altar, avoiding sight of the dark stains that covered the slab and continued, darker, down the side channels to the drain that he had known would be there. A thorough examination of the walls revealed no other doors; the only way in or out was locked, bolted, and barricaded every which way to hell and back.

He could either sit and wait out his last hours, or he could distract himself by studying the art and inscriptions.

There appeared to be a mixture of Sumerian and Babylonian influence, and although both were from the same region of ancient Mesopotamia - now modern day Iraq - there was a significant overlap in timelines and deities. The inscriptions were prayers and praises to Pazuzu. His worship was dark and sacrificial, his responses harsh and bloody, and in no man's book could he be described as good looking.

Something was niggling Josh. From snatches of conversation he had heard, Richard Vermont was linked to a secret, dark arm of the Knights Templar, worshipping Baphomet; a far cry from the serious nature of the temple in which he was now imprisoned. Where was the connection? Was there a connection? Or was Richard Vermont simply changing his allegiance in time for the big show? The latter seemed the most likely.

Further contemplation ended abruptly as the ground shook and a large crack appeared diagonally across the temple floor and the smell of rotten eggs drifted up from it in wispy tendrils of black smoke.

Josh leaped to his feet and moved well away from the fissure that had opened up in front of him. It was only an inch or so wide, but enough to tell him where it would lead to.

Time was running out at Megiddo for anyone unlucky enough to be in the vicinity and, if what they believed was true, for all of humanity. He closed his mind to the imaginings of this earth populated by every demon from the Pit, led by Lucifer himself, and brought his thoughts into sharp focus on his immediate predicament - to find a way out, as he had no inclination to be the guest of honour at this particular banquet.

There was a loud sound, like white noise, inside his head; so loud it made him clap his hands over his ears and squeeze his eyes shut. The sound was painful and he heard his own voice cry out, and then came the vision.

The desert sky was blackened with the awful insects, a swarm so thick it obscured the sun. Locusts. Josh could see them, hear them, as he flailed his arms against them, before falling insensible to the floor of the temple.

When the voice filtered through into his consciousness, it was deep and sensuous, but there was a rasping, roughness to it also. The sound of it made the hairs on his arms stand up.

He lifted his head and Pazuzu stood before him, living and breathing, in all his foulness.

"Bow down before me and I will save you from the sacrifice to come; refuse and I will fill your belly with locusts and flies and you will vomit them into eternity."

Josh drew up his knees and rolled onto his side, his hands still clasped to his ears as if they could blot out the voice that was filling his head and squirming in his stomach.

"Get away!" he yelled into the emptiness of the temple. "I won't listen to you!"

"You will listen, and you will choose. Serve me or spew my locusts!"

"I will never serve you. Never."

"Then feel the maggots writhing inside you already. Soon there will be a swarm of locusts puked with every retch and gag your body can produce."

The pain in his stomach and entrails was sudden and agonising. He screamed his pain to the walls of the temple. Pazuzu stood, a massive clay statue on its plinth again, the only companion in the temple. Another spasm of pain sent shards of exquisite agony into every part of his body. The pain gave way to a writhing and he watched as his abdomen undulated as the locusts hatched in his gut. And he could hear them, like deep white-noise.

He heaved, and they were in his throat, he retched and the vomiting of the locusts began.

Pazuzu stood before him again, satisfied at Josh's expression of abject horror and sheer terror as he was no longer able to speak. The demon of the south west wind raised his clawed hand and the vomiting stopped and so, blessedly, did the writhing and hatching in his belly.

"Shall I take them from you? Or will you spew them into eternity?"

Tears were rolling down Josh's cheeks. He was beaten, he wasn't strong enough to resist; his alternative was to continue with the abomination until Richard Vermont saw fit to take his life the following evening, and then what? Puking locusts until the end of time?

He sobbed. "I will serve you. May God forgive me and have mercy on me, I will serve you."

CHAPTER TWENTY-THREE: HER OWN WORLD

The sun was warm on her body as Beth watched with the complete love and satisfaction that only a mother can experience, as her husband and daughter ran along the beach dragging the kite behind them. She shaded her eyes against the glare to better see their happy expressions, smiling at the laughter that was drifting on the warm breeze from Adain.

She allowed herself a momentary frown; why wasn't she running along with them, joining in the fun? No matter, the thought passed as quickly as it had come and she returned to basking in her own happiness and peace once again.

Time had appeared to stand still for her and the day seemed to last forever, but she was tired now; sleepy. She waved to Mike and Addie to come back; it was time to go home.

They came back at her beckoning, falling in a happy heap onto the sand.

"Time to go," she said. "But we can come back again tomorrow. Or maybe we can go for a walk through the bluebell woods; that would be lovely." They smiled back at her as she drifted into dreamless sleep.

Sebastian was becoming increasingly concerned. This was not his doing but he knew that he would be blamed for it, despite the fact that this had been triggered by Beth's sojourn in hell. He looked again into her mind, desperate to see any indication that it was possible to heal her, but also too well aware that to bring her back to reality was even more dangerous. She had to come out of this in her own time; it was her soul's way of coping with being in the Pit, and only her own soul would know when it was ready to return to reality.

A ruthless, ambitious angel he may be, but Sebastian had no intention of harming Beth; he just wanted to use her as leverage, but he knew that to do so now would be callous and unforgiveable, and he needed Mike Travis to dance to his tune if he was going to take the credit for bringing Morning Star's efforts to a halt. And then, when he had possession of Lapsit Exillis, his goal would be even closer to his grasp. Because the stone did not only control the demons; it controlled the angels too.

He watched Beth as she slept soundly, knowing that she was in no pain or anguish, and he made a decision: he would return her when the time was right and it would have the most favourable outcome and, in the meantime, he would watch over her as she slept or let her mind tell her that she was in a happy place with her family.

*

Mike was impatient at the delay in getting back to Ben's place with the ring. He could feel it hot in his pocket, as if it had been plucked from a furnace. He put his hand in the pocket and touched the ring for the hundredth time and for the hundredth time felt it ice-cold to his touch. He had done as Lizzie Lee had commanded him and drunk the pint of Guinness and was reluctant to admit that she had been right; he felt better.

Outside in his car, she had dressed his wound.

"It will need stitches, but not here. This will keep it from bleeding all over the place until I can do a proper job. Mike, I know what you are planning to do but you can't do this on your own. There are people that want to help you."

He looked at her for several minutes, trying to see into her thoughts, trying to understand. He failed.

"Look, I'm grateful for your help, I am. And when this

is over I'll take time to try and understand the cat thing which, I have to say, I was not prepared for and still don't understand. But right now, I have to go. I have to do this." He paused, and when he spoke again, his emotions came through their fragile barrier. "They have my wife. They have Beth."

She frowned as if this was news she hadn't expected to hear. "The demons?"

He shook his head. "No. It's a goddamn angel that has her. Name of Sebastian, and when this is over I will find a way to kill an angel."

She fell silent for a moment, then, "There are ways. But now is not the time. If nothing else, Mike, let me come with you and do a proper job on that wound. The last thing you need to cope with is an infection that could take your life."

Mike laughed out loud at the incongruity of her last words. He'd been to hell to bring Beth back, had fought and killed - or thought he had - a demon, and now he was about to travel to Israel to stop the Demon Ark which could open every portal to hell; an infection was the last thing he was worried about. But there was more of Mam Thomas in the girl than even she probably knew, and because of that he nodded his acceptance to her.

"You'll have ten minutes when we get back." He was about to tell her to follow him, but she pre-empted his words.

"It's OK. I know where Ben Lovecraft lives."

Mike frowned; just how much did this girl know about him and his family? And why? He shrugged it off; it could wait for later, now he had to get back.

He drove the ridiculously short distance in dark thought. His instincts to walk away from it all were still alive and kicking and, when it was over, he was determined to take Beth and Addie so far away that even he couldn't find his way back. It wasn't fair; he may have signed up for this but *they* hadn't and he was damn sure they weren't going to pay any more of a price than they already had. He ground his teeth hard, as he contemplated what he might do to Sebastian.

When he pulled into the layby at the front of Ben's cottage he was surprised to see a beaten-up old Volkswagen Beetle parked there, and even more surprised when Lizzie Lee stepped out of it.

"How did you get here before me in that thing?"

"Don't let her hear you say things like that, she offends easily! I was born around here; I know the lanes and the shortcuts. What kept you?" Lizzie replied.

She walked ahead of him to the sound of Fred barking like crazy; a mixture of joy at his sensed return of one of his loved-ones and a hint of apprehension at the approach of a stranger - a stranger that his senses told him smelled strongly of a cat that he couldn't see.

Before they reached the door, it was flung open by Jack whose expression revealed the level of his anxiety.

"Did you find it?" he demanded. "Are you OK?"

Mike grinned at his best friend, "Yes and yes."

Jack's eyes travelled to the blood seeping through Lizzie's temporary dressing and at the blood-spatter on his face that had defied his attempts to wipe them away.

"You're hurt!"

"Jack, calm down. What's up with you? You been mainlining caffeine or something?"

"No ... I ... Bazaliel told me that you were injured."

Mike scowled. "Still listening to that friggin' demon, Jack? I told you! Cut it off!"

"It's true then, you are hosting a demon; we wondered about that." Lizzie stepped out of the shadows.

Jack looked surprised, as if seeing her for the first time. "Er .. hi there." He threw a quizzical glance at Mike. Fred, meanwhile,was still barking at what he perceived as an invisible cat. Jack quieted him with a stroke and a sharp rebuke as they stepped inside.

"Jack, this is Lizzie Lee, Lizzie meet Jack Carter. Have

you heard from Ben?" Mike asked.

Jack sneezed. "He's about an hour away. He told me not to let you go anywhere until he gets back. And he said he means it; there's stuff you need to know."

Mike nodded and sat down heavily on the sofa. "Maybe you have time for those stitches after all," he said to Lizzie.

She smiled briefly as she went to the door. "Back in a mo."

Jack sneezed twice and turned on Mike immediately. "Who the hell is that? And what does she know?"

"I told you, her name is Lizzie Lee and she sort of helped me out back there. I was attacked by a ghoul and she ... distracted ... it long enough for me to take its head off. Likewise a demon-possessed gunman. And yes, she knows more than she should, though I've yet to find out how." His words were matter-of-fact but his expression was one of deep concern.

Jack raised his eyebrows, "A ghoul? You mean a real corpse-eating dead thing?"

Mike nodded. "Yep. The very thing. This job just gets better and bloody better."

"I can't help feeling I've seen her before somewhere," Jack mused, as if Mike's encounter with a ghoul was something out of normality.

"Yeah, that would be because she's Mam Thomas's granddaughter . Oh, and you know that cat allergy of yours ...?"

Jack sneezed again as Lizzie came back through the door carrying a small case. He raised his eyebrows then frowned and shook his head. Not possible.

Mike just stared in silence.

Lizzie tossed her sleek black hair back again, a characteristic gesture of hers that they would all come to know well, as she smiled at Jack. "What's the matter boys? Cat got your tongue?"

CHAPTER TWENTY-FOUR: NO WAY BACK

Lizzie bathed Mike's open wound and applied some tea tree oil to kill any bacteria still present. It stung like a son-of-a-bitch but he made no protest; his concentration was on the one administering the torture. Neither did he flinch when she put five stitches into the wound, pulling the edges together with the polish of a professional. She finished with a dressing infused with comfrey. She was indeed of Mam Thomas's lineage.

Treatment over, she handed a round, brown pill to Jack. "Looks bad, tastes worse, but it will help with the cat allergy. Sorry about that, it happens a lot."

Jack swallowed the herbal pill meekly, his demeanour belying the fact that inside him, Bazaliel was protesting loudly as he tried to find the demon's off-switch. 'A witch! She's a witch! Get her out of here', Bazaliel was yelling in Jack's head.

Mike leaned back on the sofa, "I think you have some explaining to do, young lady. Like, how you seem to know so much about my business and why you were at Garway tonight. The cat thing, I suspect, is too long a story for now, so let's stick to priorities, shall we? Start with why you are so well-informed."

Lizzie looked unperturbed at Mike's tone. "I mentioned the Strazca to you in the graveyard. As I told you already, it's a secret organisation with contacts all over the world. It began in Slovakia in the eleven hundreds, its purpose back then was simply to watch and track vampires, though now it observes and documents all paranormal activity that it comes across. Unlike other such organisations you may have read about, the Strazca doesn't balk at interference where it deems it necessary. Our operatives are highly trained investigators, most of us with other skills, and you haven't heard of us because until now we wanted it that way."

Jack's face was a picture of bewilderment.

Lizzie continued. "We have been watching you for a long time, Mike; ever since Crowsmoor. Watching you develop your own abilities, waiting to see if you would go that extra mile against the powers of darkness that already walk the earth and soon will be joined by every legion of hell. I also told you that there was someone who wanted to meet you; his name is Roman Woolfe, and he is what we call the Eldritch, the overall head of the Strazca."

"Sounds fascinating," Mike said, in a voice laden with sarcasm. "But forgive me for not getting too excited. I've got other things pressing right now. Maybe I can take a rain-check?"

Jack had been following the conversation with great patience, but now he interrupted. "So, how do you know about the demon in me?"

"We get our information from many sources. One of them happens to work as a nurse in the intensive care unit of Neville Hall Hospital. She reported your miraculous recovery – twice – and, as this world is remarkably short on miracles but well-supplied with dark magic and its agents, we put two and two together and came up with a demon. It wasn't difficult."

Mike made an impatient noise. "Am I supposed to be impressed? As I said, there are other things more pressing right now."

Jack was still not finished. "A cat? Really? You're kidding, right?"

Mike glowered at his friend. "Jack, stay on track here."

Their conversation came to a halt at the sound of an approaching, powerful motor-bike engine. Ben was back, complete with a speeding ticket.

Fred was ecstatic and proceeded to demonstrate the

fact, by throwing himself at Ben and whimpering his gratitude that someone had arrived to make sense of the craziness that was happening in their home.

Ben ignored all but Mike. "Got it?"

Mike nodded. "Yes. And you were right, there were – obstacles. But I have it."

Ben breathed a relieved sigh and only then did he acknowledge that there were others present.

"You OK, Jack?"

Jack nodded and so Ben turned his attention to their guest. "Hello, Lizzie. Long time."

Mike was aghast. "You know her?"

Ben nodded casually. "I knew her granny better, but I met Lizzie a few times." He returned his attention to Lizzie. "I was sorry to hear about your gran. To what do we owe this pleasure?"

Lizzie pushed herself up to perch on the worktop next to the range, dangling her legs like a child. "I was sent to Garway to keep an eye on Mike."

Ben seemed to accept this with equanimity, which unsettled Mike even further. "Taken over from your gran, then?" Ben enquired.

She nodded. "Yes. Well, kind of; she was one of the Watchers, but I work for the main organisation."

"The Strazca?"

It was enough for Mike. "You know about that too? When were you going to tell me? *Were* you going to tell me?"

"Easy, Mike. I know about the Strazca because they know about me. What I am – what I was. I suspect I am well-documented and observed. Am I right?" He directed his remark to Lizzie.

She nodded. "Yep, along with other fallen or rogue angels we know about."

Mike shook his head wondering which rabbit hole he'd fallen into.

Ben ignored it. "So, before we do anything else, there's

something important." He shoved the table to one side and yanked back the rug that covered the trapdoor, obviously unconcerned that Lizzie was about to see his cellar.

He disappeared for several moments, which left an uncomfortable silence in the room above, and when he returned he was carrying a small, square, cast-iron box which was heavily adorned with protective symbols. He handed it to Mike who was unprepared for its weight.

"Put the ring inside and don't take it out again until you face the Ark. And above all, in fear of your soul, do not put it on your finger. If you do, I fear all will be lost."

The silence was heavy as Mike drew the ring from his pocket. It was a perfectly innocent-looking ring; plain gold with a gold setting surrounding a green stone of varying shades. He allowed it to sit in the centre of his hand for a moment, feeling the heat from it, knowing that if he touched the stone, it would be cold. He tried to make light of what he was feeling.

"So, if I put it on, what happens? Do I become invisible, Bilbo Baggins style?"

Ben's voice was harsh and booming. "No joke, Mike. Put the damn thing in the box and leave it there until the time comes to use it. For God's sake!"

Mike was solemn again as he pulled the box open against its magnetic closure. He dropped the ring inside and the box almost closed of its own accord.

Ben allowed himself a moment's sadness for Brother Bernard before passing the news on to Lizzie.

"I'm afraid Brother Bernard is dead. Brutally murdered. The Abbot has notified the Eldritch." He turned to Mike to explain further. "Brother Bernard was a member of the Strazca; they called him the Translator, and although he preferred the cloistered life, he served God in other ways too. I killed the demon possessing the young novice who butchered him." He waited for the inference to sink in. Mike and Jack made the connection together.

146

"Christ, Ben!" Mike exclaimed, "That means …"

Jack finished for him. "That you have no chance of your redemption now. You won't ever be able to go back."

Ben shook his head, half in sorrow, and half in relief. "No," he said quietly. "It seems I blew it."

CHAPTER TWENTY-FIVE: SURPRISE VISITOR

Roman Woolfe answered the phone in his study. "This is Roman."

"It's Lizzie. He has it. I've offered our help but it has been respectfully declined. He's taking the other one with him, and the initial report is true, Jack Carter is host to a demon. I haven't had time to witness any activity as yet and although Mike accepted my help at the scene, he's adamant ... The priest told me about the Translator. I'm sorry, Roman; I know you were fond of him."

There was a moment's silence as Roman gathered his thoughts and measured his reaction. "He was my cousin. He was the older by several years and so he knew my grandfather better than I; he remembered the trouble and why the family had to flee. It was what happened to our grandfather that instilled in both of us a deep interest in all things supernatural. He chose poverty and the cloister to pursue his research, I chose the life of a wealthy man in order to gain access to artefacts and manuscripts and contact with people possessed of 'skills', such as yourself. So, yes, I will mourn him as family and as the last of my line now he is gone. But we have work to do, Lizzie. If you cannot persuade him to let us help, then perhaps I should make an unannounced visit? Possession of this ring is most dangerous; he must be made aware of that. Is he aware of the fact that we have been watching them all?"

"I believe he is beginning to realise that, but he's a long way from acceptance. I will try and keep him here until you arrive."

"I have had word from John Barclay out of Haifa; there is much activity at Megiddo, both military and otherworldly. The demons are gathering there in preparation for the Demon Ark. And then ... and then, all hell will literally be let loose. I can be with you within the hour; I'll get Paul to checkout a landing area. I'll call you and you can pick me up. I need to talk to him. To all of them."

He disconnected the conversation without another word, and redialled the number of his private helicopter pilot, Paul Bancroft.

"Paul, I need to make a journey as soon as you can prepare. You will need a landing spot as close to the village of Skenfrith as possible. It's rural, you should be able to purchase the co-operation of a local farmer - pay him what he wants and make it happen."

He put down the phone and sat back in his chair, his lips pursed against his steepled fingers. It was time they were brought into the fold of the Strazca in one form or another. It had been all right up to now as Mike Travis had been working on the periphery of the supernatural but he was hip-deep in the major league now, where no-one and nothing played by the rules. He was going to get himself killed, or worse. His wife was already in deep trouble from his previous encounters and Roman doubted that the situation was made any easier by the interference of an angel with his own agenda. Sebastian had been on the Strazca radar before, and both times it hadn't ended well for the humans involved, and the stakes hadn't been this high.

The big picture, this time, was terrifying and he doubted that a rookie hunter and a demon-possessed friend would cut it, and that would mean devastation; but maybe, just maybe, a rookie would just pull it off with sheer guts and bravado. So, with or without Mike Travis's acceptance of it, help would be there. Discretion would be the key, but he would try appealing to Mike's better judgement first. He didn't know that Mike's better judgement was way off the charts right then.

His phone rang. Paul had secured a landing space and was ready to leave as soon as Roman was ready.

Half an hour later, they were in the air and forty minutes after that they were landing in the meadow of Pwll Ddu Farm.

And Roman Woolfe wasn't the only visitor approaching Ben's cottage.

Fred was the first to be aware of the approach and gave his usual warning, and then suddenly stopped barking and ran to the door wagging his tail and whimpering in anticipation of the greeting. Mike was on his feet instantly; could it be Beth? Ben pushed Fred to one side and opened the door into the dark.

Martha Treneglos was known for her stoicism and no-nonsense demeanour, but the vision in front of them alarmed them all. Her usually neat hair in a no-nonsense bun was bedraggled and hanging about her soot-marked face and her neat country tweeds were blackened and singed, her tights were laddered and in holes, but the most alarming thing was her expression of helplessness - a condition with which the ex-headmistress was completely unfamiliar. It was alien to her, and it was causing her the utmost anxiety.

Mike's arms were around her in a heartbeat as he guided her to the sofa. Jack was on his feet and heading for the whisky bottle and Ben was reaching for the kettle, all of them vitally aware that something desperate had happened to the old woman they loved; all guessing the obvious - that she had somehow been involved in a fire. Ben's thoughts went to Brother Benjamin. Mike's mouth was set in a grim line.

Mike sat her down in front of the dying fire, as Jack threw on a log and poked it back into life.

Mike's voice was gentle yet compelling. "Sit here and get warm, take your time and tell us what's happened."

She fought furiously to regain the composure that she had maintained throughout the drive from Cornwall, but the sight of her loved ones and the instant feeling of safety had discomposed her again. Tears threatened and, in her book, that would never do. She took a swallow of the whisky Jack had handed her and they allowed her to stand and pace the room in silence until she was ready to put into words the events that had brought her to them.

Eventually, she took a deep breath. "Demons. Filthy, black-eyed demons. They set fire to my cottage. It's gone; everything is gone. But they didn't get me, though they tried hard enough." The contempt and loathing in her voice spoke volumes. Mike supressed the hint of a smile; he had always thought that any demon taking on Martha Treneglos would soon find itself sorry.

"What happened?" he asked softly.

"I opened my door to them, which I should never have done. I should have known better; Cat was having a hissing fit, fur on end, the lot. As soon as they were in, he launched himself, claws out, into the face of one of them, gave me time to defend myself." She saw the questioning looks and explained. "Ever since you told me what was happening, I did the research. God knows I've enough … *had* enough … books on the subject." Her face clouded over at the thought of her precious books, all ash now. But it was the memory of Cat that tipped the balance and sent tears rolling down her face. "He's dead," she said. "Stupid moggie. Always knew he'd come to a sticky end." Her voice broke then and she began pacing again, sipping the whisky as she went. "Well, I had a huge pan of heavily salted water that had a crucifix sitting in it for a week. That'll do, I thought. Buy me some time if it happens. Well, it did happen, too quickly. I threw it over them, and it slowed them down long enough for me to get my father's army pistol. Yes, I know you can't kill a demon with a bullet, but if you aim it right, it brings them down for a minute or two. One of them threw flames - didn't know they could do that; thought it was fiction." She appeared to contemplate the fact. "Well, too much combustible material apparently, went up like a torch. I'm afraid they got away, ran off like the cowardly, lily-livered creatures they are. Did you know they are basically cowards? Strange don't you think?"

Mike could have informed her that the higher-ranking demons were far from that, but refrained, partly out of compassion and partly due to the fact that no-one ever argued with Martha.

She seemed to sag a little and slumped back down onto the sofa, spilling a little of the whisky as she went. She didn't notice.

Everyone reacted together. Jack poured her more scotch and Mike put a tentative arm around her shoulder and was surprised when she allowed it. Ben remained silent and made for the trap-door to the cellar. Martha didn't appear to notice that either.

Mike's expression was forbidding; his mouth set in a straight, tight line that was barely containing his fury. It came out loud and clear in an explosion of rage.

"You see! Now do you get it? I have to finish this now and for good before anyone else gets hurt because of me! This whole goddamn mess is because I took out Astaroth; it's my mess and I'm going to be the one to end it. Whatever it takes."

His face was white as china clay but the fire in his eyes expressed the determination behind the rage, and then he was suddenly and totally in control, as he flicked the switch on his emotions and set their thermostat to below zero.

The drama of Martha's arrival, and her condition, had overtaken their previous discussions and only when the heat of the moment had died, did Mike realise that Lizzie Lee was no longer with them.

Martha had regained a scrap of her usual composure as she scanned the room. "Where's Beth? I went to the cottage first and, finding no-one home, I came here."

Jack risked life and limb by kneeling in front of her and clasping her hand, and was rewarded by the warm light returning to her eyes, as she looked down at him with the expression she had always reserved for her most troublesome pupil who defied all detentions and wormed his way into her heavily-defended heart.

No-one answered her immediately, and then Mike spoke in a calm, icy voice.

"Apparently, Heaven decided, well, one of the angels decided, that I need some leverage to finish what I started and so he has taken her to a place of safety - his words - until I do just that. She's perfectly safe, apparently in her own dreamland, believing that she is with Addie and me. And, before you say anything, I intend to put an end to this son-of-a-bitch when I've finished with the demons bringing back their filthy Ark. And I will."

His cold, measured words left them in no doubt of the fact.

Jack took her hand again. "You have a home here, you know that. It will be all right. You're all right."

Her fondness for him and his soft kindness threatened to overwhelm her again. She sniffed loudly and put on her most haughty tone. "I trust you are going to, in the modern parlance, kick some ass, Michael?"

CHAPTER TWENTY-SIX: CHARM OFFENSIVE

The Strazca monitored all things supernatural; their reach was global but their agents numbered less than one would imagine. It was their state of the art technology and the infiltration of their agents in high and low places that kept their information both current and comprehensive.

Mike had been on their radar since his TV programmes investigating the paranormal, and the debunking of much of it. They watched him move away from the media as his knowledge and experience got wider. They watched him in Crowsmoor. They watched him settle into the Welsh borderlands and continue his work, gaining more and more insight into the world of the paranormal and what was considered supernatural. Now his name was in high profile in connection with information on the Demon Ark manifesting in Megiddo, along with its implications. Now they were ready to step out of the shadows.

Roman Woolfe was more used to driving in style and comfort than hunched up in Lizzie's worse-for-wear Beetle, but there was more on his mind than discomfort.

"You're certain he has the ring?" he questioned her.

Lizzie crunched the gears; Roman always made her nervous, a rare accomplishment given her lineage and abilities. "Yes. There was no way he would have left Garway without it, and I'm afraid he saw my transformation. He's still processing that. It may throw him off guard long enough for me to get hold of it. He has it in an iron box, so he's aware of how to protect it. Most of his knowledge comes from the ex-priest, but he hasn't had enough time to learn everything he needs to. Ignorance may give him the advantage, I don't know, but do we want to take the risk?"

Roman said nothing.

Lizzie continued. "He's vulnerable right now. The angel has his wife but, you know that."

Roman nodded. "We must try and persuade him to part with the ring. It needs to be in safer hands. And then it needs to disappear. It has no business on this earth once it has disabled the Ark."

Lizzie wanted to say more, but she needed the right words. Eventually she said, "You won't hurt him, will you?"

He didn't answer.

It only took a few minutes to arrive at Ben's, but it was time enough for Mike to be ready for blood. Filled with rage and guilt that those close to him were suffering just as the demons had promised, he was up for the fight - but on his terms. Roman Woolfe might as well have saved himself the trip.

He glowered at Lizzie Lee, "I told you, I appreciate your help at Garway but that's it and, yes, I knew and respected the hell out of your gran, but you're not her. God knows what you are! This is *my* problem. So, thank you for your kind offer of help, but no thanks."

Roman raised a refined eyebrow. "You said he was stubborn, but you didn't say he was arrogant too," he said to Lizzie. Then to Mike, "Arrogant indeed, Mr Travis, that you believe this to be your fight. I should remind you that if the Demon Ark is allowed to activate the consequences will be catastrophic, for all of us. You may have the Lapsit Exillis - yes, we know about the ring and its provenance – but, make no mistake we have a dog in this fight. If you choose not to join us then that is your prerogative, but I urge you to reconsider. We have vast resources, and whilst I imagine your mentor here has done you proud, we can do better, we can give you an advantage. Talk it over and call me." He put his business card on the table and turned his attention to Martha. "Miss Treneglos, I presume? I apologise for intruding on what looks like a family drama. I will leave you in peace. He smiled and nodded his farewell and left with Lizzie as abruptly as he had arrived.

Martha snorted into her drink. "How does he know me?" she demanded. "And who was that sultry young woman?"

"He knows far too much about all of us, for my liking," Mike replied, his voice laden with acid. "And as for her, well, you'll like her when you get to know her – *if* you get to know her."

Martha turned on Ben. "Benjamin? You're very quiet on all this."

Ben nodded. "Roman Woolfe is right, Mike. With the Strazca behind you, you have a far better chance at winning this. You should at least have listened to what he had to say. I have a feeling that before this ends we will need all the allies we can get. And it's true, my library and weapons may look impressive, but they are limited. The Strazca has a library that will make your eyes water and an arsenal that I daren't think about."

Mike narrowed his eyes, "How do you know this? How do you know so much about them? Seems to me that as I'm no longer your ticket back, you want to hand me over to some playboy curator."

Ben made an impatient noise and raised his voice several decibels, his anger uncontained. "Don't be a fool, Mike. I'm not handing you over to anyone; it's because I care what happens to you that I think you should at least give him a chance. As for how I know so much, I told you: they know about me. They approached me to join them years ago, but I decided to wait for you to show yourself to me in my own way. I did think about it, I even paid a visit to the headquarters and spent the day with Roman and, whilst he does no field work, he's definitely more than a curator."

Mike looked at Martha and Jack for support but their faces gave nothing away. He got to his feet and paced the room.

"You all seem to think I should give him a hearing, so, okay then." He snatched up Roman's discarded business card and his phone, and dialled. It was answered quickly.

"It's Mike. Look, I was maybe a bit hasty. The consensus of opinion is that I should at least listen to you. I'm afraid other circumstances may be colouring my opinions. Did you get far?"

"Not really." The front door opened and Roman stepped back inside.

Mike scowled. "I don't like being second-guessed, but I'll overlook it this time. So, I'm listening, what do you have to say?"

"I think you should come with me. And before you tell me you have to get on a plane for Israel, allow me to suggest that to do so ill-equipped would be folly at best, dangerous at worst. Our estimate is that we have thirty or so hours before the Ark reaches the surface; the planetary alignment isn't due to appear until the night after tomorrow and then there has to be a lengthy ritual to activate it. You have time to come with me and then, regardless of your decision, I will arrange your transport. I take it, it will be for two?" He looked meaningfully at Jack. "Or should I say, three?"

Jack appeared to be about to protest but thought better of it.

"Good. Then you should gather what you want to take, bearing in mind your travel restrictions. I will arrange for equipment at the other end; we have an agent in Haifa awaiting instructions. You should come too, Jack. Get together what you need. I will sit and chat with Miss Treneglos here, and perhaps trouble Benjamin for a glass of scotch."

He sat next to Martha, who, totally out of character, seemed flustered by his charm offensive. Mike would have expected her armour to have repelled his advances but it seemed her defences were down, courtesy of her recent trauma and even more recent glasses of whisky.

Ben handed him a generous measure of the amber liquid along with the bottle that, no doubt, would be harsh on Roman's palette after his usual twelve- year-old single malt, and sat in the chair opposite. He wasn't going to take his eyes away from Roman Woolfe for one second.

The Eldritch's urbane charm was ramped up to max, but deep down he knew it would cut no ice with the redoubtable Martha Treneglos, even if her tweeds *were* singed and she still had soot smudges on her cheeks.

"It appears that you have had some trouble, Martha. May I call you Martha? Permit me top up your glass."

"Hm. You may call me Martha because that is the name my parents gave to me at baptism, young man. And, just because I may be somewhat dishevelled, does not mean you may take advantage. And yes, a top-up will be welcome. You are correct in your assumption; I have been involved in what you would refer to as a demonic attack, the result of which is, my home and all I possess has been burned ..." she paused "... along with my cat. So forgive my appearance and no doubt I smell like a damp bonfire." She took a sip of the whisky and settled back on the sofa, her gimlet eyes locked onto his.

He smiled. She was everything he imagined her to be and he was more than a little discomforted that she had made him feel as if he had been caught out in some mischief that would result in reprisals. She would be perfect for what he had in mind for her; the trick would be to allow her to believe it was her idea. He had no idea that the situation was about to arise which would take care of that for him.

Mike and Jack reappeared with a couple of bags; Mike's misgivings still apparent on his strained features.

CHAPTER TWENTY-SEVEN: THE TEMPLE WALLS

Josh Hammond lay prostrate on the dirt floor of the temple, his stomach still heaving on locust larvae. The walls had stopped spinning but the aftermath of the attack by Pazuzu had left him devastated. Over and over again he heard his own words – *"I will serve you. May God forgive me and have mercy on me, I will serve you."*

He moaned in his own wretchedness. How could he have been so weak? But the memory of the locusts spewing from his mouth made him curl up on the floor in a foetal position. He was undone.

He had moved from the belief that he was to be the human sacrifice to the understanding that he was to be an instrument of the demon Pazuzu within the space of a few hours and, right then, he would have preferred his initial theory. He would rather be dead than serve a minion of Hell. In his desperation he cast about for anything that he could employ to bring about his end. He thought of his wife Maddie and their daughter Grace and was ashamed of the track of his thoughts. There had to be a way out and, if there was, he would find it. He brought his mind back to the inscriptions on the temple walls and hauled himself upright to examine them closely. He picked up a discarded torch and lit it from one of the burning brands on the wall.

The walls had been lined with clay so that the earliest script, the Sumerian cuneiform, had been pressed into the clay whilst wet, using blunt reeds to form the wedge-shaped impressions.

The temple had obviously been in use for millennia as the script had evolved from wall to wall, beginning with the Sumerian pictographs and evolving through the

Akkadian and into Assyrian-era writing forms. He was looking at the world's earliest known writing that dated back to 8,000 BC. For several moments, the awe of it all took away his dire plight. That was until he realised that the particular script which he was reading was a prayer to Pazuzu, to imbue the supplicant with his powers by entering his physical body and possessing him. The following pictograms were explicit in the extreme, leaving no room for speculation as to the fate of either supplicant or sacrifice.

He looked once more at the enormous statue of Pazuzu guarding the entrance; there was no way that he was going to allow that thing into his body, locusts or not. He would take his own life first.

He carried on reading the cuneiform texts, desperate to see if there was any reprieve, and the next block of cuneiform made his heart miss a beat and his blood run cold. The entire text referred to the Demon Ark. He translated it in his mind, wishing he had something on which to write down what he was translating, but he had nothing and would have to commit it to memory.

The gist of it was that the Demon Ark would rise when the Dog Star, Sirius, was in the ascendant and central to a planetary alignment which was obviously about to happen alongside the seismic activity and the plagues, illnesses, locusts and flies. That made some sense as Pazuzu, the dog-headed demon, could be associated with the Dog Star. The text further described the coming of Pazuzu to orchestrate the rising and to prepare the temple in readiness for the activation of the Ark, which would set in motion a chain reaction of all the portals to Hell being blasted open simultaneously, with the hub of the process being there at Megiddo. And it was through this very portal that Morning Star would step into the world. It was here at Megiddo that he had to be stopped.

Another passage in the text talked of a green gem that had fallen from Morning Star's crown as he fell from heaven. It was called Lapsit Exillis and it was the only thing that could shut down the Demon Ark and prevent the opening of the portals. There followed a command to all followers of Pazuzu to reclaim the stone before it could be used against them and to exploit its powers as a weapon against the angels, the purpose of which was to enable all the fallen angels that had become demons to return to heaven and claim it for their own, casting all the other angels to earth or, worse, to the Pit.

He who wore the stone would inherit the power of magic and the ability to quell all demons and angels alike. Josh sat down heavily onto the dirt floor. How could they possibly hope to stand against such darkness?

His black thoughts were brought to a halt by the grinding sound of locks and bolts being opened.

Richard Vermont and his heavies entered the temple. His step was purposeful and his demeanour dark. He nodded to two of the nearest heavies and they grabbed Josh and dragged him towards Vermont.

"Just a little insurance in case you have any ideas of leaving," he snarled, as he jabbed a needle into Josh's exposed neck, "We don't want you getting any ideas from these walls now do we?" Josh was allowed to fall back to the floor as Vermont and his entourage left as suddenly as they had entered.

Whatever the drug was, it was swift to act and he began to feel woozy almost instantly, but before he lost consciousness Vermont's words echoed around his spinning brain. They meant only one thing: there was something on the wall that would help him find a way out. And another thought followed into his fast-approaching delirium; if they had to drug him it meant that whatever was going to happen, it wasn't going to be soon. And then the darkness overtook him.

In the drug-induced dreams that followed he saw a Sumerian priest, bedecked in jewelled armlets, his beard plaited and his hair braided, his robes of the finest cloth and studded with jewels from the far corners of Mesopotamia. Before him, his king sat on a throne as together they worshipped before a huge statue of Pazuzu. The very statue that still stood at the entrance to the temple, waiting, guarding.

Even in the dream, the archaeologist was still to the fore, as he wondered about the scene in front of him. Something wasn't right - or, the accepted theories about the timelines of religious activity in Mesopotamia were off somehow. Worship of Pazuzu wasn't supposed to have been present until the Assyrian era millennia later, after the Akkadians up to about 1200 BC, and yet clearly Pazuzu had his worshippers at the time of the cradle of civilisation.

He allowed his pharmaceutically-charged thoughts to have free rein. Pazuzu was, after all, one of the fallen, cast out with Lucifer, or Morning Star as he preferred to be known. He had been Morning Star's lieutenant and his power, now demonic, had once been eclipsed only by Lucifer's. One of the most powerful angels had become one of the most powerful demons.

The drug claimed his dream and his mind then, and his unconscious visions and thoughts were of plagues and locusts, demons rising from gaping holes in the earth and possessing the bodies of anyone they came across.

And then - oblivion.

CHAPTER TWENTY-EIGHT: LINWOOD HOUSE

Mike and Jack climbed into the Augusta 109 helicopter, both of them casting professional eyes over the bird. The interior was plush and they settled into the seats, Paul lifting off as soon as their seat belts were clicked into place. Despite Mike's reticence about Roman Woolfe, he was impressed by the machine - if not its owner. Either Woolfe was personally very wealthy or the Strazca was impressively funded; maybe both.

The forty minute flight passed more or less in silence until they landed in the grounds of Linwood House. Jack mouthed 'Wow' at Mike, who simply shrugged. The house and its grounds were the classic stately home of a bygone era and, as they entered behind Roman, the interior only reinforced the impression. They followed him into the large sitting room where there was a light buffet laid out on a Chippendale sideboard.

Jack didn't hesitate, his capacity for food belying his slim stature.

"Can we just get on with this? It's good of you but I'm not hungry." Mike looked reproachfully at Jack who frowned down at the delicate sandwich and game pie on his plate, looked back at Mike, grinned and carried on eating.

Roman sat in one of the Queen Anne chairs and indicated the sofa opposite. "Please, at least sit comfortably whilst we talk. I'm not an enemy, Mike, really. If you won't have something to eat, then at least have a cup of tea. There is much I want to show you and discuss with you."

Mike sat and allowed himself to relax a little. "It isn't

sitting well with me that I may be wasting time when my wife is God knows where. I need to get this done and get her back safely. I'm sure you will understand that."

Roman nodded. "Of course. But if you will allow me, I believe that we can help you get this done quicker and safer. Why go it alone when help is right here? Please, Mike, trust me."

Jack raised his eyebrows at Mike in a way that suggested *'Go on, what do you have to lose?'*

It wasn't lost on Mike. "OK then, talk to me."

Roman visibly relaxed and began his pitch.

"The Strazca, as you have recently learned, is concerned solely with all things occult or supernatural; both studying it, and doing our best to counter the evil aspect of it, in all its forms. We can only do this by gathering and assimilating information and reacting to it. This we do via our agents who send information as and when they receive it or track it down. It's surprising how effective a few are when properly prepared and trained. The thing is, that is what we do best; we aren't front-line soldiers in this war, Mike. And, before you say anything, it is not my intention to belittle you or suggest that you are less than competent. You are impressive in the extreme, Mike, and there are few men that would still be in the game right now. I know you are thinking of taking 'retirement' when this is over but I hope I can persuade you to change your mind. You have been chosen to undertake this mission against the rising evil in Megiddo and we have no intention of interfering, but ..."

"Here comes the but ..."

" ... but there are things you should know. First, the ring you have, Solomon's ring, must never be worn; its power is dangerous and will corrupt anyone eventually, mainly because the stone - the Lapsit Exillis - is from Lucifer's crown and contains his energy. When you use it, brandish it as a weapon but do not be tempted to wear it. If you put it on your finger, it will download all of the occult knowledge that Solomon possessed from the stone. All the magic … most of it dark and all of Morning Star's corruption."

Mike sighed. "I'm not here for fairy tales; I'm not Frodo Bloody Baggins and I'm not going to Mount Bloody Doom! If this is what you brought me here for, then it's time we left."

Roman raised a hand. "Easy, Mike, I'm only just getting started here. Perhaps it would be better if we took a stroll around the place and you will be able to get a better idea of our operation."

He stood up and Mike and Jack followed suit.

From the main hallway the sweeping staircase continued down to the basement level. Mike allowed himself a happy thought that no modern lifts had been installed.

At the bottom of the stairs, the interior décor had been continued and they followed Roman through a pair of huge oak doors.

On the other side they found themselves in a panelled ante-room where state of the art technology had taken over and found its place. Roman stepped up to a retina scanner and placed his right hand, palm down, onto another scanner that was reading his fingerprints and the lines on his palm.

A buzzer sounded as a green light and digital readout of *Access Granted* flashed on the security panel. The door in front of them slid open.

"Holy crap!" Jack couldn't keep his astonishment inside.

Mike stared at the unusual arsenal before him. Row upon row of conventional guns of all calibres and categories and banks of ammunition gave way to other weapons, some of which were similar to those in Ben's cellar.

Roman picked up a plain rosary. "This belonged to Mother Theresa," he said with reverence. "Its power and authority against demons or other evil is quite extraordinary." He replaced it onto its shelf. "There are other weapons, relics and artefacts which are equally effective. For instance, your favourite wrist-activated blade – we have one similar but it works more efficiently, responding to the merest movement, almost to your thoughts. There are hollow-point bullets containing holy water from Lourdes, and we have another of the crucifixion nails. This one, we have made into an arrow head. Sometimes the silence of an arrow is better than a gunshot to allow our operative to leave the scene unnoticed. It should always be recovered, that goes without saying."

He walked on, pointing out various pieces of equipment and explaining their provenance, until they reached the end of the armoury and they were faced with another set of security doors and scanners. Roman stepped up to the scanners and repeated the procedure, scanning his retinas and, this time, both hand prints.

The green readout flashed in time with the buzzer and the door opened as before. This time however, the contents of the room appeared to be contained in iron vessels of varying shape and size. Each container was carefully labelled.

"This is where we keep dangerous artefacts; things that shouldn't see the light of day. In this iron box, we have the knife used by Jack the Ripper, and yes, I know there was nothing supernatural about it, but the evil energy that is contained within it would easily be put to use by someone with sorcery skills, and the evil would be amplified, creating an instrument of darkest magic. We have the magical paraphernalia belonging to Aleister Crowley, the black magician who proclaimed himself 'The Beast', and there are other things here which I won't list, but you get the idea. Anything that has the potential for pure evil is contained here."

He paused to allow the information to sink in.

"And you want the ring here, is that it? Is that what this is all about? What gives you the right to do that?"

Roman sighed, "I thought you would take that view. It's simply one of the safest places for it. Have you thought what you are going to do with it once the Ark is destroyed? Not only does it have the power to control the demons, but it attracts them too. It draws evil to it like iron filings to a magnet, Mike. How are you going to deal with that? Every supernatural evil will be looking for it and they can't be permitted to lay hands on it. Down here, where the entire room, floor to ceiling, over and under, is lead-lined, it won't be detected. You have it in a lead box, so you know how to protect it. Allow us to take the burden from you afterwards. What is your alternative? As you say, you can't go to Mount Doom, so let the next best thing come to you"

"Who exactly *is* 'us'? Right now I only have your word and that of a shape-shifter, which incidentally does nothing to reassure me."

"Fair question, and one which I will address when we have finished the tour. Have you seen enough down here?"

"I think so."

Jack had been silent until then, watching Mike for clues as to his thoughts; now he turned to Roman. "Do you think we could have a minute? Out of here of course."

Roman nodded his agreement. "Certainly. Let us return to the armoury and you can have another look at the equipment we can offer you."

Once they were through the security doors the room went back into lock-down. He turned at the next set of doors. "I will be just outside," he said as he left them.

Jack turned to Mike instantly. "Are you fucking kidding me? Really? What the hell is wrong with you? This is the difference between going after Goliath with a sling shot and taking him on with an Uzi! Come on, Mike, tell me what's eating you? Because from where I'm standing we don't have a whole lot of choice here."

"I was brought up to believe that if something sounds too good to be true, it probably is. And what's in it for him? He wants the ring obviously, but what for? Is he really going to keep it locked in Pandora's bloody vault down there? Why? Or is he going to use it? I don't know enough about this guy to trust him, and neither should you!"

Jack shook his head. "No, I don't, but Ben trusts him so that's good enough for me. And it should be good enough for you. I get it, Mike; you're going to be the hardass; but not here, not with me. And before you even think it, this is me, not Bazaliel. Me; your best friend."

Mike swallowed the lump in his throat. "I guess I'm having some trust issues, but you're right, you are my best friend and I should trust you, and I do, and Ben. I'm sorry, Jack. This thing is so huge, and there's Beth ..."

Jack put his hand on Mike's arm. "I know. But you aren't doing this alone. We're here now, let's at least let him finish."

"Well, we'd better do that, then. After you."

Roman was waiting in the ante-room for them and went through the process of locking down the entire basement.

"If you're ready I'll show you the rest? Or do you still wish to leave?"

"Lead on," Mike said in a voice that he didn't quite believe in.

At the top of the sweeping staircase Roman threw open a huge set of ornate oak doors into the library. It was Mike this time that displayed his amazement. Row upon row of heavily carved oak bookshelves spanned the entire length of the vast room, each and every one of them filled with archaic, arcane and occult books and manuscripts. At one end, custom-made oak filing drawers flanked a desk with a microfiche.

A glance at the nearest bookshelf revealed the depth of

knowledge to be gleaned from the collection. If Ben had a library, then this was something else. He pursed his lips and nodded his approval. "Impressive," he said.

"If it isn't here, we are in the process of acquiring it, or it isn't available. At this time." The rider at the end of his sentence said it all; their resources were indeed vast.

"If you'd care to follow me gentlemen," Roman said, his voice reminiscent of an upmarket tour guide.

They moved back to the staircase and Woolfe indicated the left and right wings. "To the left are private apartments; it's where I live, and any operatives that choose to be resident. To the right are guest apartments reserved for trusted visitors who are not of our organisation. The rooms downstairs and those apartments are the only rooms available to guests, and the library in some cases. If we carry on up to the next level I'll show you our communications hub."

Mike frowned; the whole thing was beginning to sound like a spy novel. He said nothing.

At the top of the staircase the doors were less impressive; this was obviously an area not visited by anyone from outside. Roman opened the door right in front of them, after the retinal scan granted him access.

What was inside made them both stop and stare. Computer terminals, with their own server, variously blinked and flashed at them. Sitting at one of the terminals was Lizzie Lee. She was tapping away at the keyboard and turned to smile at them as they entered.

"I've set up the video links. We're ready when you are."

Roman turned to Mike. "You wanted to know who 'us' was, well, please meet the main operatives of the Strazca."

Lizzie hit a key and several monitors flashed and fizzed into life, each linked into individual video feed.

The elderly white-haired man on the far right monitor smiled benignly. "Hello, I'm Vittorio Montagna, I'm based in Rome. How is Benjamin? Please give him my regards; he may remember me from his days at the Vatican. If not, tell him the one who dropped the books; that should jog his memory. I wish you well, Mr Travis, whether you decide to join us or not. Good Luck in Megiddo. There is a lot resting on it. *Ciao!*"

His monitor displayed static. His link was disconnected.

The next monitor displayed a face that was so young, it took Mike by surprise at the contrast to the previous picture.

The boy grinned widely. "Hey, how are you? It's great to kind of meet you, Mike. I have read all our files on you, which does give me the advantage I'm afraid. Well, here goes. I'm Niall, though for some reason I get called Niall the Geek, which is grossly unfair just because I can speak twelve languages and have a doctorate in astrophysics. Don't judge me! Oh yeah, I'm in New York. I really hope you come on board, Mike. We could surely use you. Is that Jack Carter with you? Hi, Jack! What's it like to really have a demon inside you? Anyway, that's my time up, just wanted to say Hi and to say I hope you join us. TTFN!"

His monitor went blank.

And so it continued through Florence Depardieu in Paris, Dave Radisson in the Northern Territories of Australia, Chukwuena Jaberi (Chuck) in Cape Town and finally Kimona (Kim) De Costa in Jamaica.

Mike stood in front of the terminals that had displayed the smiling faces and felt his reservations heading for the plughole.

"There is just one more that I want you to speak to, if you'd come with me," Roman Woolfe said in a quiet voice. Mike smiled at Lizzie Lee and they followed Roman back down the sweeping staircase and into the elegant sitting room again.

The older man was sitting in the armchair next to the fire, his flat cap pushed to the back of his head. "Took your time, isn'it."

Mike felt his heart leap. "Dai!"

CHAPTER TWENTY-NINE: ARE YOU IN?

"All right, boy? All right, Jack? Got yourself in deep this time, Mike. You do right to be cautious, and they thought it would take me to convince you, see. Though I did tell you to trust Benjamin. Overwhelmed, is it?"

"Where's Beth, Dai?"

Dai frowned. "Last I know, Sebastian had her in a place of safety. He's a self-serving son-of-a-bitch, but he won't hurt her. And to be honest, son, she's better out of the way while this is going on. It's going to get messy, and you need all your attention on not getting dead or worse, see. 'Spect you're wondering about me and Roman's lot. Well, you know I was part of a group that called ourselves The Watchers; me, Mam Thomas, and a few others. We were also a part of The Strazca, a kind of unofficial off-shoot if you like. Independent like, but with their backing. Our job was to watch the edges, isn'it. You know fine well how the edges are dangerous places boy, and right now it's the edges that are about to burst open. Bit of a bugger, but you should take all the help you can get. This ain't no time for stubbornness or distrust. I can't maintain this physical manifestation much longer, still a bit weak from before like, but I'll be watching you. See you met Mam Thomas's lass, don't let her ... *ability* ... put you off, I'll tell you all about that another time but, for now, you can trust her in a tight spot."

Mike's memory of her at Garway was still fresh in his mind. "Yeah, I know."

Dai faded out, his energy depleted.

Mike turned his attention back to Roman. "So, what are you suggesting?"

"Join us, Mike. Take advantage of our resources. For a start, I have you a business class flight reservation to Tel Aviv. Our agent Jon Barclay will come from Haifa to meet you with whatever you need. I can see you're wondering why he doesn't do the job. Well, as I said, it's because our agents are mainly information gatherers, historians and archivists, it's what we do; Lizzie is our main computer expert, and far too valuable to be out in the field all the time. Sometimes we unavoidably get our hands bloody but we can work more efficiently by providing the backing and the information to those that can get the job done. Like you."

Mike fixed him with a stare. "You do know how new I am to all this, right? Putting spirits to rest is one thing; taking on the demons is something else. How do you know I can do it?"

"Because if you can't then ... we're all screwed, I believe is the phrase."

"I'm doing this anyway, so I might as well accept. With the understanding that when I get Beth back, I quit. I've put her in danger for the last time. And I can walk away when I want to."

"Fair enough. And the ring?"

"Ha! I wondered when you were going to mention that again. I don't know *what* I'm going to do with the damn thing; I don't even know how to use it, though I expect you're going to tell me your resources have the answer."

Roman smiled, "Indeed they do. Lizzie has prepared everything for you in the library. Though you will forgive me if I ask Jack to just wait for you in comfort. It's not that I don't trust him, but the demon he is host to has yet to prove which side he is really on."

"Understood. Leave Jack to me. He is still coming with me though, because, while I don't know Bazaliel, I know Jack and there's no-one I'd rather have watching my back - no offence to Jon Barclay."

Jack gave Mike an appreciative smile; the feeling had

been mutual for too many years not to trust one another now. He knew that Bazaliel's presence was a sticky subject but he was going to show his friend that he could trust the demon too; after all, Jack trusted it with his life.

Roman nodded. "Understood, which is why I have made the reservations for two at the Crowne Plaza Tel Aviv Beach Hotel. And so we need to discuss airport security. Ben Gurion Airport has the most stringent international airport security in the world. Two men travelling together are bound to be questioned about the purpose of your visit, and for obvious reasons you cannot tell the truth - saying that you are visiting Megiddo to prevent the Demon Ark from opening the portals of hell will get you a strip session with a burly soldier with no mercy and a machine gun, or worse! Jon Barclay has a low profile and we would like it to stay that way, so you are tourists; which is why your hotel and flight reservations are for a week as it's easier to bring things forward to leave Israel than it is to enter. As for the ring, there is no way you can take it through security in its iron box without attracting the wrong kind of attention. Pack the box separately in your luggage. You cannot wear the ring so I suggest you hang it around your neck on this chain," he handed Mike a gold neck chain. "Many men wear rings on chains around their necks for sentimental reasons, it won't attract too much attention. It will set off alarms, I'm sure, so you will have to remove it while you are scanned. Paul will drive you both to Heathrow, all you have to do is check in. So, Mike Travis, are you in?"

Mike extended his hand. "I'm in. I guess I'll soon find out if I've done the right thing or not."

Jack nodded at him, firmly of the opinion that it was most definitely the right thing.

"Good. Lizzie will take you through what we have on the Lapsit Exillis -or 'Solomon's ring' if you prefer. Much of it has come to us via Brother Bernard after he translated it, but there are some pieces that we have acquired by other means," Roman said.

Neither of them questioned 'other means'.

In the library Lizzie had set out a couple of ancient books which she had handled wearing white cotton gloves; another pair lay at the side.

"This is the main text; it's a supplement to the original Testament of Solomon and there's some stuff on the microfiche as well," she said, in a solemn voice. "I'm glad you're joining us, Mike." Then, reading him, she added, "I don't need to eavesdrop - I know, because if you had said no, then you wouldn't be here. The files on the left of the desk are translations of other stuff you will find useful, I expect Ben has copies, but you could do worse than spend the time during the flight reading them. I'll be upstairs in the coms room. If you need anything, just press the intercom button on the desk and I'll come straight away. Roman will be here shortly."

Mike pored over the ancient texts and their modern translations. The ring had been taken away from mortal hands on more than one occasion in its lengthy history, the last time by Gilbert Belvoir. It had to be contained in iron until used; check. It could only be used once by any man; check. Above all, it must never be put on the finger. To use it, it had to be brandished in front of the user, directly at the demon. Its inherent energy would do the rest. To destroy the Ark, it had to be in close proximity and a spell chanted over it. Attached to the file was a tiny MP3 player with the spell recorded so that Mike would have no problem with the pronunciation, and fall foul of it. Spells had a nasty habit of backfiring if mispronounced or misused. The warnings at the end of the texts were dire regarding the consequences of any of the instructions being flouted.

They were engrossed in the texts when Roman appeared.

"If you're ready, the car is outside. Leave your mobile phones here, there are two pre-paid ones in the car; can't be too careful. Jon Barclay will provide you with more if you use them. Use them once and get rid. You'll make the flight with an hour to spare. Four and a half hours after take-off, Jon Barclay will be waiting for you at Tel Aviv's Ben Gurion Airport. Then, my friend, it's up to you." He took Mike's hand in his right and rested his left on Mike's shoulder. "Good luck and, it goes without saying, God go with you."

He saw them both into the car and on their way, and then returned to his sitting room where there was another visitor.

Sebastian stood in the centre of the room, his dark wings just visible.

"He has gone?"

Roman nodded. "Sebastian, I assume?"

"Yes. There is a problem with his wife. She has retreated into a world where even I can't reach her. And if I can't reach her, I can't heal her. Her mind has shut down and she spends every hour in a dream world. One where there is no evil, only sunshine and her husband and daughter, and I fear for her returning sanity. Before she retreated completely I was able to glean this much: her mental state is a direct result of being dragged into hell. Not many mortals survive there. We knew Mike Travis would because of his lineage from Michael, and we hoped *she* would because she had borne his blood-line, but it seems we were wrong. She may have survived physically, but mentally she is deeply wounded. I fear the only healing has to be done down here and with people she trusts and loves. There is one who will help, and he may prove interesting to you too. His name is Paul Beckett, another ex-priest who is also a gifted psychotherapist, and I believe, he isn't the first vampire that you have encountered."

Roman raised an eye-brow. "Really? Interesting. It is also interesting that you waited until he was gone before bringing this to me. No doubt his decision to play his part would have been coloured by the presence of his mentally wounded wife. You really *are* a son-of-a-bitch. What makes you think I won't call him back to come and take care of her?"

"Because if you do, I will remove her again."

"You must bring her here. We will provide all the care she needs, I will make the arrangements and I will contact this Beckett if you believe he is the best."

"He is the best for her, yes."

"Then it will be done. I will engage a suitably qualified nurse, until such time as Mike decides his future. Is there anything else?"

"Yes. Why are you doing this?"

"Because the Strazca takes our responsibility very seriously. We have the funds and everything that is necessary."

Sebastian prepared to depart. "It would have nothing to do with the fact, that while she is here, being cared for, it will make him even more dedicated to hunting these bastards down and dealing with them for you? Or is that just too cynical?"

The angel was gone before Roman could reply. He picked up the internal telephone.

"Lizzie, get me everything we have - or don't have - on a Paul Beckett, he's a psychotherapist, and, I'm reliably informed, a vampire. Then find me the best qualified psychiatric nurses for me to interview with a view to immediate employment. I want two; one for day the other for the night, on a temporary but lucrative engagement."

He put down the phone and stared out of the window across the vast, neatly manicured lawn. This was a turn of events that he hadn't expected, but it could be managed to everyone's advantage.

CHAPTER THIRTY: A WAY OUT

Megiddo was in the grip of a plague of flies. They swarmed everywhere and people shut and bolted their doors against them despite the heat of the day. It had even made the news. But it was the storms that had captured the camera lenses and the reporters. Heavy black clouds had hung low over the hill-top site, discharging electric blue lightning and thunderclaps at a frightening rate. The air was pungent with ozone but there had been no rain.

The fissure at the dig site was spreading outwards towards the newly excavated temple, like a finger pointing towards its own doom, and it was continually spewing out clouds of stinking black vapour. The military guards wielded their sub-machine guns and assault rifles with an air of authority that no-one had challenged. The Megiddo dig site was off limits and there was a blanket ban on all media. Israel had the power and the experience to achieve it.

Richard Vermont's eyes shone black in their sockets; he had kindly offered his hospitality to the demon that had previously occupied Ruth Weiss, and he was enjoying the feeling of power and dark energy. He would continue to do so until such time as he could eject it and claim one that was more powerful and further up the food chain.

His band of heavies had all assimilated lower-ranking demons and for now, they were biding their time. None had yet encountered the dark power of Pazuzu and they were in a state of high anticipation.

His phone rang and he dismissed his entourage and listened to the voice of Ingrid Reeves.

"He has it and is en route. I'm afraid the attempt to recover it at Garway failed. I'm sorry."

Vermont narrowed his black eyes. "No problem, my dear. Let him bring it to me." He ended the conversation with a savage click.

Inside the temple Josh had shaken off the drug-induced sleep and was intent on reading the walls. Some of the writing was so ancient he had no chance and longed for Maddie who would read her way through the temple with ease.

One of the texts was in Akkadian, which he was more familiar with. The pictographs showed something similar to the Ark of the Covenant without the familiar cherubs on top - obviously a depiction of the Demon Ark. It didn't look so powerful, could it really do what it said on the tin? He scrutinised it closely. Several words and pictographs jumped out at him. Sacrifice was heavily mentioned and he went cold. He had to get out of there before Pazuzu claimed him for his servant or Richard Vermont cut his throat; neither scenario appealed to him.

He carried on reading the text. It stated that the Demon Ark would rise with Sirius when it was in conjunction with Orion and its dimmer companion; Sirius B. Josh knew instinctively that that time was now. He read on.

Several things had to be in place for the birthing of the Ark: the Rite of the Opening of the Gates, and a human sacrifice had to be performed at the moment of the conjunction. In the meantime the Ark would rise steadily towards the earth's surface ready for the hands of its midwife.

Below the text were drawings of the sacrificial altar with its drainage channels. Channels which connected to the main ancient drains of the rest of Megiddo. The drainage channels inside the temple were narrow, but did they really connect to a later drainage system? Could it be that easy? He doubted it, but what else was he to do - sit and wait for the end, whichever end it may be?

He crossed the temple to the sacrificial granite slab and

followed the channels to their union on the ground. The main drain was covered with millennia of dust and he cringed as he scraped it clear with his foot, every fibre of the archaeologist in him screaming at the sacrilege, but his survival instinct winning out.

One of the earliest excavations in Megiddo revealed monumental engineering in the form of tunnels which brought water into the city. If these drainage channels connected to the water system, he had a way out.

He fell to his knees and began hauling the dust and debris away with both hands, then removed his boot and used it as a make-shift shovel. He breathed a sigh of relief when he encountered a cover to the drain; at least he knew now that the drain wouldn't be full of dust and detritus. The rudimentary drain began to appear and he was relieved to see the cracks in the baked clay lining. He cast around for something heavy to finish the job and widen it enough for him to see the full width of it underground. He hoped the clay would crumble so that he didn't have to make too much noise, otherwise it would be for nothing; Richard Vermont and his heavies would be on him in an instant. The whole idea depended on speed and silence.

As he scanned the place, his eye lighted on a mound within a niche in the wall. He grabbed it and was delighted at the weight of it. Dust and debris fell away from the smaller granite statue of Pazuzu that was identical in all other details to the guardian at the entrance.

The clay lining responded to the first blow that seemed to him to echo around the temple at the volume of a thunder-clap, in reality it was a gentle thud.

He examined the damage and was satisfied at the deep cracks in the baked clay; he tapped it with his boot and smiled as the thick lining fell away. He waited to hear it hit bottom and heard nothing. He hit the clay again and waited, hardly breathing to see if the sound had brought any response. It didn't and so he carried on.

Peering into the shaft, Josh believed he could just

squeeze into it; he prayed that it would open out into a wider cistern at the bottom. His jacket would have to go and he threw it onto the sacrificial slab. A thick cloud rose up as his jacket dislodged the centuries of dust; lodging in his throat and making him cough. He leaned against the slab and something hard moved beneath his hand.

Brushing aside the layers of time, he revealed a thin, wide blade, the handle of which had long since disintegrated. It was corroded in places and, where it wasn't, it was covered in dark black stains, the source of which did not require much imagination. He stuck it into his belt; it was no longer sharp but he may still be able to do some damage with it.

He halted at the head of the shaft; there was a sudden draught of air coming from the front of the temple. Had his efforts been discovered? Had it all been for nothing? He waited. Nothing. The draught had probably been caused by his opening up the drainage shaft.

The sound behind him came from nowhere; the sudden sound of stone scraping against stone. The hairs stood erect on his neck and he could almost taste the adrenaline coursing through him. Despite the fact his heart was racing, he turned very slowly to face whatever stood behind him.

Nothing had moved and no-one stood ready to attack him. Then suddenly, the pain in his stomach returned and he could hear the distant white noise of locusts.

He made a dive for the drainage shaft, ripping his shirt and jeans and grazing his leg against the jagged remains of the baked clay of the walls. The shaft was perhaps a few inches wider that Josh's shoulders and he had to force his body downwards, scraping the sides with his boots in an effort to dislodge more clay until, all of a sudden, the shaft opened out into a more modern cistern with a tunnel leading away from the temple. His old problem with confined spaces began to rear up, but he knew that wherever it led it was his only chance at escape and he took it.

If only he could get the sound of the locusts out of his head.

CHAPTER THIRTY-ONE: TEL AVIV

Security at Heathrow was tighter, for obvious reasons, than Mike remembered and the ring around his neck did indeed set alarms off, but on its removal the scanner was quiet. He also had to open his suitcase to prove to the security guard on the X-ray machine that the box contained nothing sinister but was merely a box in which to place his watch and neck chain.

On board the British Airways flight, business class was a new experience for both of them, and the four-hour flight passed easily with the attentive cabin crew and in-flight movie which they pretended to watch. They didn't converse much, both lost in thought about what they were heading into. Mike hadn't heard from Josh and couldn't raise him on the phone, but at least Roman had arranged for them to be met.

Baggage reclaim areas are pretty much the same the world over, but at Tel Aviv's Ben Gurion Airport, every area, including baggage reclaim, is flushed with armed police and military personnel, all looking as if they had bad toothache and an even worse attitude. Overhead digital information at the baggage reclaim area directed them to carousel number nineteen, where bags and cases were already beginning to do laps of the conveyor belt system.

Jack grabbed his case and stood back while they waited for Mike's. And waited. The conveyor was empty and all other passengers had retrieved their belongings and disappeared towards passport control and Mike was about to blow a fuse when two armed guards with an attendant dog approached, carrying his case.

With no preamble, the one carrying Mike's case said, "You are Michael Travis and this is your baggage?"

Mike only had time to nod before the security guards stationed themselves at either side of him.

"You will come with us please and explain the contents."

Mike's heart sank; it had to be the iron box. And then a worse thought entered his head. What if Roman Woolfe had put something else in his suitcase?

Jack made to follow them but one guard turned to him, gun across his chest. "Mr Travis only."

"It's OK, Jack; I'll see you in the arrivals hall. It's nothing." His casual words weren't a reflection of his anxiety level.

They marched him into a small room and slammed his case onto the table against one wall, both of them adopting an aggressive stance. "Open, please," one of them demanded.

Mike snapped the locks back and opened his suitcase, profusely relieved that the contents did indeed portray a holiday and also that Roman Woolfe *had* actually added something to his luggage: sunscreen, sunglasses and a couple of novels; all the trappings of someone on holiday. The man had thought of everything, but then, Mike guessed, that was one of the reasons he was head of the Strazca; the Eldritch.

The guard that had, until then, remained silent, put his rifle into one hand, and began pulling the contents of Mike's case out onto the table. He took out the iron box bearing the magical sigils and symbols and held it up for inspection. "What is this?"

Mike made a conscious effort to slow his heart-rate; the last thing he needed was for them to get twitchy and confiscate the box. He needed to put the ring back inside as soon as possible.

"It's just an antique box in which I keep my watch when I'm not wearing it." He decided to be bold then and risk everything in a wild bluff. "And this," he said, pulling the ring and chain from under his shirt. "It is a family heirloom. I wear it for luck when travelling, it's a sentimental thing. When I am not wearing it, I keep it in the box also."

They were both staring at him, hard. Neither spoke as they continued to try to intimidate him with the silent stares. The guard nearest to him lifted the ring towards him, making Mike lean forwards. "It is valuable?"

"Not really, only to me."

He didn't appear convinced, but the guard let it fall back against Mike's chest. "Come with us."

They took a step back as Mike unceremoniously repacked his case and snapped the locks back into place.

They walked one either side of him, taking him into a small room at the edge of the passport control area and sat him down at a table, standing either side of the door to wait for an immigration officer.

When she arrived and sat opposite Mike, his heart dropped as, for just one second, her eyes turned black.

"Your passport, please," she said in an expressionless voice.

He handed it over and she took it in silence. Silence which endured while she examined it, as if looking for a cure for some dread disease, lifting her eyes to him occasionally and fixing him with a hard stare. On the scale of intimidation it was close to off the charts.

Eventually she said, "What is the purpose of your visit to Israel?"

"A holiday with a friend. Just that. Why Israel? Because it's somewhere I haven't been before."

"Where are you staying?"

"The Crowne Plaza on the beach."

"Do you plan to travel around the country while you are here?"

Mike shrugged. "I haven't decided yet."

Further conversation was interrupted as the door opened and a uniformed officer entered, leaned into her, and whispered into her ear. Black eyes flashed. She stood up and pushed his passport towards him. "You can go."

She nodded dismissal at the two scowling guards as she pushed passed them, clearly unhappy with the situation.

In Megiddo, Richard Vermont smiled with satisfaction as he disconnected his call to the Chief of Security at Ben Gurion Airport. The tentacles of the Knights of the Dark Temple were far-reaching; Mike Travis and the ring would be on the way to Megiddo very soon.

As soon as Mike entered the arrivals area, Jack was at his side.

"Jesus, Mike, I had visions of you being banged up somewhere with them doing unspeakable things. And do you know how many 'Black Eyes' are around here! Baz says they are mostly demon low-life, which I can believe because they somehow sensed him and backed off, probably thinking I was one of them, which - if that's true - is going to come in handy; you have to admit that. Something is far from right here; Mike, something is brewing - something bad."

Mike rolled his eyes. "Goddamit, Jack, I thought we agreed you were going to keep that bloody demon in its place! If you can't control it … And, if calling that bloody thing by name isn't bad enough, do you *really* have to abbreviate it? You make it sound like you're bloody schizophrenic!"

Before Jack could reply, a tall man in a linen suit and open-necked shirt came towards them. He was tanned from living in the sun and he had an open face with lines from a ready smile; a smile which was currently absent, having given way to deep anxiety. He had a shaven head which suited him, giving him an air of sophistication, dressed as he was. His hand was extended and he was business-like in his demeanour, needing no confirmation of Mike's identity; Roman had emailed him with a photograph. "Jon Barclay; let's get you away from here."

With no further pre-amble he strode from the arrivals hall to a waiting taxi, which he directed to the hotel.

"To keep your story straight, they will watch you to see where you go," he explained. "Once you have checked in I'll take you straight to Megiddo."

Inside the taxi, on the short drive from the airport to the hotel, he appeared to relax a little.

"The demons that are already here are gathering to make things easier for those that will come once the portals are open. There are several of them possessing airport staff. Thankfully, most are minor demons without much clout, but they can be a damn nuisance all the same. Fucking infestation! We're dealing with it; don't normally get involved but this ... this is different. I've got a kit together for you, you not being able to bring the necessary. Did you have any problems with the ring?"

Mike shook his head. "No, but I'll be glad to put it back in its box, it has a weight to it, physically and metaphysically. What do you mean you're 'dealing with it'?"

"Old trick but an effective one. Holy Water from Lourdes is being pumped into the sprinkler system as we speak. Lizzie Lee has control of the fire alarms and sprinklers by now I should think. We're going to give everyone a Holy shower. It will be enough to send them running for cover, and maybe even finish off the really low ones in the food chain. And the ring ... you haven't claimed it as yet, I take it?"

"Pardon?"

"Claimed it; by blood."

"I didn't see anything about that in the texts and Roman said nothing" Mike was puzzled.

"Probably not in the texts; it's basic magic theory - claim your tools by blood. That way they will work for you and you alone."

Mike frowned. "Given that once this is over I'm getting rid of it, and don't ask me how or where because I don't know yet, but I don't want that kind of attachment to it. It's Lucifer's stone for Christ's sake! Why would I want to claim it?"

"Because, unless you do, it will be erratic at best and dangerous at worst. I'm Jewish, Mike, I'm familiar with magic ritual and I assure you, it's what you should do before you put it back in the iron box. This is your hotel, I won't come in with you, but I will be waiting in a café around the corner in fifteen minutes. Claim it by blood, Mike. Solomon did. I'll take care of the taxi fare. In fifteen minutes."

The taxi-driver opened Mike's door and went to the rear to hand them their baggage. Jack put his hand in his pocket; they had no Israeli shekels but sterling was usually acceptable everywhere.

The driver shook his head. "No, sir. I am Levi Bachman and I am happy to be of service to the Strazca, as my family before me, and theirs before them. I will be waiting for you, too; I am to take you wherever you need to go while you are here. It is my calling."

Jack's expression was eloquent and Mike could hear his silent comment. "Really? Fucking really?"

CHAPTER THIRTY-TWO: AT WORLDS END

Josh was able to stand upright once he hit the old water system, and put his hand on the rock-cut wall to guide him through the pitch dark of the tunnel until he felt a fork in its path. He had no idea where he was or how far from the temple he had travelled. For all he knew, he was directly below Vermont and his thugs and, he had yet to find an exit from the old sewer system. The archaeologist in him recognised the tunnels as being from the Roman occupation of Israel, and guessed they had been replaced by modern sewers much later. Even so, there would have been a way for people to enter and leave for inspection purposes. He carried on, taking the left hand tunnel, shaking his head occasionally in an effort to rid himself of the deep white-noise of the locusts.

After about a hundred yards on his knees, he stopped, feeling a draught on his face. There must be an opening not too far ahead. He picked up his crawling pace.

Another fifty or so yards and the draught was coming from directly above him. He felt around the walls and found a rudimentary ladder pegged into the wall, underneath what felt like a rusted iron door ... but how long it had been since it had been opened was something else. He stopped in his tracks again and twisted his head around to try and see through the dark; he had an overwhelming feeling that someone or something was following him. He held his breath; there was no sound and he could see nothing in the dark anyway. He waited for another minute but there was no sound except those in his head.

He reached above him and felt around the iron door

for any kind of closing mechanism. There was none, and the door didn't give at all as he heaved against it from his cramped position.

The noise of the locusts grew louder in his head and he pushed harder against the old door. It gave easily, as if his strength had come from the netherworld, but he didn't stop to wonder at it; he pulled himself through the aperture and allowed the door to fall back with a metallic clang.

He looked about him in a frantic assessment of his location; he appeared to have emerged from the tunnel on the very far side of Megiddo.

He felt strange, expanded somehow, like the time he'd taken some mind-altering substance in university, a one-off occurrence but it was still easy to recall the feeling. Expanding; that was the best way to describe the feeling - like Alice after the 'Eat Me' incident down the rabbit-hole.

Then came the pain; the searing deep-rooted pain in his gut. And the noise of the locusts. He needed to get away from Megiddo and try to contact Mike. It wouldn't take Vermont long to discover that he was missing, and his resources seemed limitless; he knew that if he was found, it would be his blood running down the drainage channels in the temple. The sky overhead darkened and a fork of lightning hit the ground.

Josh knew the risks of using his phone, but while Vermont believed him to be safely locked in the temple he decided to risk a brief conversation with Mike. The white-noise in his head made thought processes difficult and he fought to get his mind in order to find a place to meet Mike. He realised that he was incredibly thirsty as the screen on his phone showed several missed calls from the same number. It had to be Mike.

He dialled the number.

Mike answered it quickly; they had checked in to the hotel and met Jon Barclay at the café.

"Josh? At last! I've been trying to get you for hours.

Are you all right?"

Josh replied in one short phrase. "Bar at world's end." He disconnected the call; no-one would have the time to triangulate it and he hoped with everything he had that Mike would remember their joke at university when Josh talked about life in the kibbutz; Mike called it 'world's end'.

Mike took a minute to stare at the phone as if it could give him answers. World's end? What the hell did that mean? Josh was clearly in trouble. He sighed. As if bringing an end to the demon Armageddon wasn't enough. He brightened at the thought that this would be the last time he would stand against them.

He squinted against the sun. "Josh is in trouble somewhere. He wants to meet at the bar at world's end, wherever the hell that is. Any ideas Jon?"

Jon Barclay shook his head. "Haven't a clue. But I do know we need to get moving. If my astronomy is correct, Sirius will be in the ascendant tonight and it won't be long before the ritual to birth the Ark and open the portals begins. If your friend is in trouble, I'm guessing he's going to find himself at the business end of a ritual dagger."

Jack looked thoughtful, "World's end? Is it related to the final battle at Megiddo?"

Mike shrugged. "I don't know. Let's get on the way, I can think in the car."

Jon Barclay signalled to Levi Bachman who was sitting in his taxi on the other side of the street. In seconds they were on the way to Megiddo.

Highway six, the toll road, also known as the Yitzhak Rabin Highway, was fast with its electronic tolls making the journey to Megiddo just about an hour. Mike fought to compose himself. Nothing that had come before this compared to his current anxiety level. His past encounter with demons had been sudden and unplanned; this felt like he was going into battle unprepared and, not for the first time, he wondered why the hell he was there when there were other, more experienced, hunters out there. Surely, just because he was of Michael's bloodline wasn't a good enough reason.

He was fingering the ring around his neck unconsciously, searching for an answer to Josh's whereabouts. His mind was totally focussed and Jon Barclay's voice had taken on a distant quality. But suddenly, he tuned back into what Barclay was saying to him.

"Sorry, what was that?"

Barclay frowned at him. "I said that I hoped the archaeologists and the students were well out of the way at the kibbutz."

Cogs turned and tumblers fell into place in Mike's head. "The kibbutz. The bar at the kibbutz; that's where Josh is."

Barclay's frown deepened. "There's more than one kibbutz."

"He won't have gone far. It will be the one nearest the dig site. At least, that's where I think he'll be."

"I'm not sure we need him. Why not leave him safe out of the way? After all, what can he do?"

"Yeah, I agree, but I believe he's in trouble and that counts. I need to find him and make sure," Mike replied.

Barclay made an impatient noise and accompanying gesture. "Very noble. I hope it won't be your undoing. In the meantime, I want you to familiarise yourself with the weapons I have brought for you - not that any of them will stand against the high-ranking demons alone, but with the Lapsit Exillis…"

The weapons were similar to those in Ben's basement, only more refined and of high-tech origin, except of course the rosary that had belonged to Mother Theresa. Mike took immediate comfort from holding the rosary and put it carefully into his pocket.

The wrist-activated blade was designed to deploy much faster than his and the machete-like blade that Barclay handed him last infused him with more confidence. It was heavy and finely balanced; its edges honed to razor-sharpness and polished to a blinding finish.

"Impressive," Mike murmured.

"Made of the finest Damascus steel and blessed by the stigmata blood of a saint. Have a care with it, lest you become its victim and not its master. You know that wounding the host of a demon is not enough; it must be decapitated."

Lovecraft's Rules played in his head.

Lovecraft's Rule No.7: It ain't dead until it's really dead, and that means taking its head off. He couldn't afford to wonder if the host could be saved; this was kill or be killed – or worse. Lovecraft's Rule No. Eight: Demons can jump bodies.

He shoved the blade into its leather scabbard and under his belt.

The remainder of the journey passed with him plugged into the MP3 player and the spell that Roman Woolfe had provided him with. It was in Aramaic and Mike knew from experience what missing a word, or mispronouncing it, could bring about. He had the spell written down but listening to it burned it into his consciousness. It was the spell to use in conjunction with the Lapsit Exillis to disable or destroy the Demon Ark. If he made it that far.

Barclay gave Mike a pistol, loaded with bullets made of silver and iron. A bullet wouldn't kill a demon but it may slow it down long enough to buy him time.

Jack looked across at Mike to make sure he was listening to the Aramaic intently enough not to hear his conversation with Barclay.

"What about you? Are you in this, or not?"

Barclay grimaced and made an expression of distaste to Jack. "Yes, I'm in it; I have my weapons, don't worry. I will do my part."

Jack wasn't convinced; there was something niggling him. He had tried to shut Bazaliel out until now, determined to keep a clear head, but the demon was clearly rattled.

CHAPTER THIRTY-THREE: STILL THE REBEL

Ben was deeply unhappy. He should have been the one at Mike's side, not Jack, but someone had to stay and watch over Martha and be there in case Beth came back. Jack's demon may swing the balance, but he wasn't sure which way. He felt responsible for Mike and, despite the resources of the Strazca, he felt as if he had abandoned him.

He had to keep busy, and to that end, he had begun work on Mike's new vehicle and had started to strip it down. Yet, at the back of his mind was the thought that it may be for nothing; Mike was intent on walking away from all of it. He allowed Martha to lose herself in making him tea at more regular intervals than he cared for and, as he sat in the barn behind his cottage with the car doors and all other removable panels on the floor, he stood up abruptly, spilling the tea on to the ground. He threw the cup down in frustration, spinning around as the Archangel Metatron appeared in a blast of air.

"You!" Ben said through clenched teeth. He stood to his full height, not intimidated by his old adversary. "What the hell do *you* want, Metatron? Whatever it is, the answer is no."

Metatron's dark complexion and steely grey eyes would have moved mountains, but Ben stood his ground.

"Still the rebel, Seraquel. I should remind you to have more respect for your betters."

Ben's face was a picture of scorn as he snorted his disdain. "It's only your opinion as to whose better you are. Get on with why you've come and get out."

Metatron narrowed his eyes and paused before

speaking in a voice of ice.

"Have a care, Seraquel, I can terminate this arrangement and you will be back in heaven's jail faster than you can say 'angel'. You are fortunate that, in your mistaken belief that you killed the demon, you allowed the Abbot to remove his head. It was in fact, that act that killed the boy who was its host. You are perilously close to violating the terms of your duty down here. You see your redemption in this man, helping him, mentoring him, but *I* see how close you are to wielding a weapon and striking a fatal blow to help him. Remember this; if you take a life, it's game over. In addition to which, you are living with a man who has a demon inside him. You walk a fine line; have a care you do not cross it."

Ben's fury was written on every part of his face.

"Is that it? Good. Now piss off and leave me alone. Crawl back under whichever rock in heaven you've been under. If I was wanted back there, you would have come for me before now. You have no need to remind me of my position. So, if there is nothing else?"

Metatron allowed his presence to almost fill the barn before returning to seven feet in height.

"No. That's not all. You should know that Beth Travis is mentally wounded. It has nothing to do with Sebastian, much as I would like to have seen him brought down to size. It was her time in hell that has scarred her mind. She has taken herself to a place of safety in her soul and whether she returns from it is up to her. She has put up a barrier so thick in an effort to protect herself that even the angels can't reach her."

Ben let out a cry of anguish which quickly turned to rage. "I swear, Metatron, that if this is your doing …"

Metatron looked down at the great bear of a man whom he dwarfed. "You'll what? You have no powers down here, remember that. I told you, this is a result of her time in hell. There is nothing we can do for her where she is and it has been decided that she would stand a better chance of healing down here. I recommend you say nothing to him until his task is accomplished; it would be folly to distract him."

"You bastard! Bring her to me!"

His words fell on empty space. Metatron had gone.

He kicked out savagely at Mike's car and with tears in his eyes and a lump in his throat he slammed the barn door so hard it almost came off its hinges as he went to break the news to Martha. Her previous trauma hadn't been enough, apparently.

In the few yards from the barn to the cottage, he came to a decision. He was going to join the fight against the demons and take the consequences. The words kept going round in his head – Revenge is an act of passion, Vengeance is an act of justice. Well he would see to it that justice was served. The gloves were off now.

Martha had gone to bed exhausted, so he was spared telling her the news of Beth immediately. He knew what to do. He picked up the phone, scrolled through his digital directory and dialled a number.

When it was answered at the other end he said, "I'm in. I need your help."

Roman Woolfe raised a surprised brow. "Benjamin?"

"Yes. You have asked me to join you before, now it's time for me to accept. I need your help. I should never have let Mike go without me and I know I am four hours behind him, but I need you to get me to him. I can, hopefully, be with him at the end of this mess."

Roman's tone was measured. "I take it you no longer care about the consequences of such action?"

"If you mean I will never be able to regain angelic status and will remain human and mortal, then yes, I accept that. No, dammit, I *want* that. I've had my fill of angels!"

"One minute." There was a pause while Ben heard Roman's muffled voice giving instructions to his helicopter pilot. "Paul is on his way to you, we will get you to him as quickly as possible. We were cautious with Mike not to attract attention, but I may have a way to speed things up at the other end for you; you have no time to lose if you are to catch him up. We have a contact at the embassy, perhaps some diplomatic papers can be obtained in time."

"I don't want to know the details, just get me there."

"There will be a car waiting for you at the airport. May I ask what has brought about this change of heart?"

"Beth. She's … injured …"

"I know. I have received a visit from Sebastian; quite an experience I have to say. We will take great care of her. I have engaged nurses and one of the guest suites is being made ready as we speak. She will receive the best of care until such time she can find herself again. I promise that much. There is a place with us for Martha Treneglos too. We have need of a librarian and archivist; Lizzie has far too much to do these days. If she is willing, she can be resident here, close to Beth Travis whilst she is recovering and being among what she loves best, her precious books. At least let us care for her while you and Mike are away."

"Thank you," was all Ben could manage to say.

"I rather think, it is us that should be thanking you, if you're sure that your future lies in this direction. I can't help feeling there will be blood on your hands before too long."

"I have never been more certain."

CHAPTER THIRTY- FOUR: SUMERIAN WRITINGS

Mike scanned the bar but could see no sign of Josh.

"We have to get a drink if we don't want to attract attention," Jack murmured. "Are you sure this is the place he meant by 'World's End'?"

"He definitely meant a kibbutz and if he's in trouble he has two choices; run for hills or hide in plain sight. Knowing Josh, he won't be running. I'll get us a table; you get two coffees and keep a look out for Josh."

Mike sat at the back of the bar, scanning the room constantly; his anxiety levels spiralling. When Jack returned his face was pale.

"There are two 'BlackEyes' behind the bar, plus that girl in the red dress and the lad in the corner with his head in a book; demons. What do you want to do?"

"Nothing. Sit down and look as though you are enjoying your coffee. If we take them on now, we tip our hand. They are already giving us the heavy once-over. I'm thinking they are sensing Bazaliel and backing off, thinking we're with them. That's a good thing for the minute. I hate to say this, Jack, and I thought I never would, but I think you are going to have to let him through when we are looking at the big boys. This lot are minnows in the pond. Small fry."

"You trust him? You trust me?"

"I always trust you, Jack. Him? I'll let you know later. Heads up, here's Josh – Christ he looks rough."

Josh kept his head down as he approached. He pulled out the chair opposite Mike, his back to the bar, sat down heavily and, when he lifted his head Mike couldn't hold back a gasp of shock.

"Josh, what the hell? I thought you were in trouble mate, but ... seriously ... you look like hell on earth. If you'll forgive the expression."

Josh's face and clothes were torn and dirty from crawling through his make-shift escape tunnel before reaching the water system and hiding in an old shed until he knew Mike would be at the bar. His eyes were ringed with dark shadows, and they were beginning to be blood-shot and sunken.

"I'm about to be toast, and you too, if they find me." Josh's voice was gruff. "So I'll make this brief. They are going to perform the Opening of the Gates ritual in an ancient Sumerian temple that they uncovered; it's a long ritual that has to be precise. When Sirius, the Dog Star, is in the right position in the sky tonight, probably around ten, the ritual should be at its conclusion and the Ark will surface. The temple is dedicated to the demon Pazuzu, and it is he that will activate the Ark. Pazuzu was Lucifer's left hand before the fall, and he plans to be so again."

Jack leaned forward and lowered his voice. "So why don't we just go in and take them out now?"

Mike had a sudden moment of clarity. "Because we need them to birth the Ark so that it can be destroyed, not just shut down. There can be no second chance for that thing. I'm guessing the temple is well guarded?"

Josh nodded. "They kept me prisoner in there because I believe I was to be the human sacrifice for the ritual's conclusion."

"So how did you get out?" Jack asked.

"Drainage tunnels. They start in the temple as small channels for the blood of the sacrifice to run down into an underground cistern, and from the ground down they are big enough to squeeze through, just. You may find it tight, Mike. From there they join larger drainage tunnels built during the Roman occupation, and they come out on the far side of the dig site."

Mike looked at Josh's reddening eyes and growing

pallor. There were two small pustules on the side of his face that he hadn't noticed before.

"Josh, are you OK? I know you've had it rough, but you look ill, my friend. You should see a doctor."

"There has been a lot of sickness here, Mike. I'll be OK; it's just the noise in my head. Deep white noise, like a swarm of bloody locusts. I can't get it out of my head since the temple. I'll be fine."

Mike wasn't convinced. "Josh, you can take us to the tunnels and then you clear out, and I mean it. You've done your bit and you really should see a doctor. For all our sakes. If you are with us you could put us all in danger. Are we clear?"

Mike's tone was compassionate but authoritative and Josh appeared to crumple in front of them.

Jack looked at his watch; it was ten minutes past eight. "You said it was a long ritual, how long?"

"If my memory is correct from the Sumerian writings I saw, about an hour. They have to call on many of the Ancient Ones in turn; the Opening of the Gates requires the presence of all of the most important Gods. Nanna, Anu, Enki and Enlil, Marduk, Tiamat and Pazuzu to open the gates, and they have to make the sacrifice at just the right moment; like I said, it has to be precise so they will take their time."

"We need to be there before it kicks off; we should move," Mike said in a quiet, level tone which portrayed a calm he didn't feel. "Is there any cover in the temple?"

Josh tried to think beyond the white-noise of the locusts. It was like trying to walk through treacle. Finally, an image settled. "Yes, at the rear of the temple where it's cut into the rock, there is an alcove and a minor altar, big enough to conceal you, if we can get you there in time. What are you thinking?"

"Nothing you should worry about. Take us there now, and then get yourself to a doctor." He put his hand on Josh's arm. "Thank you for waiting for us. Many would have run."

"You wouldn't have."

Mike tried a casual grin and failed. "No, but then, I'm crazy."

Outside, Levi Bachman was waiting for them.

"Mr Barclay had an urgent call; I am to take you to him. He asked me tell you that he has important information. Come."

Josh was alarmed. "Who is this? Who is he talking about?" His voice tight with anxiety.

Mike tried to reassure him. "It's OK, Josh. He's a good guy. It's a long story, but we have help, let's leave it at that." He began to reconsider keeping Josh with them. "Can we find the entrance to the tunnels without you?"

Josh was becoming unsteady on his feet. He swallowed hard. "Maybe. Let me think ... OK ... about a hundred yards from the eastern edge of the site there's an old goatherd's hut with the roof collapsed in and a sheet of corrugated tin acting as a door. Just past that, probably thirty yards or so, there is what passes for a Roman version of a manhole cover, nothing more than an inspection opening. It's rusted to hell and a bitch to open. About half way the tunnels fork; coming out I took the left hand tunnel so, going in, it will be the one to your right. When you get to the cistern it's directly above you. I should ..."

Whatever it was that he felt he should, he didn't say, as he collapsed in a heap at their feet.

Levi was swift to pick him up and look around to see if there was anyone around. His reactions were like lightning. He could see, from his expression, that Mike was surprised.

"Living in Israel, you learn to react quickly to any situation," he explained. "We'll have to take him with us; Mr Barclay said it was urgent he speak to you. I'll take him from there to a doctor."

Jack caught hold of Josh's other arm, hooked his own arm under his shoulder and, with Levi, they dragged him over to the waiting car in the car park.

As they got to the car, the girl in the red dress from the bar stepped in front of them, black eyes wide. She opened her mouth and her jagged teeth reflected the light streaming from the bar.

The next seconds flashed by and, ten or twenty years on, Mike would not be able to describe it, it all happened so quickly.

The girl-demon launched herself, all teeth and claws, towards them. Jack dropped Josh onto the ground and met her full on. There was blood on Jack's throat and they heard the sound of her neck breaking. Jack swung around to Mike, his hand on his throat, trying to stem the blood. "Finish it," he gasped.

The blade was out and slashing at her neck, severing flesh, sinew and bone before Mike had time to think about it. Levi grabbed the torso and dragged it around to the rear of the car and threw her into the boot, turned back to grab the head, tossed it in and slammed the boot shut. "Get in!" he yelled.

Mike yanked Josh onto his feet; he was coming around and easier to manhandle into the rear of the car with Jack.

Mike spun around to see Jack. "Drive to the nearest hospital!" he snapped at Levi.

Jack took his hand from the cut on his throat. "No, it's all right, she missed anything major, it's almost stopped."

He took his bloody hand away and looked at Mike meaningfully. Bazaliel was already on the case and Jack hadn't lied, she had missed his carotid and jugular vessels.

Levi had his foot down and in seconds they were outside a house on the edge of the kibbutz. He opened the rear door and helped Josh out, guiding him into the house. Mike and Jack were only one step behind.

"We don't have time to mess around, Levi. Where's Barclay?"

Levi turned to them, pointing a 9mm pistol directly at them. He inclined his head to the left and they stared at the bloodied mess on the floor that had once been the Strazca agent.

CHAPTER THIRTY- FIVE: IF SOMETHING'S RIGHT

As Mike and Jack had been getting off the plane at Tel Aviv, Ben was checking in at the British Airways desk at Heathrow Airport.

The clerk at the desk handed him his boarding pass. "You will have to hurry, sir. The gate is closing in eight minutes."

He nodded his thanks and checked his watch; the courier from the embassy should have been there. Without the diplomatic papers he would face delays at Tel Aviv. He checked his watch again.

A red-faced, flustered young man rushed up to him. "Ben Lovecraft? You have ID?"

"From the Embassy?" Ben asked, handing over his boarding card.

"You could say that. Papers are in order and there are two burn phones in the envelope. You should know that the papers have a shelf-life of twenty-four hours. Do not attempt to use them after that and we would be grateful if you would burn or shred them at that time. Have a good flight, sir."

"Passenger Lovecraft, please report immediately to your departure gate, your flight has now boarded," came over the public address system.

Breathless he shoved his passport and boarding card towards the woman at the gate. "Sorry. Last minute arrangement."

"That's all right, sir, have a pleasant flight."

It wasn't until he had settled into his seat and the plane was in flight that he realised how exhausted he was. He closed his eyes and pondered his actions. In one fell swoop he had consigned himself to no way back from his human life. And he was glad.

The Strazca had made themselves known to him years previously, though he never knew how they had discovered him and his secret, and probably never would, and he had refused all their advances to him to join them. The last few hours had only served to demonstrate their far-reaching abilities in the administration of the organisation that had stayed in the shadows; now what they needed was hunters. Previously, he had been focussed on one thing; getting things ready for the one that would be his redemption. Well, that was out of the window now so, what the hell, he would become the hunter that had been inside him all the time.

He spent the flight between contemplating his move to join with the Strazca and sleeping. Surprisingly, when he slept, it was peaceful, dreamless sleep and, although short-lived, he woke refreshed and ready for business.

True to Roman's prediction, his diplomatic papers made his passage through Ben Gurion Airport a smooth transition, although he attracted long looks from officials. At the Hertz desk, a clerk handed over keys with a smile and directed him to the Orchard Parking garage on the ground floor, where he would find his Kia Picanto, fuelled and waiting.

Ben had always believed that if something is right, it is problem-free; a sentiment that was reinforced by the ease of his arrival so far. He allowed himself a sardonic smile then; things might be easy now but, when he arrived in Megiddo, it was going to be a whole other ball-game. He wondered why he had taken so long to make the decisions he had, and concluded that it had taken the injury of the innocent so close to home that had given him the final push.

Thinking about Beth made him feel cold; he would have to break the news to Mike. When he would do that exactly, would be dictated by the circumstances on the ground. If Mike was worried about her at a critical moment, it would be *his* head separating from his body and not that of a demon, or, the other side of the coin was that he may be enraged and it would fuel his fighting skills. Either way, he would have to play it by ear.

His hire car had an electronic tag on its windscreen, allowing him to drive straight through the electronic tolls on Highway Six. He put his foot down, hoping that if he was stopped his diplomatic papers would get him out of any delay by the Israeli police for speeding. He wasn't stopped.

Ben drove in the belief that he was four hours behind Mike, when in fact, Mike's delay of two hours at Ben Gurion Airport, then the check in at the hotel for the sake of their cover, had actually reduced that to under two hours. He made the hour drive in forty-five minutes; now he had to find Mike and he needed weapons of any description.

He had brought his old rosary and crucifix with him and pages torn from the Holy Bible and the Koran; contrary to initial thought of desecration and sacrilege, these pages were a powerful weapon against demons. On more than one occasion he had shoved a page or two into the mouth of a possessed person and the demon had fled. He wasn't under the illusion this was going to be anything like that easy, but he had them ready, all the same.

He took the junction onto Highway 65 and drove until, close to Megiddo, he turned off left into the town of El-Biyar, where he wasted no time in finding an iron-mongers. There he purchased a machete after staring down the eyes of the shop-keeper, who eventually decided that three times over-the-odds sterling was better than turning his customer away. Tensions were high enough between the Palestinian and Israeli factions without taking on a stranger, and one with cash to boot.

The hill-top dig site in Megiddo was off limits up front, he knew that, and finding Mike was going to be next to impossible. He had the burn phones but instinct told him not to call him. He had only one option. He was going to find a demon that had been drawn with the others and make it talk. He had discovered in the past, a couple of pages of Psalms and a page from the Koran when scrumpled together and shoved in the mouth did wonders to loosen a demon's tongue.

He drove through the Megiddo kibbutz looking for somewhere to leave the car without attracting unwanted attention. A club in the centre looked promising and there were several cars already parked there. The rest of the way was on foot. Strategically, the guards were in an excellent position to see anyone approaching, but dusk was falling and he hoped he could use it as cover.

He sat for a few moments, casting up a prayer, then he closed his eyes, reached into his pocket and bought out a white circular collar. In the rear-view mirror he checked it's position. He was a priest again. No church, no dogma, no rules; he was just a priest, standing with Mike against the demons.

CHAPTER THIRTY- SIX: BECKETT

Roman Woolfe was energised; it had been a while since he had done anything of a practical nature, spending most of his time in meetings designed to increase the influence of the Strazca, or in recruitment. Very rarely was he in the field, and even more infrequently organising the minutiae of an operation. It felt good.

Lizzie had given him several phone numbers, all of which belonged to highly qualified psychiatric nurses. The first two he discounted due to their location; the third and fourth he put to one side. In the space of an hour he had chosen the two, and offered them a salary they couldn't refuse. Neither of them did.

Beckett was next on his list.

The atmosphere in the room changed rapidly, making Roman feel as if all the air had been sucked from the room; the angel was back. Sebastian appeared, head down, dark wings outstretched, carrying Beth in his arms. He folded his wings and lifted his face that was etched with concern. Roman allowed himself the thought that if an angel was concerned then, maybe, he should be too. He suddenly felt foolish in his belief that he could throw all the resources and finances of the Strazca at a problem and the outcome would be solved. He felt humbled and was glad of it.

Sebastian followed Roman upstairs to the suite that had been prepared for Beth. It was a sunny room with large bay windows and pretty, primrose damask curtains and bedcover; antique mirrors reflected the warm rays around the room. Late-blooming roses filled a crystal vase at the side of a comfortable sofa and Sebastian nodded his approval as he sat Beth down. All the time her eyes had been distant and a small smile hovered around her mouth but she had not reacted to any of the stimulus around her.

"Hello, Beth. I'm Roman Woolfe and I'm a friend of Mike's. We hope you will be comfortable here until he gets back."

There was no reaction, and if he thought her smile had broadened, he knew deep down it was wishful thinking. He turned to Sebastian.

"If this has anything to do with you, I guarantee you that there will be several hunters that you will need to look for over your shoulder. I guarantee it and the Strazca will support it."

Sebastian gave Roman his most haughty expression. "It has nothing to do with me, and I should tell you that your empty threats mean nothing."

Roman smiled. "You want to be sure you are right, because when Mike Travis returns and finds her like this, you will see how empty those threats are."

Sebastian drew himself up to an impressive height and scowled at Roman, who remained unmoved. He had seen at first hand his grandfather's lunar transformation on more than one occasion, and an arrogant angel didn't shake him.

There was a sudden shift in the atmosphere again, and Sebastian was gone. Roman picked up the internal telephone and dialled Lizzie's extension. She would be the best person to keep Beth company and make sure she stayed safe until the nurse arrived.

He went down to his study to telephone Beckett; fascinated that a vampire could be off the Strazca radar and working as a successful psychotherapist. Clearly there was much to learn from Paul Beckett; if he gave them the chance.

Beckett's phone was answered by a young voice with a slight Eastern European accent.

"Hi, the Cedars Clinic, can I help you?"

"Am I speaking with Paul Beckett?"

"No, 'fraid not. This is Darius, Beckett's ... assistant ... Can I help you?"

"It is rather urgent. If he is there, please tell him that Beth Travis is in need of his care."

There was a sharp intake of breath on the other end of the call. "Hold on, man, I'll get him right away."

Seconds later a very professional voice reached his ear.

"This is Beckett. To whom am I speaking? Is Beth Travis with you? Is she ill?"

Obviously, Beckett had not been apprised of her condition.

"My name is Roman Woolfe and Mrs Travis is currently under my care whilst her husband is away ... on business ...." He didn't know how much to divulge about how her condition had come about. He decided to play it safe.

"I'm afraid she has fallen prey to some form of psychiatric condition, and you have been recommended to me to help her. Do I take it from your demeanour that you know Beth Travis?"

"Yes. Where are you? I'm coming straight away."

"I see you are in Abergavenny, just over an hour's drive. This isn't an emergency, you understand." He gave Beckett the address, thought about sending his helicopter to pick him up and decided against it. Better let the good doctor get to know him and his intentions first. This was going to be interesting.

Exactly one hour later, Beckett brought his partner's MG Roadster to a gravel–spinning halt outside the front door of Linwood House. The door was wide open.

Inside the beautiful hall, he called out. "Hello?"

Roman came from his study at the far end of the hall, hand extended; he couldn't take his eyes from Beckett's face, looking for any nuance that would give away his true nature.

Christ, he knows, Beckett thought, then dismissed it as unimportant. "Please take me to Beth," was all he said.

He followed Roman up the sweeping staircase, hearing every minute sound in the entire house. His vampire senses picked up three other people in the building and the one he was interested in lay directly to his right. Roman stood aside as Beckett brushed past him.

Beth hadn't moved from the position Sebastian had left her in, but her demeanour had slightly changed in that she appeared even more distant. Lizzie got up from the chair as Beckett knelt down in front of Beth and took her hand.

"Beth? Sweetie? It's Beckett." He brushed some stray hairs from her face and tucked them behind her ear. "Beth? It's me, Beckett."

Beth gave no indication that she was aware of his presence. He stood up, his face flooded with anxiety and fury.

"Tell me how this happened. The truth. Because I will know if you lie to me, and I can see you know what I am, so don't let's play games here. What the hell has happened to my friend?"

"Perhaps we should go downstairs, I am not the doctor here, but I think if she hears us discussing this, it will cause her more harm. Come. Lizzie will stay with her." Lizzie smiled at Beckett, appreciative of his slim body and elegant, handsome features that would never age, under a mop of dark hair that was heavily-streaked with silver; his eyes drew her attention and she tried to hold his gaze but he looked away.

Beckett shook his head. "I want to be alone with her, please. If you would both leave, I will find you when I have finished examining her."

Roman nodded and indicated to Lizzie that they should comply. "Lizzie will return to sit with her when you are done, she will be just across the corridor. I will be in my sitting room, to the right of the hall. Is there anything you need?"

Beckett shook his head and turned his attention back to Beth. He needed no instruments to measure her heartbeat

215

or her blood pressure; he could hear the blood being pumped around her arteries and veins in a slow, regular symphony. He tilted her head up to meet his gaze and found his way into her locked-off mind. The barrier was there, protecting her from whatever memory or trauma lay behind it, and even though he knew he could tear it down to see what was haunting her, he dare not. She had erected the barrier from her own sub-consciousness and to destroy it would be to destroy her.

He kissed her gently on the forehead, allowing her to remain in her world of sun, flowers and butterflies, populated by herself, her beloved daughter, and her husband. In her world there was no hell, no demons, and no monsters.

His steps were slow as he made his way back to Roman's sitting room. Now was the time for questions.

Roman sat, relaxed, in a comfortable armchair by the window, gazing out across the manicured lawn at the bank of rhododendrons at its edge.

He stood when Beckett entered. He had already made a decision: a man who was a vampire, with his own secrets to keep, could surely be trusted with basic information about the Strazca.

"Please tell me you can help her," he said. "I wonder if you would care for some tea?"

Beckett took a minute to get his measure, flirting on the outskirts of Roman's mind. "You are very tactful. Thank you, I would love some tea. I do, in fact, drink many beverages." He smiled at his and Beth's host, allowing him to see the tiny points on his canine teeth. Enough to make it known who was actually in charge there.

Roman understood the subtle message. "What is your diagnosis, doctor?"

"Beckett," he said. "Just Beckett. She is suffering from a very extreme form of Dissociative Disorder, the extremity of which I have not encountered. The condition is usually accompanied by a loss of identity but from what I can tell she knows exactly who she is and who her loved ones are. She has completely relocated her reality and blocked from it all outside influences and stimuli. There is no medication that will help her; only constant reassurance and contact with family and friends. I can't say how long she will remain in this state, and only she can bring herself out of it. I have no doubt that, at some point, she will, but only when the trauma that caused this has healed. I can help her, but it is she who will dictate how much and how quickly."

"Then there is hope, and that is good. Ah, here is the tea."

A smart woman in her fifties entered bearing a tea tray. Beckett stood to take it from her - the third soul that he had detected on his arrival; Romans' cook and housekeeper left as quietly as she had entered.

"Mrs Cooper, my cook and housekeeper as you will have guessed," Roman said. "She is also my friend and counsellor. She will help to look after Beth."

"You presume a lot. What does Mike have to say on the matter? He may want her at home," he paused, picking up Roman's thought. "Oh God, he doesn't know," he said.

Roman poured tea and told him how Beth had come to be there, filling in the blanks after Mike had left Beckett's home. "I had a visit from an angel; Sebastian. A thoroughly unpleasant character, so arrogant, but what an experience."

Beckett smiled at Roman's next thought. *And now I'm sitting drinking tea with a vampire.*

Roman continued to appraise Beckett of Mike's current location.

Beckett sighed. "He told me about the Demon Ark, but I didn't know he'd gone to Israel! But if Jack is with him and Ben is on his way, then I hope he'll be back soon. He's had a pretty rough go of it lately and his own mind is very fragile; I hope this won't hit him too hard. I can't be sure how he will react."

Roman's expression was impassive, his voice steady. "Oh, I think you can be very sure. He is going to go after every demon on the planet and make it his business to see they have a very bad day."

Beckett grinned, despite his initial caution. He was beginning to warm to Roman who was as easy to read as any book in his library.

"How do you come to be involved with Mike? He has never mentioned you."

"No, our relationship is of recent origin."

"And what is the nature of that relationship? I ask only out of concern for a friend."

Roman leaned back in his chair. "I am the head of an organisation called the Strazca; I am known as the Eldritch. Our organisation is not known outside of its members and for very good reason." He continued to tell Beckett about the organisation and how they were progressing from pure scholarship and study of the paranormal or supernatural, to actual intervention in the evil side of such phenomena. He was careful not to mention any involvement with vampires which Beckett noted with pleasure.

"The world is out of balance and it is time to stand against the evils that come from the dark side of nature or other realms, but we are students, librarians and archivists, not warriors. Mike and Ben are warriors and they have agreed to join us in as much as they will work with us and benefit from our resources."

"I'm not sure how Mike will react when he knows about Beth. He is full of guilt about the demonic attacks on his loved ones as it is; he will see this as his fault. There will be fallout."

CHAPTER THIRTY-SEVEN:
REMEMBER AFGHANISTAN

Levi Bachman stepped over the bloodied body of Jon Barclay, the gun steady in his hand, the glint in his eye steely, his free hand outstretched.

"Hand it over and live; makes sense, eh?"

"You black-eyed bastard!" Jack yelled at him.

Bachman was unmoved. "I am not one of your so-called Black Eyes. But I will have the Lucifer Stone. Call it severance pay."

Mike's expression was impassive. "I don't think so. Can you kill both of us before one of us kills you? Are you that good? Do you think we are stupid enough to believe that if we hand it over, you won't kill us? You have no option, have you? I imagine the Strazca won't be too happy at your betrayal. Have they not paid you well? And what about your family? Your father and grandfather? Why would you trample on their loyalty?"

"The Strazca! Yes, they pay me for my services, but why should I settle for a pittance when I can take this and live comfortably?"

Mike laughed at him. "You think it's valuable? It isn't. It's a low-grade semi-precious stone."

Levi's face grew dark with anger; he stepped forwards and the gun was levelled directly at Mike's head.

"Give it to him, Mike; he means it. Remember what happened in Afghanistan," Jack said quietly.

The synapses in Mike's brain fired in quick succession as the memory of the situation Jack was referring to came forward: a Taliban had gone rogue and held up Mike and Jack. Mike had made to hand over his wallet and, as the gunman's eyes were fastened on his prize, they launched themselves on him simultaneously and overpowered him. This time, the stakes were higher than a wallet and its contents, but Levi Bachman was no hardened Taliban fighter.

Mike raised his hands in a gesture of submission. "OK. Just take your finger off the trigger, you're making me nervous. It's in my pocket so you either have to trust me to reach in and take it out or you can come and get it."

Bachman hesitated, weighing up his options. The possibility that this wasn't going to end the way he'd planned made itself known. He didn't know what Mike may have in his jacket pocket besides the ring. He should have taken the advantage while he had the element of surprise and he knew it.

"Slowly, and no funny business," he said, pointing the gun at Mike's pocket and then back at his face. "I *will* kill you; I have nothing to lose now."

"All right, take it easy. I'm going to put my hands down now and take it out of my pocket. Just cool it."

Neither Mike nor Jack took their eyes from his. It was all about his eyes not the gun. If they saw a millisecond of hesitation, they would take him. His eyes didn't waver.

Mike began to lower his arms.

"Slowly!" barked Bachman.

Mike slowed the descent. "OK, OK." He reached into his pocket and in a split-second Bachman's eyes followed Mike's hand. It was enough. Jack threw himself on him, followed immediately by Mike, and they took him to the floor.

The first gunshot was muffled by the body on top of the pistol, the second was louder.

It seemed as if time had ceased.

The dark pool of blood was spreading out from the tangle of bodies in the deafening silence.

Suddenly galvanised, Mike leapt to his feet, looking at his blood-covered hands and chest. "Jack?" he demanded as he bent to turn his friend over. Jack groaned and levered himself to his feet. In the struggle, Levi Bachman had managed to shoot himself; the second shot was a reflex action that had put the bullet into a wall.

They both exhaled loudly.

"Well, there's one thing," Jack said. "I've got a gun now."

"Barclay didn't deserve that," Mike said, nodding towards the dead Strazca agent.

"No. But there's nothing we can do for him right now, and if those two gunshots don't bring people running, I'll be damned! We need to get the hell out of here. Mike! Come on, let's move."

Jack picked up Levi's pistol and stuffed it into the waistband of his jeans and grinned at Mike, "I was always a better shot than you on the range."

Two gunshots in Israel were not enough to bring people running. There had been no ensuing commotion so people tended to mind their own business.

Together they hauled Josh into the back of the car to get him away from the carnage in the little house.

Jack threw himself into the driver's seat and grinned at Mike. "I drive faster than you, too."

Mike acknowledged him with a smile and climbed into the passenger seat, ramming his seat-belt home. "Jack, I just want to say …"

"Don't, Mike. There's nothing to say. Don't get all mushy on me; I'll cry like a girl. You *do* know I'm gay, right?" He laughed harshly at his own joking words as he slammed the car into reverse and spun it around. "Let's go and fuck up some demons."

Mike laughed as well then; it was, in fact, ridiculous. How he had come to this was unimportant, but he was there now, with a job to do and he was going to do it, regardless of the outcome. One way or the other there was going to be a mess at Megiddo in the morning.

He looked at his watch. "By my reckoning we have about half an hour to get into the tunnels and into the temple before everything kicks off."

Jack said nothing; he just stamped on the accelerator.

They parked the taxi back at the car park to the bar, hoping it wouldn't be noticed among the other customer's vehicles. Mike dialled 101, the emergency number for an ambulance.

"Please send an ambulance to the car park of Club Megiddo, in the centre of the kibbutz. There is a very sick man here." He disconnected the call before the operator could ask for any details, and tossed it onto the back seat next to Josh, who was still semi-conscious and unaware of what was going on.

"Sorry, mate; gotta go. Help is on the way. I'll find you when this is over. Ready, Jack?"

They ran through the darkness to the edge of the kibbutz where they found the old hut with its tin door and, walking then, scouring the ground, they came to the tunnel entrance.

"Let's hope they don't go into the temple too early. Once they find Josh is missing the balloon will go up. We have to hope they find the escape route immediately, because then they won't be looking around the temple and find us."

Mike dropped into the tunnel first and began feeling his way through the darkness. Jack was right behind him.

At the fork, they took the right-hand tunnel and picked up their pace, becoming accustomed to the dark and finding the ground more level.

Mike felt and heard the crunch of the baked clay pieces under his boot; Josh's debris from the temple drainage channel. He put out a hand to bring Jack to a halt behind him.

He lowered his voice to a whisper. "OK, this is it; we keep silence until we know what's up there. No point in announcing our arrival if we can help it. Give me a shove up and I'll pull you up from the other side."

"OK, and just so you know, you owe me a new shirt."

Mike grinned. "You've got it. OK?"

"OK."

Jack interlaced his fingers to form a foothold to shove Mike up into Josh's narrow tunnel. He heaved, and Mike scrabbled for a foothold. He only just fitted into the tunnel which was useful as he was less likely to fall back down. The rough excavation made for hand-holds and footholds, and as he neared the top he paused, listening. There was complete and unnerving silence.

He made a grab at the opening and hauled himself through it, and relieved to find the temple still lit, he took off his belt and leaned into the hole. He felt Jack's weight immediately and braced himself as Jack searched for hand and footholds and seconds later the belt went slack as he hauled himself up through the hole in the floor.

They took a minute to look around for the altar that Josh had described, and both took a spontaneous step back as their eyes alighted on the statute of Pazuzu.

"Ugly bastard, isn't he?" Jack whispered.

Mike didn't reply, as he set about making the mess around the hole more obvious and dragging the ancient drain cover into a more visible location before they both crouched behind the stone side-altar that Josh had rightly assumed would be big enough to conceal them.

They didn't have to wait long, as ten minutes later the sound of heavy locks being turned and bolts drawn back announced the arrival of Richard Vermont and his entourage.

The scream of rage from Vermont told them that it was playing out as they had hoped and it was swiftly followed by a scuffle and a cry, as one of the minion demons came upon the opening and drain cover.

"Grand Master! Here!"

Richard Vermont, or rather the demon possessing Richard Vermont, lapsed momentarily into an archaic language, the tone of which gave ample illustration as to the gist of it: he was pissed off.

He composed himself long enough to return to English. "Get after him; and if you don't find him, you would be well advised to disappear. Permanently."

The tension was palpable as each and every one of Vermont's heavies knew the score; they were in need of another sacrifice.

Vermont retreated to the arcane language that some of the others obviously understood. There was sudden movement and a cry as one of the lesser demons was grabbed and hauled in front of Vermont. The language would have been recognised by Josh as Akkadian, ancient enough, but more recent than the Sumerian of the demon Pazuzu. Josh would perhaps have understood Vermont explaining to the defenceless demon in front of him that he should be honoured to be the sacrifice to Pazuzu that would begin the cycle of birth of the Demon Ark. He would be remembered, Vermont said.

The honour was obviously not appreciated as the demon being held by two of the heaviest of the thugs began to whimper.

There was the sound of a heavy fist connecting with flesh and bone, and the whimpering ceased. Mike and Josh didn't need to see the scene as they could put mental pictures to the sounds of an unconscious body being dragged along a dirt floor towards the sacrificial granite slab.

They felt the temple grow cold and the pervading smell of a foul blend of incense.

The ritual of the Opening of the Gates was about to begin.

CHAPTER THIRTY- EIGHT: OPENING THE GATES

From their place of concealment they could see nothing, and by mutual and silent agreement they moved very slowly to the edge of the stone altar where, with difficulty, they could just see what was happening. They held their breath; had their movement been seen or heard?

It hadn't. They allowed themselves to breathe again.

Richard Vermont carried an ornate staff and faced the statue of Pazuzu, beginning to recite the ritual, not in the arcane language of the demon possessing him, but in his mother tongue; English.

Mike didn't know when he was going to use the Lapsit Exillis but he had to be ready. He fingered the ring in his pocket and let it fall into his hand, closing his fist around it.

Vermont's voice had power and he was obviously used to ritual.

"I call upon Pazuzu, guardian of this temple, destroyer of men, bringer of plagues and storms: stand guard upon this temple as the gates to the underworld are flung wide!"

He began to draw with his staff in the dirt floor; it was the seal of Nanna. It was complex and painstaking, nothing could be wrong or out of proportion; everything had to be exact.

"Nanna, Father of all Gods. In the name of your promise to the race of men, I call you. Before the gate to the underworld I call you. You who made kings and Gods, I call you.

"Master of the Gates I entreat you to open wide the first gate."

He turned to the unconscious man on the granite slab

and drew a shining blade from within his robes. He leaned across the man and opened a small vein, allowing the first blood to flow.

"This is the blood of the first gate. Nanna, open wide the gate!"

He repeated the supplication, now in Akkadian.

There was a heavy silence and from deep underground a tremor made its way to the surface.

Jack's eyes were wide; Mike's were closed in prayer.

Vermont drew another seal in the floor; the seal of Shammash. Then he returned his attention to the statue of Pazuzu.

"Pazuzu, guardian of this temple, destroyer of men, bringer of plagues and storms, stand guard upon this temple as the gates to the underworld are flung wide!

"Shammash, God of the Sun, bringer of fiery light, I call upon you to fling wide the second gate to the underworld. Shammash, Render of the dark, Lamp of Wisdom, open wide the gate!"

He turned again to the sacrifice on the altar and opened another vein.

"This is the blood of the second gate. Shammash, open wide the gate!"

Again, he repeated his supplication in Akkadian.

Another tremor rippled beneath them and this time there was a distant cracking sound of rock being rent apart. The temperature in the temple fell another few degrees.

Vermont drew the seal of Nergal and continued the ritual.

"Pazuzu, guardian of this temple, destroyer of men, bringer of plagues and storms, stand guard upon this temple as the gates to the underworld are flung wide!

"Nergal, God of War, I call you. Defeater of Armies, Slayer of Men, I call you. Open wide the third gate, in the name of the covenant sworn and made between Gods and Men!

Another vein was opened.

"This is the blood of the third gate. Nergal, open the gate to the underworld."

The ritual was having an effect. The temperature was dropping rapidly as Vermont's voice was beginning to rise to fever pitch. One by one, he repeated the seals and supplications to each and every one of the Ancient Ones, and each time the tremors were stronger, the smell and taste of sulphur, thicker. The blood flowed from the cuts in the body of the sacrifice.

After the final supplication to the God, Marduk, he invoked them all again.

He turned to the statue of Pazuzu and fell to his knees.

"Pazuzu, come forth! Manifest to greet your Master, Morning Star and all the Fallen Ones, Demons all! Come Pazuzu, come at the last blood!"

He rose and turned to the sacrifice and, with one smooth motion he cut open the blessedly still-unconscious victim's throat.

The ground trembled and a huge crack appeared in the floor of the temple. Outside, thunder and lightning raged suddenly in the night sky and the temple filled with the deep white-noise of locusts.

The statue of Pazuzu was covered with the swarming insects. From hell they had materialised in the temple. The huge statue was now a writhing mess of fat, feeding, locusts.

Jack looked at Mike, beseeching him – *Now?*

Against all of his instincts, Mike shook his head. They had to wait for the Ark to break through into the temple. They had to destroy it at its birth.

The swarming locusts began to form a black cloud in front of the statue; a black cloud that was gradually taking the shape of a man.

And as they watched, half in disbelief, the locust figure raised its arm and pointed straight at them and gave an unearthly shout in Akkadian.

Vermont's demon followers reacted instantly and ran

towards them en- masse. There was nowhere to go.

The ground gave a final birthing shudder, and the Demon Ark rose through the fissure into the temple as Josh Hammond stepped out of the mass of swarming locusts; the white-noise was no longer in his head, incubating the demon Pazuzu, making him ready for the possession, it was all around and he was now fully the vessel of the demon. The ambulance had arrived at the abandoned car to find Josh no longer there; demons had no need for paramedics.

CHAPTER THIRTY-NINE: HITTING THE PAUSE BUTTON

Constructed from black metal that was not of this earth, it rose into the temple; two and a half cubits long, a cubit and a half wide, and a cubit and a half high. The Ark of a different Covenant. A covenant made between Lucifer and men at his fall.

It was then or never, and Mike knew what he had to do and what the consequences were; he closed his eyes and said a silent goodbye to all that had been.

And put the ring onto his finger.

Jack muttered a prayer that they wouldn't kill him instantly, giving Mike time to do what he had to, and ran to meet the oncoming thugs, shooting 9mm rounds in every direction. Some of the demons fell, temporarily, but others grabbed him and pushed him roughly to his knees in front of what had once been the mild-mannered archaeologist, Josh Hammond and who was now the host of Pazuzu.

Before Mike's heart could beat again, in a millisecond of space and time, the ring claimed its new owner and the Lapsit Exillis began its instant download.

Solomon's dark magic was in him, in his every cell, empowering him, shielding him, blinding him, torturing him, corrupting him. The Key of Solomon, The Legemeton, The Testament of Solomon, Grimoires of dark magic, and all manner of ritual and knowledge, were downloading into his head.

The Ark began to tremble and its domed lid broke open and fell to the floor. The noise of a thousand hurricanes came from it as demons began pouring out it from every portal; purely evil spirits rushing out of the temple in search of hosts. Incandescent light and fire spewed from the Ark as it began its final activation.

Mike raised his trembling hand, the download still pouring into his brain, blotting out all rational thought and intention; he fought against it, and began the spell to shut it down.

Josh was in front of him then, speaking in a voice that sounded like deep white-noise. Mike looked into his eyes and saw nothing of his old friend, only visions of Pazuzu.

He fought with the last ounce of his being to keep the ring pointed at the Ark while his free hand brought the blade from out of its sheath and plunged it deep into Josh. He twisted it, pulled it free and swung it sideways, taking Pazuzu's head from Josh's body, before letting the blade fall to the ground. He would mourn Josh later; he had died long before Mike had taken off his head; Josh had died in the back of the abandoned car when a demon from the bar had possessed him and delivered him to the temple.

Vermont had fled from the temple and, before Jack could get after him, the door slammed open again and the massive figure of a priest, complete with dog collar and biker gear, strode in dragging Vermont behind him like a sack. He threw him to the floor and hit him out cold, planting his foot on his throat.

Pazuzu had lost his host and Richard Vermont had failed him. The choice had been simple. The dog-headed, leather-winged demon roared in triumph as he returned to spirit-form and, as a dark cloud he entered Vermont through his eyes, his mouth and his nostrils. Vermont's eyes shot open, his coal-black eyes of the demon inside. Possession wasn't enough for Pazuzu; he wanted revenge for the failure. Vermont screamed in agony as the demon ripped through his internal organs, inflicting the utmost suffering that he could before he turned his attention to the great bear of a man that was holding his host down on the floor under a massive boot. Pausing for revenge was his undoing though, as the machete swung through the air with a force that brooked no argument. Vermont's head rolled to the side of his body, still bearing the look of surprise. The biker-priest stepped over the body as demons began pouring from the Ark and Ben Lovecraft did what he had waited years to do; he began killing demons.

Chaos erupted in the temple as more demons came out of the Ark which was now glowing with electric blue light. Mike couldn't hear or see anything; his actions were automatic, coming from a time lost to man.

Jack's eyes turned to the blackest black of midnight. Bazaliel had joined the party.

It was the voice of the Shadow Demon that came out of Jack's mouth speaking in Latin; deep commanding tones that brought some of the lesser demons to their knees, covering their ears, as he began the rite of exorcism, turning on his own.

"Exorcizamus te, omnis immundus spiritus, omnis satanica potestas, omnis incursio infernalis adversarii, omnis legio, omnis congregatio et secta diabolica. Ergo, omnis legio diabolica, adjuramus te ... cessa decipere humanas creaturas, eisque æternæ perditionìs venenum propinare ... Vade, satana, inventor et magister omnis fallaciæ, hostis humanæ salutis ... Humiliare sub potenti manu Dei; contremisce et effuge, invocato a nobis sancto et terribili nomine ... quem inferi tremunt ..."

We exorcise you, every impure spirit, every satanic power, every incursion of the infernal adversary, every legion, every congregation and diabolical sect. Therefore, diabolical legions, we adjure you ... Cease to deceive human creatures, and to give to them the poison of eternal damnation; ... Be gone, Satan, inventor and master of all deceit, enemy of man's salvation ... Be humble under the mighty hand of God; tremble and flee when we invoke the Holy and Terrible Name at which those down below tremble ... ...

Demons were screaming and leaving bodies to fall onto the dirt floor of the temple, exiting the temple as dark shadows in the night.

Mike was speaking again now; the spell to destroy the Ark of the most ancient evil. His hand was glowing as if on fire and the beam of energy from the Lapsit Exillis was directed like a laser onto the Ark.

A dark mass emerged from the Ark and rose as a thick black cloud to the roof, hanging over the temple like a pall, as another rose from the ground to join it.

Mike continued.

A tempore ad tempus, et astra de terra coram Deo omni virtute Angelicos placant. Sicut Daemones orientem et manes reliquerunt portas miseras et perdere verba eloquor arca pactum sempiternum. Lucifer solutum. Hoc ego pronuntio maledictionem!

From a time before time, from this land beyond the stars and in the presence of the God, I invoke the power of all the bright angels. As the Demons rise and the spirits of the dead have left the gates, I utter the word of their misery and destroy forever the Ark of their Covenant. Lucifer unbound. I pronounce this curse!

"Ego sum praedo!" In nomine Domini quia ultus sum in ... EGOSUMQUISUM!"

I am the destroyer! I destroy you in the name of God ... EGOSUMQUISUM!

The laser-like beam from the ring intensified to a blinding brightness. Ben raised his hand to cover his eyes and Jack fell backwards as if he had been shot. The pure power of Lucifer himself was acting against its own creation.

The light expanded; exploded in a wave of energy that sent ripples out into the temple, engulfing it, stopping time.

Mike looked at the scene in front of him; it was as if someone had hit the pause button. Ben was motionless, Jack hadn't quite hit the floor and was suspended a foot or so above it. Bodies of demons were turning to dust, as the Ark imploded in on itself, creating another flash and wave of energy that should have destroyed everything, if time had not been suspended, shielding the world from the blast, containing it and turning it in on itself.

In the centre of the temple, a large molten mass of black metal sat where the Demon Ark had been.

And still nothing moved except Mike; slowly, as if in a vacuum.

He stared at Ben, frozen in time; at Jack suspended above the floor; at the mess that had been demons and their hosts. Was it over? If so, why was this happening? And then he thought he knew.

The blast had to take a victim, and he was it. Time had been suspended for him.

He was dead.

CHAPTER FORTY: MORNING STAR

He ought to be moving on, wherever that was, but he was still watching the scene, frozen in a moment.

Something else was moving. The black shadow that had clung to the ceiling was drifting down towards the floor, swirling around in a vortex of black energy. It divided into two; one half seemed to evaporate before his eyes. The other remained.

He watched transfixed as it coalesced into human form, and particle by particle materialised into a man; a handsome man – no – a beautiful man, a man that Mike couldn't take his eyes from. The man smiled and the temple illuminated with his sheer presence.

An angel. One of the good guys, come to take him from there. He felt an overwhelming sense of relief. It was over.

The angel smiled again and held out his hand.

"Yes," he said. "It's over. You can rest now and hand over your burden before it burns out your soul. An object such as this has no place here."

Yes, Mike thought, *it has to go back to God. Where else would it be safe?*

He felt so tired, exhausted, it was time for him to rest.

The voice jolted him wide awake. Adain. *'No! Daddy! No! It is The Deceiver!'*

He recoiled, refocused and directed the energy from the ring directly at what he had assumed to be an angel.

Nothing happened. The man shook his head.

"Yes, I am Morning Star. Mine, I think."

He held out his hand and Mike felt the ring slacken its grip on his finger, burning into flesh and bone as it did so.

Mike screamed out in agony as his finger turned to

scorched flesh. He grabbed the ring in his fist as it fell.

Morning Star sighed, but it was a contented sigh.

"I have reigned in what you humans call Hell for too long. Quite frankly, I'm bored. There is so much more here for me to enjoy. The potential here is vast. Watch me rise. Watch me corrupt. Watch me reign. Oh, sorry, you can't, you're dead. So I'll take my ring and I'll be on my way."

There was no conscious thought, no physical effort, as Mike reached into his pocket and brought out the rosary that had once been the comfort of Mother Teresa. He threw it into the beautiful face, which contorted in rage.

The change in the atmosphere was subtle but Mike felt the savage rip at his solar plexus as Sebastian materialised between him and Morning Star. Mike knew what he had to do in the short space of time he had.

He gave the Lapsit Exillis to Sebastian.

Morning Star let out a scream of fury that made the ground tremble and the walls of the temple shake.

Sebastian was gone. And so was the lump of black metal.

The shift was immediate; time expanded and caught itself in a loop. Jack fell to the floor with a heavy thump, and an expletive that was both new and creative. Ben lowered his arm, and Mike fell down next to Jack.

Ben's reaction was immediate. He took advantage of the chaos.

"Begone Serpent, begone defiler, begone thou vile corruption! Return to Hell whence you came and disturb no more the servants of the Most High God! In the name of Christ, the first exorcist, I command you in his name!"

He picked up the fallen rosary and threw himself at Morning Star.

Too late.

Particle by particle, Morning Star was once again a moving shadow. His laugh echoed around the temple; the temple that was beginning to collapse into rubble.

Ben and Jack grabbed Mike's inert body and dragged him outside as the final tremor reduced the entire temple to dust and clay once again. Except for the huge statue of Pazuzu.

"Do something!" Jack yelled at Ben. "For God's sake, it can't end like this!"

Ben was giving Mike CPR, praying in between life-giving breaths. Mike was unresponsive.

"I can do something."

Ben turned his face to Jack whose eyes were black and shining. His voice was deep and harsh.

"Yes, it's me, Bazaliel. I have communed with Jack Carter and you know I can jump bodies. I can save Mike Travis, but leaving Jack is not without risk. He is almost healed but more time would be beneficial. I can stay in him and heal him completely or I can leave him and save the other life. It goes without saying that you have to decide quickly."

"What did Jack say?"

"He is predictable. He told me to jump. You have the decision to make Benjamin Lovecraft: Jack or Michael?"

Ben's mind and heart had plunged into a torment of despair, but he kept on praying and breathing into Mike, compressing his chest in the futile hope that, like in the movies, he would take a gasp of air and sit up, but knowing down to his entrails that it wasn't going to happen.

Bazaliel continued in the harsh voice of the demon, "If I jump, this time there will be no going back. You should know I will give myself over to him completely; in effect, I will be no more as my life-force drags his back and melds with his to keep it anchored in his body. It will be a one-time deal; I won't be able to heal every subsequent injury, and, if he rejects me, he will die. And he will always carry the darkness now. It has been building in him for a long time. But from now on he will always have a piece of hell inside him. I don't know how much of the dark magic will remain; not all I suspect, since the disconnect with the Lapsit Exillis was so violent, but some will remain. I believe the corruption will not. I have proved that you can trust me and you should. I will have no control over him because I will allow his soul to consume me, as I must consume part of him. I will destroy my own seal. This will be my ultimate sacrifice, my redemption."

"Jack! Jack, tell me! Tell me what you want me to do!" he pleaded.

Jack closed his eyes and when he opened them, they were his own, twinkling in their sockets, peace written on his features.

"Bazaliel is wrong. It isn't your decision; it's mine. And I have already told him to jump. I wanted to give him time to speak to you first, because once he's in Mike, he will be no more. And we should agree, right here, right now that this stays here. *It never happened and he can never know.* Don't worry, I'm healed enough to survive this."

He bent over Mike and pushed Ben away from him, taking over the CPR. He breathed his own and the demon's life-force into his best friend and felt something give at soul-level. He breathed into him again, and again, feeling weaker with every breath.

He stopped and sat back, breathless and pale, Mike was still unresponsive.

"We need to wait a minute," Jack said quietly. "Just wait."

As he spoke, tendrils of dark smoke began to rise from Bazaliel's seal on his arm. His skin puckered as if it had been burned but he felt no pain. The seal had been destroyed.

There was no dramatic intake of breath; instead Mike simply opened his eyes very slowly. Eyes that were darker than before, that flashed black for a second, and then it was gone.

Jack nodded to Ben who swallowed the lump in his throat but still couldn't speak, his eyes flitting between the two most important people in his life.

Mike tried to sit up. "Give me a hand here," he said, in between bouts of coughing. "What happened? Ben? How the … f….? What the …? What's with the collar?"

Ben laughed his deep, booming laugh. "What part of 'don't put the fucking thing on your finger' didn't you understand? You scared the shit out of me, you bastard!"

Before anyone could say anything further, Jack tried to stand up and staggered forwards. Ben was on his feet instantly, supporting him, helping him to keep his balance. Mike was up and at his other side.

He had taken Jack's arm and now he was staring down at the puckered skin where the seal had once been.

"Jack?"

"Well, you know, when you exorcise a temple full of demons it's not selective. He's gone, Mike. So you don't have to lecture me anymore. And before you get all freaked out, I'll be OK. Have to take it easy for a while, but most of the healing was done. It's just time now."

Mike looked around at the destruction of the temple and at the lights that were approaching the hill-top site. "Speaking of time; we shouldn't be here."

By common agreement they moved quickly in the opposite direction of the approaching lights.

Once out of sight, they slowed their pace. Mike was quiet, his mood darkening with every step. Finally he stopped and turned to them.

"He's out there. Lucifer, Fucking Morning Star, whatever he called himself; he's out there. Loads of demons escaped before I could shut it down. I shouldn't have waited." Memories came flooding back, dark memories prompted by his realisation. "I killed Josh; he was possessed by Pazuzu. And I have to tell Roman Woolfe that Jon Barclay is dead. And … Oh Christ! Look back at the site. Where is the statue? It survived the goddam wreck… now it's gone." He recalled the dark shadow splitting in two. "Pazuzu is out there too. I failed."

"No, Mike you didn't fail. You shut down the Ark. You destroyed it. The portals are closed again. Yes, some demons got away, but if you hadn't waited and destroyed it, who knows if it would have been activated again. You did what you had to do."

"And Morning Star? I let him go. And that son-of-a-bitch Sebastian has the ring."

"There's another day," Ben said, trying to calm him.

Mike shook his head. "Not for me. I quit. I said I would walk away when this was over. I'm going home to get Beth from that bastard Sebastian, and we're going to start again somewhere off the grid ... What?"

He stared into Ben's eyes. "What?" he demanded. "*What* ...?"

CHAPTER FORTY- ONE: FALLOUT

Mike had spent an hour with Beth, holding her, talking to her, trying to get a response out of her, kissing her on her cheek, her forehead, her hands. She smiled at him but her eyes were a blank canvas.

Now he was pacing. Silently striding up and down the length of Roman's sitting room. No-one spoke; no-one dared. He had to fight so hard to contain the explosion that was threatening, they all held their breath. His face was taut, and the scar that ran the length of his cheekbone stood out against his pallor.

Every now and then he would look at them, and every now and then they saw the merest hint of black, flash through his eyes and then disappear as quickly as it has shown itself. Roman looked questioningly at Ben, who shrugged and shook his head in a way that said, *'I don't know what you're talking about, and if I did I wouldn't tell you.'*

Eventually, Mike stopped in front of Ben.

"You know how to summon an angel?" he demanded, in a voice that would chill a furnace from Hell.

Ben hesitated, he knew what was coming next and it scared him.

"There may be a way. I would need to do some research."

"Do it. And, when you know, you tell me. I want that bastard here and then I'm going to kill him. I will find a way. You can research that while you're at it!"

Jack stood up and made a tentative move towards him.

"Mike, Beckett is on his way back to see you. He knows what's wrong with her. And ... and, it wasn't Sebastian."

Mike's fury spewed out then, in a lava stream of rage

and there was a fragment of a second that Jack saw the darkness behind his eyes.

"How can you say that, Jack? How? For Christ's sake, she wasn't like that until he took her! What are you saying, eh? You think it's my fault? How can you think that? How? Tell me. Because I'm lost. It's too much, too bloody much!"

He pounded his fist into the marble fireplace, leaving a blood trail in its wake, and started pacing again.

Jack didn't sit down again, despite the fact that he was still weak from losing Bazaliel's life-support; he leaned against the wall, trying to adopt a casual stance. Anything that may calm, Mike, though he knew nothing would.

Mike continued to rant and rave and every now and then he would stop and stare out of the window in silence.

It was during the louder part of the process that the door opened and Martha appeared in the room.

"Michael Travis! Come here! How dare you behave this way? The people around you love you and care about you and will support you and Beth through this. *I* spoke to Beckett too, and there is hope. You only disrespect Beth by this behaviour, not help her. Now, are you going to carry on letting this rage fester and boil inside and alienate everyone dear to you, or are you going to do something positive? Like getting the hell back out there and killing every goddam demon you can find. I have lost my home and everything I owned and I am going to make a new life here. I will stay with Beth and earn my keep as the Librarian of the Strazca. I will watch over her while you, Michael Travis, stop feeling sorry for yourself and be what you are meant to be: a Demon Hunter. Or am I mistaken about you? *Am I?*" she demanded.

The room had suddenly filled with the atmosphere of high octane anxiety, as the unstoppable force met the immoveable object. Mike and Martha were staring at one another. All bets were off.

His face suffused with rage and his eyes were darker

than a thundercloud; Martha appeared not to notice.

"*Am I?*" she demanded again.

She stood her ground, waiting for a response.

When it came, it shocked them all. He crumpled into a heap on the floor at her feet and sobbed. She patted his head in silence.

Jack looked away, unable to watch. Ben shook his head and lowered it in mutual sorrow and Roman remained impassive. Mike's heaving sobs eventually stopped and that silence was worse than the sobbing. After five or so minutes, he took a deep breath and stood up, put his arms around Martha and kissed her on the cheek.

"I'm sorry," was all he said.

As he pulled away from her, his expression had changed. His eyes seemed permanently in the eye of a storm, he had a determined set to his jaw, and a cold, hard-boiled coating to his demeanour.

"You are not mistaken. I will be the demon hunter. And I will show no mercy. I will hunt them all to the ends of the earth if need be. And I won't stop until I get each and every one of them, especially Morning Star and Pazuzu. I am Strazca now, one of your hunters," he said in acknowledgment to Roman.

Ben stood up, impressive in his biker gear and dog collar. "*One* of them, yes. I'm with you."

"And so am I," Jack said. "And I'm still a better shot than you, Travis."

Mike turned his attention to Roman. "Looks like you've got yourself a team. You'd better take care of her while I'm away."

"The best," he said, "the very best.

FIVE MONTHS LATER

Mike was sitting in her sunny room, reading Beth's favourite book to her. It seemed right that she should be listening to a world populated by hobbits and elves and dwarves on a quest, lost as she was in her own world. She looked sleepy, so he closed the book and laid it down. He took her hand.

"I'm going to be away for a short while, Wife. Lizzie has a lead on something I need to do. Will you be good while I've gone?"

Her smile never wavered and he thought that there was a faint glimmer behind her eyes. Was he mistaken? Was it a sign that she was coming back to him? Whatever it was, it was gone again. But he had seen it, and that meant there was hope.

He kissed her on the cheek and went down to Roman's study where he joined Jack and Ben. Jack was stronger, leaner and impossibly more handsome than ever. Ben still wore the collar; he had spent the first month cloistered in the abbey on Caldey Island in the care of the Abbot; finding his faith again, finding his way back to the collar. He answered to no Church, no Bishop; only to God. But he was a priest in every sense of the word, and probably the hardest and meanest exorcist walking.

All of them had been studying for impossibly long hours and when they weren't studying they had been training hard. They studied demon lore and ancient grimoires; grimoires that felt strangely familiar to Mike, his understanding of the dark magic contained within a remnant of the download from the ring. One day, he knew, he would use it. And they always had a full kit packed and ready to leave at a moment's notice. Demons didn't wait.

Roman handed them a file each.

"We have a lead on Pazuzu and there is definite demonic activity in Paris."

Mike didn't look up from the file. "I'll take the lead on Pazuzu," he said in a voice devoid of expression.

"OK, we'll take the Paris trip," Ben replied. "Ready, Jack?"

The grin was wider than before, "You betcha."

They both clapped Mike across the shoulder and made for the door.

He nodded at them. "Back safe," he said.

He watched out of the study window as Ben straddled the massive bike, turned the throttle, and slammed his visor down. Jack climbed on behind him and waved at the window. There was a flurry of gravel and they were gone.

"I'll be off too," he said to Roman. "Just want to see Martha before I leave."

He headed for the library where Martha was always to be found, reading, cataloguing, and sorting, when she wasn't sitting with Beth. She wasn't there, and he decided that if she was with Beth he would leave her there since it would unsettle him to see his wife like that again just prior to a case.

He felt pressure on his chest, and suddenly it was as if the air had been sucked out of the room. He ground his teeth and spun around.

"Sebastian. You've got a fucking nerve. You're lucky I haven't found out how to kill an angel yet, but it's in there somewhere," he tapped the side of his head. "And I'm kinda busy, what do you want, you son-of-a-bitch?"

The angel folded his dark wings and looked at Mike steadily for a good few seconds before speaking.

"I know you will always blame me for what has happened to her, and I will always have the knowledge that you are wrong. That won't change things. But I need you to know something. I am no longer one of the so-called

Greeting Angels. I have another assignment."

Mike made a sound of disgust. "Of course you do, you sycophantic bastard. You got your brownie points by taking the Lapsit Exillis, and taking the credit for it. We could make good use of it down here, did that ever occur to you?" he snapped.

"It is deemed far too dangerous in the hands of mortals. But yes, returning the stone did bring its rewards."

"That it? You come to gloat? Well, you've done that now piss off."

"I came to tell you my new assignment."

"Go on then, I'll play. Then you'd better go before I forget I'm in a relatively good mood today. What's your new assignment?"

There was a ruffle of dark feathers. "You. You are my assignment, to watch over you and help when I can."

"Ha! A guardian fucking angel! Well, no offence, pal, but I can do without that kind of help. And just so you know, when I find out how, I *will* kill you."

The room filled with light and air again as Sebastian left without another word.

Mike grabbed the vintage, black leather flying jacket that he always seemed to wear these days, grabbed his bag and his keys and left through the side door.

His four-by-four was sleek and black, customised by Ben, to conceal weapons and equipment that would get him incarcerated for longer than he cared to think about, if he was stopped and his car searched.

The spring sun was hitting him square in his darkened eyes and he put on a pair of mirrored aviators completing his new look.

He threw the car into reverse, turned it around and headed down the drive.

It was going to be a bad day for some demons.

THANK YOU!

To my Reader:

Many thanks for buying *The Demon Ark*, I hope you enjoyed reading it.

If you did enjoy it, please post a review at Amazon, Goodreads or your favourite social network site and let your friends know about The *Demon Ark*.

I hope that this has whetted your appetite to read the other novels in the Mike Travis paranormal investigation series. You can find details of these in the next page as well as the short stories collections.

And don't forget to sign up for my newsletter for details of my latest books and a FREE short story at:

janmcdonaldemailsign-up.gr8.com

Happy Reading!
All the best
Jan

ALSO BY JAN MCDONALD

Mike Travis Paranormal Investigations
The Crowsmoor Curse: getBook.at/Crowsmoorcurse

Long Shadows: getBook.at/longshadows

The Sacred Ark: getBook.at/sacredark

The Haunted Diary of Victoria Little:
getBook.at/haunteddiary

The Merlin Manuscript: getBook.at/merlin

The Sin Eater: getbook.at/sineater

Mike Travis Demon Hunter
Fallen Angels and Demons: getBook.at/FallenAngels

Mike Travis short stories
Beginnings: getBook.at/Beginnings

Halloween: getBook.at/halloween

Christmas Spirits: getBook.at/christmasspirits

The Beckett Vampire Trilogy
Midnight Wine: getBook.at/midnightwine

Lycan: getBook.at/lycan

Part 3 coming 2016

ABOUT JAN MCDONALD

Jan lives close to the Welsh borders which have their own mystical quality and provide endless resources in the way of legends and folklore surrounding paranormal experiences. She loves all things paranormal and has read the best: Dennis Wheatley, Stephen King, Edgar Allan Poe, Bram Stoker and all those authors that excel in the creepy or downright scary world of paranormal events.

When she embarked on the Mike Travis series, she realised that the field of paranormal investigation is more than we see on the popular TV programmes. So in order to provide compelling ghost hunting tales but with the greatest accuracy, Jan trained as a Paranormal Investigator and has studied parapsychology.

CONTACT DETAILS

Visit the authors website:
    jan-mcdonald.co.uk

Follow on Twitter:
    www.twitter.com/janmcdonald1

Cover designed by: Raven Crest Books
Cover art: © Dusan Kostic - Fotolia.com

Published by: Raven Crest Books
    www.ravencrestbooks.com

Like us on Facebook:
    Facebook.com/ravencrestbooksclub